Ficti
Evans
First fruits
5/29/01

W9-CUH-614

WITHDRAWN

FIRST
FRUITS

ALSO BY THE AUTHOR

The Last Girl
Freezing

FIRST
FRUITS

Penelope Evans

Carnegie-Stout Public Library
360 West 11th St., Dubuque, IA 52001-4697

FICTION

3 1825 00369 6971

Copyright © 200∪ by Penelope Evans

All rights reserved.

Published in the United States by

Soho Press, Inc.
853 Broadway
New York, N.Y. 10003

Library of Congress Cataloging-in-Publication Data
Evans, Penelope, 1959-
First fruits / Penelope Evans.
p.   cm.
ISBN 1-56947-188-6 (alk. paper)
I. Title.

PR6055.V215 F57 2000
823'.914–dc21   99–048520

10 9 8 7 6 5 4 3 2 1

For Anne Bryant Evans,
my mother

❧ Chapter One

I MADE A NEW FRIEND today. Her name is Lydia. Now I'm wondering how I'm going to get rid of her.

That's the trouble with the new girls. They promise more than they deliver. Although it's not all bad. It just depends on what you need them for. Look at Hilary. Hardly what you would call ideal material, but she's come in useful in all sorts of ways. It's only that, well, I hoped for more.

But Lydia, she had potential. Or so I thought. The signs were all there. Mrs. Chatto brought her into the classroom, leading her by the hand like some small animal she had lassooed and then stunned. Lessons hadn't started and the din was tremendous. Hilary was there of course, glued to my side as usual, whispering into my ear the hundred and one things she had done since she had got up this morning. That includes cleaning her teeth and folding up her pyjamas. You see the problem.

But what can I do? If I let her go, she'll be off to attach herself to Fiona McPherson and all that lot. And we don't want that. Because who would that leave me with? I'll tell you who. Moira MacMurray. In which case, need I say more?

Two reasons to sit up and take notice then; one, just to have a distraction from Hilary and two, because you only had to look at Lydia to see she would be easy. You felt that the moment Chatto took her hand her away, she would fall over. I mean, the girl was shaking.

'Class.' Mrs. Chatto removed the hand so as to clap for our

attention—and see what I mean? For one astonishing moment Lydia actually seemed to hang in mid air, like a baby that's been dropped. 'Class, this term we have a new girl, Lydia Morris. Lydia has moved up all the way up from . . .' She paused, frowned and turned to Lydia,who had recovered her balance. 'Where was it again, dear?'

The girl beside her gasped. She was wearing thick glasses, and you could see her eyes start swimming frantically behind them like two small fish panicking. She muttered something none of us could hear.

Mrs. Chatto turned to us again. 'Hole. Lydia has just moved all the way up from Hole in Devon.' There was a hush, and then the entire room exploded. This is Scotland, for Heaven's sake. And it wasn't going to occur to anyone here that the name of Auchtermuchty might cause just as much mirth down where she came from.

Mrs. Chatto of course had recognised her mistake. She clapped her hands again. 'Girls!' She had that look in her eye, so we stopped laughing—all except for Moira MacMurray, for the simple reason that she hadn't been laughing in the first place—and stared at Lydia instead. And that was even better in a way, because you never would have thought it possible for a human to turn so red, and all the while staring at the floorboards as if searching for a crack wide enough to take her.

See what I mean? Easy.

Meanwhile Mrs. Chatto was casting her eye over the class. 'Lydia, I think you should go and sit with . . .' Her eye landed on Fiona McPherson. Just in time I realised what she was had in mind and shot my hand into the air.

'Mrs. Chatto,' I cried. 'Lydia can sit here, next to me.'

Note the sharp intake of breath from Hilary. She had been under the impression that she would be sitting next to me, just like she always did. So it served her right—she could go and sit beside Moira MacMurray for thinking she could take me for granted. Note also the approving glance from Mrs. Chatto; it never did any harm to get on the good side of her. But, most important of all, do you see what I'd done? I'd snatched the new girl right out from under the nose of Fiona McPherson!

Only trouble is, Fiona McPherson didn't seem to care. Now she was making a great show of wiping her brow for all to see, and pretending to be relieved. So there you are; less than five minutes into the friendship, and you had to wonder if being kind to Lydia might not be a mistake after all. I mean, if Fiona didn't want her . . .

Too late though. Mrs. Chatto had already turned to Lydia. 'All right, dear, you can go and sit next to Kate Carr.'

But, would you believe it, Lydia didn't move. She took one look at me and bit her lip. And *that's* the thanks I get for putting up my hand when not a soul in the class wanted her. But it gets worse. Now the whole room had grown quiet, watching as Mrs. Chatto actually had to push her in my direction before she's willing to move. That's when I noticed her sneaking a glance over at Fiona McPherson, as if she had known that was where she might have ended up and was sorry she hadn't.

Finally she began to make her own way between the desks, bumping against chairs and tripping over school bags, moving like someone twice the size she was, which actually was no size at all. Imagine a head with straggly thread for hair and a body made of pipe cleaners. Got it? The full horror of it? Now you've imagined Lydia.

Hilary whispered in my ear. 'Did you ever see anything so *skinny?*' She stood up straight and stuck out her chest to show what a proper fourteen-year-old was like. As if Hilary would ever know.

But Lydia didn't even look at her. She was standing by the desk now, staring at the floor. Was it my imagination, or was there suddenly the faintest whiff of ammonia in the air? Yet I didn't say a word about that. I just smiled, giving her one of what Hilary likes to call my goofy grins. (Hilary adores words like *goofy* and *loony*.) It means smiling at someone with every inch of your face and letting your eyes crinkle up in the corners. It never fails, at least not on Hilary.

'Hi,' I said, and patted the seat beside me. But still she didn't move. Maybe it was Hilary glaring at her, putting her off. I sneaked a hand up to Hilary's waist and took a large pinch of all the spare flesh that was there and squeezed. Hilary smiled. Sort of.

And at long last, Lydia sits down.

'Well,' I say. 'This is nice.' No answer. She had her hands bunched in front of her, so tightly clenched you could see the whites of her knuckles. At the same time, I looked up, and what should I see but Fiona McPherson across the room grinning from ear to ear. Well, that did it. I just lost all patience with her, with Lydia.

'Where did you say you were from again? I don't think I've heard of it before.'

Above me, Hilary snorted, like one of the horses she always claims she wished she had. At the sound of it Lydia's arms seemed to twitch and something tinkled. That's when I noticed it, the bracelet of metal links, hanging off her wrist like half a manacle. I picked up her arm, and had a better look. The bracelet had one of those tabs you can get inscribed, like this one.

'Good Luck Lydia,' it said. 'From all your friends in 2A.'

Fancy that, she had had friends then, before she moved up here, to the very top of the country. I bet it felt like a hundred years ago, and a thousand miles away.

'Oh, that is nice,' I said. Dad says if there's nothing you can think to praise in a person, praise something they're wearing instead. That way there's no end to the gratitude. 'You'd better take it off though. Mrs. Chatto can't stand folk to wear jewellery.'

Well, I couldn't let praise go to her head.

Finally, however, a reaction. Lydia's head shot up to look at me, eyebrows arching above her specs. 'Oh,' she said. 'Oh?' Her hand moved across to touch the engraved tab as if it was all she had to ward off evil. 'Oh,' she said again, faintly.

As I said, a reaction—of sorts. But really it wasn't good enough. Not after the effort I had put in. After break, she'd find herself sitting next to Moira MacMurray. We'd see if that didn't teach her to be more appreciative. And better still, I wouldn't have to look at her. You could hide the Rock of Gibraltar behind Moira MacMurray.

After assembly, and the usual Welcome to the New Girls, it was history. For once, Mrs. Chatto ignored us, continued to read what was in front of her long after we had sat down. People started to exchange glances.

Finally she looked up, glared at us. That's when it occurred to me that whatever she had been reading had put her in a thoroughly foul mood.

'Girls,' she says. 'I've just been looking over Lydia Morris's report from her last school. You may be interested in hearing a little of what is here for yourselves.' Then she made us listen to all this stuff about Lydia's genius for history—not to mention maths, French and every other subject under the sun. And to make matters worse, Lydia's last school hadn't even been a private one, not like ours. Not so much as a penny had changed hands.

Of course, it rebounds on us, with Chatto telling us we're going to have to pull our finger out, that we're costing our parents the earth, and for what? We've to look at Lydia, see what hard work can do for us.

Tell that to Moira MacMurray, who could work till there's no ink left in the world and still not be able to spell her own name. In fact I noticed that Chatto let her eyes slide right across her as usual, as if none of this had anything to do with her. They all do it, all the teachers. I think they gave up on Moira years ago. If it weren't for needing the fees, I reckon they would have bumped her out into one of those places where they don't even try to teach folk like her. They just make them do basket weaving instead. That's how Moira can get away with it, sitting there, eyes bulging, taking nothing in, letting nothing out.

Meanwhile everyone else is looking at Lydia with a kind of horrified interest—with the sole exception of me. Dad says it doesn't do to let yourself be impressed. There's always going to be something to detract.

And when has he ever been wrong?

But what about Lydia? What did she do with all this praise flying about? I'll tell you what she did; she just sat there gazing at the desk as if trying to ignore it—Mrs. Chatto, people's stares, everything. Yet she had to be secretly pleased, having all that attention. I mean, she must have been. Surely.

Later, at breaktime, the inevitable happens. Fiona McPherson moved in. Lydia was sitting beside me as before, but we were just doing our best to ignore her now, bring her down to earth where she belonged. Hilary was leaning over from behind, breathing loudly in my ear, whittering on about something and nothing. And Moira . . . Moira of course was just . . . there.

Moira.

I don't think even Dad would have anything to say about Moira. Not that I've asked him. Somehow, I've just not got round to it. Some things you just don't want to discuss. Right at this moment she was opening her mouth to insert a sherbet lemon, the kind of sweet all the old ladies eat in church, sweetening their breath before closing in on Dad at the end of Service. Dad, who is a proper scream about these things, says they have cups of tea which they keep ready for him in their handbags, but that's not true of course. You can't keep pots of tea in a handbag. All he's saying is, you can't escape old ladies when they're determined to give you tea.

But why should anyone want to be old before their time? Moira does. Or rather, Moira doesn't. Care that is. Moira doesn't seem to care about anything.

Where was I? Not thinking about Moira, that's for sure.

So *where* was I? Oh yes, Fiona McPherson moving in where she isn't wanted.

And the first thing that happens is that Hilary shuffles out of her way because folk like Hilary will always be impressed by Fiona. But Moira, Moira stays exactly where she was. Fiona has to move round her, which she does, without seeming to mind, as if Moira were just part of the furniture. That's how they all treat Moira. But they haven't noticed, have they? They don't see what I see, how there's something very wrong with Moira.

'Oh, Lydia,' says Fiona, face smooth, hair shining. Lydia looks up and the faintest of blushes begins to spread across her cheeks. Did she know then, even after this short time, about Fiona? How she's a boarder, and how generally boarders stay over by the radiator under the window, and never cross a room for anyone? Yet here she was, standing right in front of our pair of desks, come all this way just to speak to her.

'Lydia,' Fiona says again. 'We hardly heard you in class just now. You've got such a little voice. I wasn't even sure if you got the answer right, you know, to the question Mrs. Chatto asked you.'

Lydia pushed her glasses up her nose. Suddenly she was thoughtful, as we'd never seen her before. Which means she *did* know, about Fiona. How is it people always seem to know?

Meanwhile, Fiona carries on, voice suspiciously calm, that posh Edinburgh accent of hers adding a little extra polish to every word. 'What was his name again, the man who jumped off the bridge to escape the Duke of Argyll's men?'

Lydia swallowed hard. Opened her mouth, but nothing came out. Opened her mouth again, and this time there comes the answer. . . .

'Rob Roy.'

Or rather, *Wob Woy*.

The room which had grown quiet at the sight of Fiona leaving the radiator, suddenly erupted. Too late, Lydia has realised what she has said, understood for the first time how she sounded. She should have listened harder to Kenneth McKeller on the radio, learned from Moira Anderson and the TV specials at Hogmanay before she ever thought of moving North. A huge swathe of red sweeps over her face, as she stares around at an entire room laughing.

And that's all she can do—stare, her head turning every which way, cheeks flaming, lips pale and twitching. Until. Until she comes to Moira. Because as usual, Moira isn't laughing. As usual, Moira has failed to see the joke. Yet something about her has its effect. A moment later Lydia stops staring and shaking. She even stops blushing. It's as if suddenly, she isn't so much upset as confused, asking herself why Moira is the only one here not laughing.

And it didn't stop there. The confusion seemed to lead to something else, a kind of unexpected confidence. Suddenly she lifted up her head, stretching that long skinny neck of hers and mumbled something.

'What did she say?' This was Jackie Milne, who's deaf as a post because even at her age she doesn't clean inside her ears. I'd heard though, and so had Fiona McPherson. Who had stopped laughing, and now was simply smiling. She turned to Jackie. 'Lydia says if we ask her nicely, she'll say "Round and Round the Ragged Rock the Ragged Rascal Ran." Just for us.'

At which, at long last, Lydia actually smiled. And that's when we saw it, the logjam of metal in her mouth. She was wearing dental braces, gigantic ones with bands and knobs and claws, the sort that made you wonder what sort of man could have done such a thing to anyone. No wonder she had barely opened her mouth before.

Only now here was another point of interest. Everyone bent

forward to have a really good look. And once again, she didn't seem to mind. The smile just grew broader, more metallic.

Watching her now, you'd have sworn she was the only interesting person in the room.

That's when I jumped to my feet. 'Stop it, stop it all of you. Stop staring at the poor girl. How can you be so unkind? She can't help being ugly. Just leave her alone.'

The effect was instantaneous. All the smiles stopped together. A couple of people—like Helen May and Pamela Wilson—even appeared to be quite upset. But it was all you could wish for. In the bare twinkling of an eye, Lydia had become quite invisible. There was a new centre of attention.

Me. You see, it was me they were staring at now—even Moira MacMurray and let me tell you, not even Lydia had managed that. It's a moment to savour really. Because it's at times like this that you know, that you remember what it means to have It. Something no-one else has. I haven't mentioned It before, how It changes things. But then I haven't had to, have I? It has a habit of making itself known, all by itself.

One by one, then, they drifted away, even Fiona McPherson, till there were only the three of us left. Four if you count Moira MacMurray.

Hilary however was still gazing at me. Her eyes were shining, and her nose had gone quite pink. 'Kate,' she said. 'Kate, I never saw anything so brave. You were just like something from a book. Lydia, wasn't Kate brave . . . ?'

She was casting round her, looking for Lydia. But she couldn't find her, not at first. Yet Lydia was right there, exactly where she'd been all along, beside me, in my shadow. It's just that for some reason or other, she had made herself so small again, so insignificant you could hardly see her.

Sad really. Some people just aren't made for the spotlight. Better for everyone that they stay invisible.

• • •

Down in the cloakrooms after lunch, Hilary was still going on about it. So brave, she kept saying. So headstrong, *so in control*. She was beginning to sound like a broken record. Still, it's nice to be appreciated. Without Hilary it wouldn't happen, not with the sort of people we have in our class. It's one of the things she's good for.

It helps, you see, having someone to remind you that you're special. That you're not just anyone—or worse.

Remember Lydia, back there in the class room the first time, looking at me as if I was something she had discovered under a rock? Biting her lip. Believe me, a lesser person might want to make her pay for a look like that.

And that's what I'm up against.

Something about me. People can see I'm special. Something about my eyes perhaps, out of the ordinary. Something *he's* put there. That's why you have to remember to smile. Smiling makes the world a better place. It puts people off their guard, makes them easier to . . . deal with.

And anyway, why not smile? I have reason to smile. I'm *his* daughter. The luckiest girl alive. Except for the one thing.

I suppose I have to mention it. If I don't someone else will. Except for my leg, then. The one thing that stops me walking on air, stops me walking like other people, like Hilary. Like Fiona MacPherson.

Actually, we prefer not to talk about it. *He* doesn't like it. And why should he, when he can't bear anything not to be perfect, least of all me?

It's the reason I can't ask him. How it happened that I have the one leg shorter than the other. A leg that no-one is allowed to see. Not even me. It's the rule. Every family has to have rules. There's a way of getting dressed, having a bath even, without looking down, without having to be reminded. I get dressed the way *he* showed me, so as never to catch sight.

Except that, every so often I *do* catch sight. Streaks of brown, tinged with pink. And in bed I can feel it, below the knee, softer than the other leg, softer than the tips of my fingers. It's what happens when something burns, when skin has been fired to become something different from skin. Something beyond repair. Something lost. Something I can't even remember. Something no-one will tell me.

Don't dwell. It's unhealthy. And I can walk, can't I? I could even run if I wanted, as fast and as far away as I wanted, if I weren't so happy where I am.

And anyway, none of it matters. None of it. I've got him and I've got *It*. When you've got *It*, nothing else counts. Especially if you know how to use It.

So brave, Kate. So in control.

Hilary will have to stop going on about it soon. Even she can't keep it up forever.

I told Lydia to go and sit next to Moira. It took a moment to get through to her, but she did as she was told. She was tired. Behind their glass panes her eyes looked sunken. Three hours at a new school had taken it out of her.

But there couldn't have been anything brighter than my smile when I said kindly: 'I wonder what they're doing back at your old school right this minute. Your friends in 2A. Getting on without you, do you think?'

She just stared at me then, but her eyes seem to sink even further into her face, like people going slowly down into quicksand.

Hilary, who is no slouch when it suits her, chipped in. 'Funny how you can forget a person when they go. One moment they're there, and the next moment they're not, and then it's as if they never existed.'

She gave me a nudge. And that's Hilary for you. Nobody had

told *her* to go making the poor girl's day more miserable than it was.

So I ignored her.

'Actually,' I said—nice and clearly because Lydia was trying to look away—'Actually, I should think they're missing you terribly.' I pointed to the bracelet which, despite my best efforts on her behalf, she was still wearing. 'You must have been *really* popular to be given something like that when you left.'

I glanced round then and there's Hilary wearing a look sour enough to turn milk, and it's irresistible. 'Do you think anyone would club together to buy *you* a bracelet if you left, Hills?'

Of course they wouldn't. Not unless I organised it.

Lydia is the one to watch, though. Putting Hilary in her place has had its effect. That teeny flash of metal was the signal, the first time she's smiled since Fiona started to make fun. In other words, the first sign of gratitude I've seen all day.

And as Dad would say, it doesn't do to ask too much of people. Not everyone has it in them to rise to the occasion. You've got to take them as you find them.

Meanwhile, the room has grown quiet suddenly. Someone must have noticed the time and signalled it to the others. Yes, it's time. You won't catch anyone moving now, not for anything.

Or would you? Behind me, a rustling noise. Completely unexpected. I turn round, and believe it or not, Moira is busy offering a crumpled bag of sherbet lemons across the desk to Lydia. It's as if she hasn't noticed the time. Or doesn't care.

And to make matters worse, Lydia takes one.

Meanwhile, far away, in a distant part of the building, comes the sound of footsteps, hailing closer. And is it my imagination or is there also the warning flap of gabardine, cracking in the bone-dry school air like a ship's sail? There's danger here, and yet Lydia and Moira are oblivious, busy with their sweets. Lydia pops hers into her mouth.

Serve them right then when the door bursts open and there it is, standing in the entrance, the reason we've all been waiting.

The door slams and a poisonous cloud of chalk dust—twenty years of it, rising from those same black folds of gabardine—moves across the room, scattering particles. Mandy Edwards—who swears she's allergic—immediately begins to cough. But it doesn't get her anywhere. In the middle of the cloud, a hard black figure—Miss Jamieson—stands, tapping her foot, glaring with chips of flint for eyes, and waits for her to stop.

Silence falls. Then she is off again, this time striding between the desks till she arrives in front of Lydia. There she judders to a halt, black gown swirling and, finally, settling around her. Lydia lifts her head, slowly, unwillingly; takes one long look—and gulps. She has just swallowed her sherbet lemon. Whole.

'Lydia Morris,' says Miss Jamieson. 'New girl. Good at Latin. Very good at Latin. Well, we'll see. We'll see.'

There's another silence. Miss Jamieson is examining Lydia, taking her in. You'd think the girl would be all of a shiver. But here's a surprise; after that first involuntary spasm, Lydia is staring back at Miss Jamieson with a look none of us has seen before. A look that is partly terror, but also partly of naked admiration, the look some folk will have when they watch a thunder storm.

Miss Jamieson continues to stare, then, almost imperceptibly, nods her head. Something has passed between them, Lydia and herself. An understanding you might say. Not that anyone else would have noticed it. You would have to know how to look properly, how to read the glances that pass between people. In short, you would have to have *It* to be aware of anything at all.

For the moment though, Miss Jamieson is brisk. Whatever went between her and Lydia, it doesn't show. She turns away and makes her way to the front of the room. The word is she's a Catholic, but you wouldn't know it from looking at her. Dad has taught me how to recognise every Catholic I am ever likely to meet, told me how you can be friendly, but never trust them. Because they've got it all wrong, haven't they, with their idolatry and being such fools for Mary, who is only a woman after all. That's what he says, so it must be true; yet still I can't imagine Miss Jamieson being a fool for anyone.

Nothing I've done has ever worked.

She turns her back and starts to sweep the blackboard with the eraser, arms outstretched so as to be sure to catch all that stray chalk in the folds of her gown. 'Pages open, girls. Book three. Lydia, you can start.'

And so Lydia starts. Reads the Latin, then translates it into unfaltering English, sentence by sentence, never stops for breath, or to think even. Around the class girls are catching each others' eyes, and opening their mouths in mock horror. Hilary however dreams up another tactic of her own, and sticks two fingers down her throat, pretending to be sick.

But Lydia, she doesn't notice a thing. Lydia is enjoying herself. The tiredness that had her slumped in her seat has completely disappeared. It's as if someone has come and slipped ice-cubes down her neck, given her oxygen, put the bubbles back in her brain.

And the effect goes on. When it comes to other people's turn to translate, Miss Jamieson is like a crocodile that has eaten its fill, allowing small fish to swim between her claws without harm. Time after time, people make mistakes and Jamieson just sits there, smiling, doesn't bite off a single head. You can feel what folk are thinking. Lydia Morris is an asset to the class.

Unless of course, you're Hilary. Who hasn't forgiven Lydia for sitting in her rightful place all morning, for taking up my time.

And it's not over yet. As we're putting away our books, Miss Jamieson raps her desk. She has an announcement to make. She tells us that she is considering teaching Greek as an extra subject to anyone who is interested. She needed two pupils at the very least. Lessons would have to take place in free periods and some lunch breaks. Was anybody interested?

I suppose I should have warned Hilary. In her book, friends

know everything there is to know about each other. No secrets. But that's Hilary for you, not understanding that we don't belong on the same page, she and I, let alone the same book. As if it was planned, I put up my hand to be the first to volunteer. Miss Jamieson merely nods.

'Yes, Kate, I know all about you. That's been discussed with your father.'

You see, it *was* planned. Hilary looks at me, piggy eyes wide. I knew this announcement was coming. They talked about it at the end of last term, Miss Jamieson and Dad. Worked the whole thing out between them. It was Dad who suggested it actually, the one who had the vision.

You'd think Miss Jamieson could have shown a bit of gratitude then, managed something better than a nod. Instead, she looks straight past me, mouth twitching, impatient because no-one else has put up their hand. Her face is browner than usual, hair curlier, though just as grey. She'll have just come back from Greece, goes there every long vacation. Next week, after the brown has begun to fade, she'll be bringing in her photographs. She always does, passing them round as if it's some kind of treat. But they're all the same. Ruins and lots of blue sky. Usually there aren't even any people to make them interesting—except the odd fat person maybe, bursting out of his holiday clothes. Or just occasionally, this one woman who crops up time and time again. Miss Jamieson says she's only there to give a sense of scale.

Meanwhile she is still waiting for another hand. But who in their right mind would want to give up their free periods, not to mention lunch breaks? There's no-one here with a dad like mine to steer them in the right direction. All the same, suddenly I become aware of a little local difficulty beside me. It's Hilary, taking gulp after gulp of air as though in distress.

And you know why, of course. Ever since I had put up my hand, she had been struggling. I can read her mind. Hilary *likes* her lunchtimes. She even likes school mashed potato and rice pudding, though she tries to pretend otherwise. Best of all, she likes doing absolutely nothing—and yet even that is difficult for her. One lunch break is taken up with piano lessons, and another is Sewing for the Disabled in the domestic science block, which she does because there are biscuits provided.

Now there's Greek. Yet it's not as if she's even any use at Latin. But Hilary has read all the books about girls at school, going through everything together, sticking close no matter what. No wonder she's having problems.

And I can't resist it.

I lean across the desk and whisper, 'I thought you were supposed to be my friend.'

Well, you have to have fun sometimes. Poor old Hills-are-alive. A slow despairing look at me, then up goes her hand.

Miss Jamieson looks surprised, pursing her lips, which just for now are pale next to her skin, tanned by so much unScottish, not to say Mediterranean, sun. Come to think of it, she looks quite handsome, though you couldn't imagine anyone actually falling for her. Right now, she's regarding Hilary in almost kindly fashion, the way she might some poor animal she has found run over—before she pulls herself together and puts it out of its misery. Miss Jamieson likes animals. She has a cat called Cassandra that she mentions now and then.

Then she remembers that Hilary is not a cat and she frowns. 'Hilary Cross, I can't believe you have time for Greek. You'll have no lunch breaks left to play with, child.'

Now there's a surprise, Miss Jamieson letting someone down lightly. When she could so easily have said, *Hilary Cross, you don't have the brain for what Kate is doing*. Hilary however puts down her hand, and begins to perspire with sheer relief.

But the relief only lasts a second. Because now, behind us, we become aware of another hand climbing upwards, calling attention to itself. Hilary freezes, then forces herself to turn around.

Sure enough, Lydia is holding up a scrawny wrist as though to test the air.

Miss Jamieson smiles briefly. 'Lydia?'

But the only sound that answers her is the soft thud of Hilary's head hitting the desk in despair.

Which Miss Jamieson ignored. She writes down Lydia's name, and then drops the subject. I don't believe she wanted more than two anyway. This was to be her treat to herself, teaching Greek. Can you believe it?

Trust Dad to know it. One conversation, that's all he needed. He can do that, get people to tell him things they would never dream of letting on to anyone else. He knew Miss Jamieson was just itching to teach Greek.

The trouble is, then you have to ask yourself why I have to be the one who has to go and learn it. I mean, who in their right mind would *choose* to learn Greek? (Well, there's Lydia of course. But then, she's hardly what you would call normal.)

The answer is simple. Anyone can go to school and learn French, or German or whatever. But I'm his daughter, and that changes everything. That's what he says. It changes *everything*. That's the reason for the Greek. It's important to have something special, something no-one else has got, something that marks you out. *He* realised this when he taught himself Greek years ago, Hebrew, too.

So that's why I will be learning Greek. Greek will make us even more special than before. We'll be able to read the New Testament together as it was first written. It will put us in a class of our own.

Except, now there's Lydia, too. Which makes you wonder. Maybe I'm not the only one. Maybe there's someone else with a dad like mine.

Silly me. That's impossible. I know very well, better than any-one. There's no-one like my dad, not in the whole wide world. And I'm his daughter, the luckiest girl alive.

❧ Chapter Two

TIME TO GO HOME, AND here's Hilary—who has been ready for the last ten minutes—insisting on waiting for me. The idea is to walk out of school together, arm in arm just like the rosy-cheeked schoolgirl pals on the covers of her books. As if she didn't know, with my leg the way it is, that people would take one look and think she was needing to help me.

So Hilary, who keeps on having to wait, has to walk unaided.

What she can't understand though, is the reason for the wait, for why we invariably have to be last out. And that's where I despair of Hilary. Because she wouldn't get it, not even if I told her.

He will be waiting for me.

In other words, it's no good making my exit along with everybody else, just another person in the crowd. You may as well be an ant among five hundred other ants, he says. When I walk out of school, he wants to be able to see me, standing out, unmissable.

Like him.

It means I have to keep *him* waiting too, but he doesn't mind a bit. He parks the car next to where the sixth formers come out, stalking past on legs way too long for skirts that haven't fitted them since the fourth year. Well, you can imagine what they look like. Yet he doesn't complain—or look away—ever. He just stares and stares, never takes his eyes off them. He says it's a God-given opportunity to spot souls.

That's what he's so good at, you see, identifying souls. My dad, he can spot them from a hundred yards, the folk who are destined for Heaven and the folk who aren't—the Sheep and the Goats. Though of course you can't tell them that, not nowadays, not even at his Service. Nobody wants to hear how, in God's eyes, they are no more than livestock. But that's what it's all about; and my dad can sit there in the car and spot them, the ones who are chosen and the ones who are not.

Appearances have nothing to do with it, not even amongst the tiny ones, still clutching the hands of their older sisters, straight out of nursery, all big cheeks and curls. They look like angels already, don't they? But it makes no difference. It's been decided. If they're not chosen they'll go the same way as the others, finished before they've even started.

And of course they don't suspect. Bad teaching in the churches, he says, the reason that those girls in the sixth—the ones who pass by him the closest, the very people who would have the most to learn—can carry on walking, pretending he's not there. But *he* knows. Everything's temporary. In the next world it could all be different.

I only wish he would tell me who they are, the ones who haven't been chosen. I always have. Once when I was little I had the idea that I could go round warning them, not understanding it was the worst sin of all: wanting to interfere with God's will.

I shouldn't have told him what I had in mind. I was old enough to know better. It was my fault, then, forcing him to take steps, making sure it never happened again. Some people have to be saved from themselves, including even a child of his. Especially a child of his.

Yet even now, I'd still love to know. Especially about Fiona McPherson, and where she's headed. There'd be no danger of me trying to interfere with God's will.

In the meantime, today, as every day, Hilary thinks she is the first to see the car. 'Oh, there's your dad,' she says, trying to sound casual. As if I hadn't managed to spot my own father. He sees us coming and winds down the window. It makes an awful scraping noise, the car is that old. One of the things it doesn't do to mind.

Hilary bends down and inserts her nose through the gap. Her bottom sticks out, blocking half the pavement. It's the sort of thing Hilary forgets. Just how much space she takes up.

And so I have to wait while she has her time. Everyone has to have their time. Hilary, the old ladies, everyone. He'll not turn anyone away. And when she stands up again, her entire face is red. Even her neck is glowing. And you know why of course. He'll have found something to say to her, something that will have made her blush. He can do it with the most unlikely material.

Sometimes I think that's the real reason she hangs on after school. Just for those few words which will have her believing she's special, something no-one else would give her. Nothing to do with me.

But she has to stand back now, go home to her mother and a life so ordinary it makes you wonder how she can bear it. Meanwhile I get to go with him. The luckiest girl in the world.

Poor old Hilary, she's still standing there as we swing out into the road. Horns blare and lights flash, but it doesn't matter. Nothing ever touches us. Once I overheard Miss Jamieson say to Mrs. Chatto: 'Kate Carr's father drives in accordance with his beliefs.' Those were her exact words, and she sniffed as she spoke them. As if driving in accordance with your beliefs was something to disapprove of.

Meanwhile, I have a last sight of Hilary, shoulders drooping under her duffle coat, wistfully shrinking as we leave her behind.

One final thing though, just before school disappears altogether; I catch sight of Lydia. She is walking with a little girl of six, maybe seven. The kid is everywhere, skippety hopping along the pavement, all dancing curls and milk teeth. Lydia meanwhile is plodding along behind her, her mouth pursed, grudging every minute of her time.

I didn't know Lydia had a sister. Not much alike, though, were they? But really, it's only of passing interest. This is not the moment to be distracted by either of them. I have to think about *us* now. We've been apart a long time, the whole day in fact. He worries about me; all those poor influences. Those bad lessons to be unlearned and learned again. So think hard, Kate. Say the right thing. Try to forget the times when you've got it wrong, save yourself another lesson.

NEXT morning, just as Lydia is about to slip into the seat next to mine, Hilary slams her own bottom down before her and glares up, daring her to say a word about it. Lydia looks confused, then bites her lip. Satisfied, Hilary spreads her bottom over the seat. She's making sure you couldn't slip so much as a pencil between us.

What else can Lydia do but turn and drift away to sit next to Moira?

Who didn't say a word. I suppose that's the best you could say for her; Moira will scarcely ever speak unless spoken to. It must be the one thing her granny remembered to teach her. Shame about the rest of it, like washing her hair and changing her tights. Everyone knows about Moira's granny. They say if you go to their house she'll give you sour milk in your tea. That's what they say. They say even Moira's own mother doesn't go near them, Moira and her gran.

The funny thing is, I've seen them walk away together, away from school towards the wrong end of town, Moira and her gran, and they look quite happy. More than happy. Watch them from a distance and it looks as if there are two old women, instead of just the one. Both with carrier bags, both rumbling along the pavement towards home and a cup of tea. A perfect pair.

LUNCHTIME and Hilary is sniffing the air. Something fishy and fried. And chips naturally.

'Come on,' she says, trying not to sound too urgent, and careful not to include Lydia.

To which I reply, 'You'll have to go without us. We've got Greek, haven't we, Lyd?'

And behind us, Lydia sits up, blushing a little. It was that *Lyd*, so familiar sounding, so friendly. Hilary hears it too, and visibly flinches.

'Are you ready?' This is me addressing Lydia again. And not so much as a glance at Hilary. We have a lesson to attend, and everyone knows Miss Jamieson hates to be kept waiting.

You can feel Hilary watching us as we walk away, sense the disbelief following on behind. Just for fun, I slip my hand under Lydia's arm, schoolgirl fashion, so there could be no doubting it; Lydia and I are the very best of friends. Lydia naturally looks a mite surprised, and scans the floor, blushing more than ever.

A moment later, though, we've turned a corner and are out of sight. I can have my hand back. Hilary can't see us any more.

IN the time it takes for Miss Jamieson to arrive, Lydia insists on keeping herself busy, emptying out her pencil case, changing the cartridges in her pen, arranging two small furry animals on the front of her desk. She's as bad as Hilary, who needs a herd of soft toys just to get through a lesson.

'You're looking forward to this,' I say to her—and yes, I'll admit it. There *was* a touch of surprise leaking into my voice. Then again, it's not every day you meet someone all fired up at the thought of doing Greek.

Lydia swallows, tries to be a little more discreet. Already she's learning from Hilary's mistakes. It doesn't do to give too much away. You're anybody's then. People can do what they like with you. But it's no good, the seconds tick by, and the smile just creeps back to where it was.

All I can say is, I wish I was looking forward to it.

What's more, there's that same question growing in my mind. About Lydia. Why feel the need to do to Greek? Hilary I could understand. She put up her hand because I had put up my hand, because of all those books she reads. But Lydia, what reason has she got?

Sometimes, even a person who has *It* occasionally has to ask a question, just like anybody else.

'What's he like then?'

'Who?' Lydia looks at me, blinking.

'Your dad, of course.' Good grief, who did she think I meant?

'My father?' And just listen to the surprise in her voice. You'd swear her father was the last person she was thinking of. Which makes you wonder; *what sort of home life does she have?*

'Your father,' I repeat. 'Is he the reason you put your hand up to do Greek? Does he . . . does he expect things. Of you, I mean?'

The way mine does.

But now something has happened. Lydia's frowning. At the same time she begins fiddling furiously with the nib of her pen, stabbing ink into her finger. 'My father . . .' she says again. Then she makes the biggest effort she's made since she came to school. 'My father doesn't expect anything. He doesn't care what I do. He's much too busy.'

No more to be said.

So that's the answer. Lydia's father has more important things to think about. In fact, Lydia and Greek are the very last things on his mind.

Lydia is doing Greek for herself. She really is odd. Question answered. Still, it seems a shame to leave it there.

'You have a sister, don't you? I saw her. Pretty little thing.'

'Yes,' she says. And that's it; the last bit of jigsaw slips into place. In one little word, everything you would need to know about Lydia, her father and her sister. Lydia is clear as daylight after all.

And is it any surprise? If you were a father, who would you prefer to think about? Poor, stringy, brainy Lydia—or that curly dancing kid I saw on the pavement?

Makes me glad I'm an only child. That way, you get all the attention. No end of it. You never have to feel invisible. Unlike Lydia.

Except. Except . . . oh and here's a thought to conjure with suddenly; what if I hadn't been the one and only? What if there would have been someone else for him to watch? Someone else to take his mind off me?

Someone else to make mistakes?

So odd, what a single thought can do, one tiny germ of an idea, suddenly making your brain tingle. One moment sensible, and the next imagining all sorts of impossible things—such as what it would be like not to be the one and only. To be invisible. Because attention shared would be attention halved. . . .

But then, almost before the idea is planted, it gets nipped in the bud. Lydia has grown perfectly still. This time she has heard it before I have, the sound of footsteps beating down the corridor.

MISS JAMIESON stops in front of our two desks, looks down at us. Together we make a triangle, the isosceles kind. Come to think of it, that's Greek, isn't it?

She's going to give us a talk first, is prepared, drawing breath even as I speak. She did the same thing when we were beginning Latin, delivered a great long speech about the Romans. About the buildings they left behind, the amphitheatres and the viaducts. Stuff you'd know already—unless you were Moira MacMurray, in which case it would have floated right over your head. I had to repeat it to Dad, just so he could be happy for once. Sometimes they teach us the right things. Things he can approve of.

Only let's hope this speech isn't going to be about those gods and goddesses. He doesn't like any of that Pagan stuff, not at all. That's not what he learned Greek for.

But it turns out that I didn't have to worry—at least not about heathens and such. It turns out that Miss Jamieson doesn't seem to want to say a thing about the gods or even the goddesses.

'The Greeks,' she says instead, and draws another breath, 'are dying.'

Well that was an odd thing to say for a start. Makes you won-der if you've heard her right. The Greeks aren't dying, even Hilary could tell her that. They are already dead. Dead as the dinosaurs you could say.

But just as I'm trying to catch Lydia's eye, Miss Jamieson goes and says it again.

'The Greeks are dying.

'Their thoughts, their words, their history—in short everything that reminds us that, despite the passage of the years, they were never so very different from ourselves—are passing away. And why? Because Greek itself is dying, that remarkable language which came to contain every original thought known to Man. People don't learn it any more. They say it is difficult, or worse, irrelevant. They say we don't need it now, not in this day and age.'

She turned and reached for a chair, brought it right to the edge of Lydia's desk and sat, changing the shape of what had been an equal triangle.

'But, believe me, they are wrong. Because people who have no knowledge of the Greeks are like people with amnesia, who have forgotten everything that happened before today. People who don't know the Greeks are like children who have never known their parents.' She leaned on the desk, bending towards us, towards Lydia. As a matter of fact, almost every word she has spo-ken so far has been addressed to Lydia.

'Think about it. Imagine yourself as you are, but without

any memory of your parents, of the people who taught you your first words, who loved you, who showed you how to see the world. Imagine that you know nothing about them. Every word, every thought you have reflects them, but you can't remember them. You don't even know what they looked like. And so here you are. You see, but how do you know if you are seeing with your parents' eyes—or your own? You think, but how would you know if the thoughts are their thoughts, or your thoughts? In short, how could you ever explain yourself to yourself? You would be an enigma, a perfect mystery. And yet that is what I mean. The Greeks help explain us to ourselves.'

At this Lydia laughed aloud. It was a soft, bobbing kind of laugh. It's the thought of being an enigma. Poor Pipe-cleaner Girl would like nothing more.

But I don't laugh. Miss Jamieson is talking as if it was in everybody's power to know themselves, and anyone could tell her it's not possible. There's only one Person who's made you who you are. One Person who knows you. Miss Jamieson should remember to read her Bible more. Or come to the Service and have it explained.

And now there's something else to worry about. How am I going to repeat all this to *him*? To Dad, I mean. This is not the sort of thing he wants me to learn.

Sometimes you have to know when to call a halt. Lydia for instance is sitting there, positively half-baked, ready to believe everything she's being told. And it's going to get worse, you can tell. Miss Jamieson is just getting into her stride.

Something had to be done, and I know *he* would agree with me. Only what? Actually it's not a problem, because no-one is looking at me. Miss Jamieson is all caught up with Lydia, pleased to have someone lap up every word. I can reach across, draw the compass out of my pencil case, pass it from one hand to the other under the desk. . . .

. . . And ever so gently, nudge it into Lydia's side.

A moment later she squeals, piglet-like, almost leaps out of her seat. Miss Jamieson stops mid-sentence, taken by surprise. Lydia sits very still then, hardly knowing where to look.

'Lydia?' It is as if Miss Jamieson has been woken out of some happy dream—of uncalled-for mysteries and enigmas, probably. She's not going to like this, being interrupted in the middle of her stride.

The only question is now, will Lydia betray what just took place, point her finger at me? But no. She must have read the same books as Hilary in the dim and distant past, before she got onto French verbs and rocket science. Instead, she mumbles something about an inexplicable pain in her stomach. Miss Jamieson looks disbelieving, but there's nothing she can do.

And so she turns to me, infinitely suspicious.

But I haven't done a thing, have I? No more than put the lesson on the right track.

Because now Lydia's attention has wandered and Miss Jamieson has lost much of her concentration. She starts again, trying to talk about the ideas some of these Greeks seem to have tossed around but presently she gives up. Goes on to talk about the Olympic Games instead. And that's much better, just the sort of thing I'll be able to repeat to Dad.

THE moment Miss Jamieson left the room, Lydia turned on me. 'Why ever did you stick that *thing* into me?'

Gosh, little Miss Fierce she was all of a sudden.

'Oh well,' I say. 'Oh *well*. I didn't realise you couldn't take a joke. Golly, I mean *golly*, Hilary would have laughed and laughed. She's *fun* that way. I should have stuck with Hilary.'

Lydia looks at me then. Watch her eyes behind their specs. She's fast, faster than Hilary. You don't have to spell things out word by word, which is something in her favour. Already she's thinking about the consequences of not being able to take a joke. Of Hilary and me having fun, just the two of us. Leaving Lydia with what?

With Moira MacMurray, who else.

I wait, patiently, because Patience is my middle name, and don't say another word.

And then it comes. She shuts her eyes and then opens them. The spark has disappeared. Finally, she manages a smile—of sorts. Part of her lip has become snagged on a claw of her brace. 'Ha,' she says, and the word seems halfway to choking her. 'Ha ha ha. You're right. What a joke, hahaha.'

Which means, when Hilary finds us, on our way to our own late lunch, we are laughing like drains, like people who have never had so much fun. As if Greek was the best fun lesson in the world.

Later, before Hilary has time to ask about the lesson, I say, 'How about me coming back to your house this afternoon, Hills?'

It's a Wednesday. Dad hardly ever picks me up on Wednesdays. And he likes it when I go to Hilary's.

Hilary's face glows, the brightest she's looked all day. 'Of course you can, Kate. Of course.'

Then her face clouds over as she tries to remember if this is the day her mother has arranged extra piano. But it's not, of course. I know the days of Hilary's week even if she doesn't. Her face clears. 'Of course you can,' she repeats, louder this time.

'Great,' I say, and punch her arm in friendly fashion, the way they do in those books of hers. 'Oh, *and* Lydia,' I add. 'We can't leave Lydia out.'

Lydia lifts her head, surprised. Flustered, she manages another smile, while Hilary scowls.

'COME away in, my dears,' says Hilary's mother. 'Come straight in.'

It's what she says every time, but just try putting it to the test. She's worried about our feet. Hilary's mother has cream carpets running through her house, and lives in fear of what might be brought through the door. Imagine her face then when Lydia, not realising that some invitations aren't to be taken at their word, clumps straight into the hall—*and doesn't stop to take off her shoes.*

Mrs. Cross swallows once then twice, but doesn't say a word. She can't. It's never been necessary before. It's up to me to save the day.

'Hey, Lydia. Take your shoes off.'

There, simple. Lydia turns, momentarily surprised, then without another word, nods and shakes off her shoes. Mrs. Cross throws me a glance of eternal gratitude. And that's good, isn't it. There's nothing so useful as gratitude.

Hilary takes us upstairs. She is proud of her bedroom. She has flounces on her counterpane and window, and even more of them round her dressing table. Pink carpet, pink cushions. It ruins it really, having frogs everywhere, frogs in all shapes and sizes. Hilary will tell you she collects them. But that's only because I give them to her, every birthday and Christmas, making it official; Hilary collects frogs.

She nods to Lydia to go and sit on her dressing table stool. Meanwhile she and I collapse on the floor, yards away. No doubt who is being left out.

A moment later, her mother appears with a tray of weak orange squash in unspillable cups. Tells us there are biscuits if we want them, but we have to come to the kitchen table to eat them. The carpet, you see. Always the carpet.

None of us moves though, not even Hilary. She waits till her mother disappears, then turns to me, 'Well, go on. Tell me all about it. Was it terrible? Did Miss Jamieson stand over you with a whip? Have you got loads of work?'

I open my mouth as if to let it all flood out, every precious detail that would bring her right into the picture. Then close it again. And sigh.

'I don't know, Hilary. I just don't know if it's the sort of thing we ought to talk about it. What do you think, Lyd?'

I've turned to look across at Lydia, who is sitting, clutching the sides of Hilary's stool as if in danger of falling off. We've kept her at such a distance, I don't think she's heard a word we've said. Now, though, her head shoots up. It was that *Lyd* again, so . . . friendly.

But not knowing what we're talking about she can't think of anything to say, so it's up to me to carry on. 'You see, Hilary, I think Greek is going to be sort of private. Something just between the two of us—Lydia and me. I mean, we don't keep asking you about your piano lessons, do we? Not that we'd want to, mind.' I give a little laugh to remind us that we've all got a sense of humour, even Lydia, if she would only work at it.

Meanwhile Hilary just stares at me, then goes bright red. She is seeing the way it's going to be from now on, and there's no saying what the shock might do to her. To be honest, she looks as if she might be about to have a fit.

And that's just what her mother thinks, too. Because it is at this very moment that she walks into the room to collect the cups. She takes one look at Hilary, who appears to be having difficulty breathing, and almost faints with horror. Next thing we know, Hilary is in bed and Lydia and I are being bundled out of the house.

But really it doesn't matter. Beside the pavement a familiar car is waiting, with the window wound right down. I never said I was coming to Hilary's but he always seems to know where I am. It's like having someone locked into your mind. Something no-one else has—least of all Lydia, whose father doesn't care.

He has noticed Lydia of course, and has leaned his head out of the window with a view to having a chat. He hasn't seen her before today, so naturally he'll be interested. But then something very peculiar happens. Lydia glances at the car, and of course, its occupant, then looks away.

And that's it. She didn't even change her expression. After that one quick glance, she mumbles a goodbye to me then plods off along the road, weighed down by a great big satchel that looks heavier than she is. Yet she must have seen him, my dad, smiling out of the window at her, ready to give her all the time in the world. How could she not have seen him?

It's shocking, how self-centred some people can be. Hilary now, she would have given her right arm just for a glimpse of him. But Lydia, she wasn't interested, didn't give him a second thought, as if he wasn't there, as if he was just anyone. She took one look and she walked away.

It's the shock that keeps me watching her, trudging along, shoulders bent, pipe cleaner legs getting thinner and thinner. Then I hear a sound beside me. It's the window being wound up, so fast it meets the top with a small thump. Which reminds me, I should have been getting into the car.

It's going to be harder this evening, finding the right thing to say. She's turned everything upside down, has Lydia, walking away like that. Not giving him the time of day. Acting as if he was nobody. Nobody at all.

Even before I climb into the car, the bad leg begins to ache, the way it does at times like this, as if to remind me of other times when everything's gone wrong. But it's important not to limp or do anything to show. Do nothing, say nothing to remind. Less than perfect, remember. Less perfect than ever now. He'll think it's my fault. My fault that she didn't notice him, my fault that she didn't say a word. Two days she's been at school and I haven't said a word about him. Not to Lydia.

And no good telling him that the reason I didn't mention him was because she didn't ask. That she wasn't interested. That she's just one of those people who can only think about herself.

In other words, not my fault at all.

✍ Chapter Three

THEN AGAIN, THERE NEVER WAS anyone like my Dad for surprises. Surprising me.

It must have been something that's different about Lydia, something about her walking past. Even before he's started the car, he's begun asking questions, *and not one of them is about me.* Instead, he wants to know who she is, where she's from, why I haven't mentioned her before.

In short, he wanted to know all about her.

But it was when I told him about Greek, how she had actually volunteered, that something deeper took place. Suddenly he was so quiet it was impossible to tell if he was glad or upset. *Then* I told him how her father had had nothing to do with it. How he didn't care what she did. Which is when I went quiet too, so he'd see that I could see it, the enormity of it. A child whose father didn't care what his daughter did. A father who looked the other way.

But even then the silence didn't last; a moment later he's started up again, one question after the other, so in the end, there's only the obvious question left unasked. The one question I couldn't answer.

How she could have walked away, and never given him a second glance.

But he never did ask. Something unexpected has happened. My dad, he never forgets to show an interest. It's the secret of his success, the reason Hilary and the old ladies fall for him. He's convinced them that they're special, something that couldn't be further from the truth. And he does it without even having to try.

But Lydia is different. Lydia has made him stop and think, and not even Miss Jamieson has ever done that. (He found his own way round *her*, didn't he, fingering her weak spot, bringing up the Greek.)

But now there's Lydia, and it's not the same. The interest is real. And suddenly here, in the car, on the way home, something has eased if only for a moment. There's been a shift. Like having a beam of light that should be trained on Kate Carr suddenly change direction, putting the focus on someone else, leaving me . . .

. . . Invisible.

I don't know that this has ever happened before. And of course it doesn't last, it can't last. But it makes you wonder. What would happen if they were ever to meet properly, Lydia and my dad? Who would he focus on then?

NEXT day, they are at it again, Hilary and Lydia, both expecting to sit next to me. Or to put it another way, neither of them wanting to sit next to Moira.

Well I solved that one. *I* went to sit next to Moira.

I'd been meaning to anyway. Some things have to be done occasionally, and one of them is reminding myself to sit next to Moira, just to show I can.

Now that might sound as if I had some kind of difficulty with sitting next to Moira, as if there was a problem. And the fact is, nothing could be farther from the truth. No, the only problem with sitting next to Moira is that she smells. A kind of vegetable odour, like the fug which collects at the bottom of a bag of potatoes. Damp, musty. Fleshy. That's the one problem with Moira.

That, and the sheer size of her.

And even the size isn't a problem, not in itself. Handsome is as handsome does, Dad says. And friends with that kind of handicap are almost the best friends to have. Gratitude again. Show a bit of interest and people can't believe their luck. I mean, you should see the shape of some of the folk who turn up at the Service. You'll never catch them turning their back on Dad.

So you'd think Moira would show a bit of gratitude, but it doesn't happen. So *then* you find yourself wondering if she even knows there is a problem—or if maybe, just possibly, her gran's been telling her that she's fine, perfect just the way she is.

No, if there was a difficulty with sitting next to Moira, it wouldn't be the size of her. It would have to be the stillness. God surely never made any of us to be that still, as if time and motion had got lost in all that flesh. That's the stillness of Moira. Something not quite awake—but not properly asleep either. Something you can't quite ignore in case . . .

. . . Well, just in case.

It doesn't bother me, though. Nothing about Moira bothers me. Not even the way she stares.

Moira stares at me all the time.

I keep expecting somebody to notice, the way she never takes her eyes off me. But nobody ever does. Notice, I mean. That's because nobody ever looks at Moira. It never seems to occur to them; I've watched people's eyes slip over her as if she was part of the furniture. And *that* is why no-one has ever noticed. While no-one is looking at Moira, she is looking at me.

Watching me with eyes that have no centre to them, like tablets on the point of dissolving.

But, so what if she wants to stare? It doesn't bother me. Not one little bit. And just to show how much it doesn't bother me, I'll remember to go and sit next to her now and then. Cosy up to that bulk and stillness and faint smell of vegetables. She can stare until the cows come home, until she's seen what she's waiting to see. But it won't mean a thing. It simply doesn't bother me.

And that's why, when I plump myself down next to Moira and she turns to me with that slow, dissolving beam of hers, I give her just the brightest smile you could imagine. No-one could fail to get to the message. Kate Carr couldn't give a fig for Moira and her stare.

Meanwhile, Hilary and Lydia think I'm just wonderful sacrificing myself like this. But they had better make the most of it. After break I'm going back to my own seat, and then I'll decide which of them sits next to Moira.

I think it will have to be Hilary. She's bigger, takes up more space—much better built to get in the way of Moira and her eyes.

THEN it's lunchtime again and we have to go for our Greek lesson with Miss Jamieson. Lydia is almost quivering with anticipation. She's told me about her homework. The entire Greek alphabet memorised, and a few dozen words as well.

Let's hope she can work hard enough for both of us. After the commotion she caused last night, it was bedtime when I finally got to look at the alphabet. And even then there was no peace. Sometimes things just seem to conspire against you, stopping you doing the things you should, feeling the way you ought.

In other words, I had the dream again. The one I keep thinking will go away. After all, surely no-one was meant to dream the same dream, time and time again. That's not what people go to sleep for.

It's hardly worth talking about really. But I'll mention it now, just this once, just in passing, even if it does make me like Hilary, who does it constantly, insisting on describing every dream she's ever had. Mostly to do with sitting exams, or playing music on a piano that won't keep still.

Never the same dream though. I asked her once, and the silly girl just gave a me a funny look, as if she didn't understand the question.

My dream then. I'm small and lighter than a feather. But my father is a giant, holding me to his chest as he strides through a house where the walls are threatening to fall in upon us. Yet nothing touches us. And as he walks, he shines, lit up by the brightest of lights that glows on me as well, so both of us are brilliant, dazzling, with pure light flickering up around us.

So much light, and his arms around me, it should feel like heaven. But it never seems that way. And maybe, that's the worst of it. Knowing I should be thankful, and feeling—nothing.

Is it any wonder then, when Dad comes to wake me in the usual way, I've forgotten every word I'd tried to learn? After a dream like that it's hard work remembering who *I* am, let alone a few Greek letters.

LAST two periods of the day, and we troop outside into the cold for P.E. Not that it is any concern of mine. No-one could expect me to run around a netball court with a leg that won't do what it's told. I get to sit on the sidelines and pretend to keep score.

Who would want to play ball at our age anyway? Fiona McPherson and Jackie Milne apparently. It must be the stupidity of it that makes me stare the way I do, sitting here next to the fence, watching them so hard that something goes wrong with my eyes and I seem to be seeing them in slow motion. When they run, it is as if they are dancing, long legs kicking patterns in the air, while the ball appears to hang by a thread from the ends of their fingers. Feet that do as they are told. Watching them, the leg that's wrong begins to throb. And even then I can't look away.

Only today it's different. Moira has been told to play.

Miss Botham must have put her foot down, and dismissed that stuff from Moira's gran, about her having asthma, and being too frail to play. Moira, *frail!!!* I'd bet Miss Botham is regretting it now, though. Moira is standing there in the middle of everyone, like a piece of furniture someone has dragged onto court; something massive—like a double wardrobe say—getting in the way, stopping everything.

And that's without mentioning Lydia, on court for her first ever game of netball. She's standing there, miles apart from everybody else, yet impossible to ignore. Her arms and legs are pulsing as if her braces were receiving invisible signals and transmitting them to every nerve in her body. She has all the fingers and toes a person could wish for, but can she use them? Don't ask.

But the funniest thing of all is Miss Botham herself. She must believe so deeply in the benefits of Sport. You see, even though it's impossible for someone in my position ever to play, she'd like to have me on the court. I can tell from the way she looks at me every now and then—as though she has temporarily forgotten the ball and Moira and Lydia and everything. Some days, like today, Miss Botham can't seem to take her eyes off me.

Especially when I give her that certain smile, the one I keep just for her. The one that makes her look flustered and turn quickly away.

AFTER school, Hilary is showered, dried, dressed and standing next to me before certain others have even got their gym shoes off. The black stuff blobbed around her eyes is mascara her mother doesn't know she owns. It's Service in the City night, and again Dad won't be picking me up. I'll be catching a bus from Aberdour Street Station, and as usual, Hilary will be coming to keep me company. In fact, I'd go so far as to say that coming to the bus station is the very highlight of her week.

It may even be mine. We can walk out of school at the same time as everybody else. There's no need to stand out, not tonight. No-one is watching. The next best thing to being invisible.

As for the other stuff—what happens at that busy place, the bus station, week in, week out—that's just practise, a way of reminding oneself exactly what it means to have It.

NEXT morning though, the impossible has happened. Lydia is even less of a pretty sight than usual.

Her specs are sitting all lopsided on her face, and one of the panes of glass is cracked. Hilary snorts and whispers what it was she had seen in the changing rooms last night. Lydia had been on her knees in the showers, fumbling in all the steam for her lost spectacles while everybody else had stood by and screamed with laughter. Incredible that Hilary hadn't stayed to see the end of that. But then, she does so love the bus station.

Lydia must have found her specs—but just look at them now. And just look at her. The living, breathing picture of misery. All because of a pair of glasses.

Or is there something else? When I slip a hand through her arm, and whisper *Time for Greek* in her ear, she doesn't stir. Doesn't even seem to hear. She just continues to stare into the distance, fascinated, for all I know, by a world divided into two unequal halves by that crack running through the glass.

But as Dad says, there's nothing worse than folk who don't listen, so I naturally I try again.

'Lydia, what*ever*'s eating you?'

And finally she deigns to pay attention. 'Nothing,' she says, though sulky with it. 'Nothing's eating me.'

So I just look at her.

Sure enough, a moment later it comes pouring out: 'It's my parents. They've said they have to go away next week, to Venice. There's a conference. Daddy wasn't going to go, but he changed his mind when they kept calling. They said it wouldn't be the same without him.'

'What do they want him for?'

This is Hilary butting in, too nosy for her own good. You wouldn't have caught me asking. My dad gets invited to conferences all the time. Good grief, he was in Scarborough only last week.

Trust Lydia to have a reply ready, though, as if it mattered. 'Trompetto. They want him to talk about Trompetto.'

It's a surprise she can get the word out, with all that metal in her mouth. And look, she's lost Hilary.

'Tromp-*who*?'

'He's a painter, goofball,' I tell her. 'Fancy not knowing that.'

It has to be said, though, I wouldn't have known myself, not in the normal way. We don't hold with pictures in our house. It's the Catholics who like that sort of stuff, Jesus and Mary and all, trying to make out it's always Christmas. A bad case of the graven images, Dad says. But there's still that picture above the desk in his study, the one I've known since I was a little girl, showing Moses coming down from the mountain to find the Israelites worshipping false gods. That's by him, this Trompetto person. It's got his name on it. So you see, I know all about him. Yet no-one has asked me to go to Venice to give a talk.

But hark at Lydia. 'My father knows more about Trompetto than anyone in the whole world.'

Suddenly, there's no mistaking the note in her voice. Pride. One of the Seven Deadly Sins.

'So what's the problem?'

Lydia's face, lit up a moment ago, becomes decently miserable again. 'I've got to go and stay with our Aunty Jane. All the way down to Carlisle.'

So there we have it. Her parents are getting rid of her—if just for a while. And who could blame them? If it's charm you're after, Lydia's always going to be the one that's left behind, the first person out of the balloon. The one no-one would miss.

Still, you have to look on the bright side, even if it's for her sake.

'It can't be that bad,' I say. And it's true. She'd miss school *and* she wouldn't be in Scotland, the country where she can't open her mouth without sounding like an alien.

But Lydia's not having it. 'It is, it is that bad. I mean, *Laura* loves it, but that's because she's young. She doesn't mind the cats or Aunty Jane fussing. She doesn't even care about Aunty Jane's friends. In fact *she* likes them. They give her fifty pences and tell her she's wonderful.'

Silly of me. I'd forgotten Laura. Then again, clever Laura, knowing the value of old ladies. Cleverer than her big sister, that's for sure. Listen to her now, still going on, complaining about the smell, the draughts and tinned macaroni cheese. As if these were the worst things ever.

A proper moaning Minnie, that's what she was being.

Then suddenly, out of the blue, a voice cuts in, stopping her saying another word.

'If it's that bad, then why don't you come and stay in the boarding house?'

It's Fiona McPherson, appeared from nowhere, cool as a cucumber, a copy of *Just Seventeen* folded under one arm. She must have been listening to every word. But on whose say so? I give her one of my special looks, the sort that would chop the legs out from under Hilary. The kind of look that has no effect whatsoever on Fiona.

Instead she's having an effect of her own.

'What?' says Lydia in a voice gone all faint. 'What did you say?'

Fiona gives a smile, the sort anyone else would have to practise in front of a mirror five times a night. Chilly, but with just the correct touch of warmth—*if* you were the right person. 'I said you could always get your parents to let you board for a while, here at the school. People do it. You could sleep in our dorm.'

She raises an eyebrow (plucked, you can tell) and pauses, waiting for a reply. But Lydia is speechless. Fiona smiles, even more coolly and, as a final gesture, places that copy of *Just Seventeen* on Lydia's desk. 'Have this' she says, *so* casual. 'It's this week's. And ask your parents about the boarding.'

Then she was gone—leaving Hilary and Lydia to stare at the magazine as if it was a gift from high.

'Well,' I say, brisk as anything. 'Well, *really* . . . '

But this is bad. Because neither of them seems to have heard me. Hilary reaches out a hand, touches the magazine, then withdraws it, remembering it wasn't meant for her.

'Lydia,' she says, all breathy. 'Oh Lydia, would you . . ?'

It's those books she will keep reading, having their effect.

Midnight feasts and talking far into the the night. All girls together, having fun. Best of all, getting to sit with the boarders over by the window day in, day out.

And Lydia? She doesn't even answer. She's too busy staring at *Just Seventeen*, eyes dreamy behind the broken panes, a tiny smile on her lips. Golly, it's like a disease, and she's got it worse than Hilary. You can see it would be no good saying anything to her now. You might as well try talking to the wall.

I think we may have lost her. And she was turning out to have so much potential. Attention shared might have been attention halved. Now Dad will never get his chance to meet her, and I'll never see them together. It will just be just the two of us, as it has always been. I'll be his one and only for ever.

Unless.

Unless I do something about it.

🐝 Chapter Four

A PHONE CALL, THAT'S ALL it took.

Monday morning, and Lydia is back to normal. No more far-away looks, no more secret smiles aimed at the window, just as if she was safely there already, one of the gang. A single telephone call and Lydia is herself again, one of us, where she belongs.

But does she appreciate it? Saved from her Aunty Jane, saved from having to sleep among strangers—who wouldn't want her anyway—and does she appreciate it?

The moment she walks into the cloakroom, you can see the way it is. Barely able to raise a smile. And after all I've done for her. She's still thinking about those midnight feasts and chats and a place by the window. Things that just aren't going to happen now.

But I don't hold it against her, not yet anyway. Instead I punch her in friendly fashion and say, 'Isn't it just the best? You coming home with me every night. Can you imagine the fun we're going to have?'

Behind us a familiar figure looms, the shape of a duffle coat approaching. I need to raise my voice now, just a little. 'Poor old Hilary. She's going to be *so* jealous.'

Hilary stops dead in the cloakroom doorway, tenses up, sniffing trouble.

'What?' she says. 'What am I going to be jealous about?'

Time for a sideways glance at Lydia. Surely she won't be able to resist. All she has to do is imagine the look on Hilary's face when she tells her.

But Lydia doesn't say a word. I don't think she was even listening. The silly girl still has no idea of how lucky she is. Almost the luckiest girl in the world.

UPSTAIRS, in the classroom, Fiona McPherson rests one hand lightly on Lydia's desk. 'Well, did you talk to your parents?' Smiling because she thinks she knows the answer.

And Lydia freezes. Poor thing, I have to do the talking for her. 'Lydia won't be coming to the boarding house. She's made other arrangements. She's coming to stay with me. My father has sorted it all out.'

It's worth everything just to see the look on Fiona's face. Or it would have been. In fact, Fiona didn't bat an eyelid. She never does. That's her secret. She just shrugged and carried on to join the others by the window. Lydia stared after her, but Fiona never looked back, and why should she? Lydia has made her choice.

Or rather her parents have. Dad says they were so surprised to hear she had made a friend, they didn't even think they had to ask her.

Lydia is coming to stay with us.

ALL the same, it's important for Lydia to see how lucky she is—and show it. So everybody can look at her and know.

In the end, nothing could be simpler. It starts in French. Hilary is sitting right next to me, so when I pass along the note, naturally she thinks it is for her. She's wrong of course; it is addressed to Lydia. She hands it on, pretends to concentrate on her book. But it's no use because I have another note for her to pass after that, then another, and another, till they are coming at her thick and fast. And right beneath Mrs. Chatto's nose, which takes some doing.

Before long, even Lydia has caught the spirit of the thing. Who could resist messages like *hope you don't snore* and *if your feet smell, you're not coming*? It's a taste of things to come, fun only we can share. And if even that isn't enough, all she has to do is look at Hilary, see how it feels to be left out.

By the end of the lesson, it seems Lydia has come full circle. I reckon she'd be heart broken now if she couldn't come. Mission accomplished, you might say.

BUT it goes to show. You can't take anything for granted. Not even a creature like Lydia.

We are sitting in Greek when Miss Jamieson decides to rock the boat.

'Kate, I've not heard you open your mouth in a long time. Not asleep, are we?'

This was rich, coming from someone who from the very first lesson has behaved as if Lydia was the only person worth talking to.

Instead of answering then, I just stared at her.

Which in this case simply makes things worse. Jamieson's eyebrows plunge into a downward swoop, always a bad sign. 'Kate Carr, I want to hear the verbs you've been learning over this weekend.'

Again, I just stared at her. What was there to say? I didn't know any verbs. Greek's turning out to be more difficult than I thought. I need careful, special attention, something to spur me on. The sort of attention Dad expected I would receive. The sort of attention Lydia is getting all the time. He's being cheated.

But the silence is having its effect. Miss Jamieson has started to breathe hard now. I suppose I should be worried. But I'm not. You could compare it to being an expert sailor out on the ocean, bored with flat seas and gentle winds. Hilary is easy, Lydia is easy. Sometimes a person needs a *challenge*. Sometimes it's all she wants.

Then, something happens. Something unexpected. I become aware of Lydia.

Her arm is touching mine, and all down one side, I can feel her body grown tense. More than tense; the girl has actually stopped breathing, as if any movement, any sound could be dangerous. So what's wrong? It's Hilary of course, filling her head with stories about Miss Jamieson, and legends of the Lost Temper. And the people who are never the same again—well, not for several days at least. But why should *Lydia* worry? It's nothing to do with her. This is about me. And Miss Jamieson finally showing the proper attention.

Then it hits me, the reason she's trembling. It isn't herself she's thinking of. Lydia is frightened all right. But not for Lydia. For me.

Not like Hilary then. Hilary would be shivering with delight. She belongs to those audiences who used to fill the Roman amphitheatres Miss Jamieson tells us about, drinking in the sight of other people's blood. The only thing she'd fear would be that, like any storm, Miss Jamieson's temper might suddenly veer uncontrollably in her direction. But Lydia is different. Lydia is behaving like someone who is on my side.

Suddenly I hardly know what to do next. It's the surprise factor, you might say, complicating things.

Back to Miss Jamieson. She is standing very still, hands square on the lid of my desk, fingers splayed, keeping her steady. It's the hands you have to watch. You can see other teachers using up half their temper just throwing their hands around—and anything else they happen to have on them. But not Miss Jamieson. That must be *her* secret; her hands stay still, and nothing gets wasted.

In a way, it's interesting, being forced to notice them, properly, for the first time. Her hands I mean. They are small, but with strong brown fingers. There's a sense in which they don't look like a woman's hands at all. But they don't look like men's either. They just look, well, useful. I bet she puts up her own shelves. Not even Dad can do that.

Something about her hands then. Something that causes me to

lift my head and look at her, straight in the eye. And for the first time ever, smile that certain smile, the one I use for Miss Botham.

'I'm sorry, Miss Jamieson. I haven't learned any verbs. But it won't happen again. I promise.'

The word 'promise' makes my lips come together as if in a promise of their own. I can feel it happening. Something to do with having It.

Miss Jamieson's eyes widen, and for a long second we continue to stare at one another. Then suddenly she is moving backwards, away from the desk, away from me. A moment later she's scrubbing the blackboard as if all our lives depended on it, gathering clouds of chalk in her arms and her clothes, and her hands don't look brown or steady any more.

The storm has blown itself out, just like that.

Beside me though, Lydia is still holding her breath. She doesn't know it's finished, over. Yet I have the strangest urge to whisper in her ear, tell her everything will be all right and not to worry, not for my sake.

And even when the lesson's done, and Miss Jamieson has left the room, I still feel as if there's something I have to say. Something important.

'Look,' I begin. 'Look . . .' And then I have to stop. Well, it's not easy, is it, doing something that makes no sense, not even to yourself. 'Look, you don't absolutely have to come to my house, you know. Not if you don't want to. Not if you would rather go somewhere else.'

Because if she came it would be the beginning of something. Nothing will be the same for Lydia, not after that. Now I'm giving her the chance to stop it, before it's even started.

But look at her, blinking at me. Lydia might know a lot of Greek, but she hasn't an ounce of what I have. She hasn't got It. Give her a Situation, and she'll walk blindly through—and out the other side, never knowing it was there.

So I say it again, different words this time, same meaning.

'What I'm saying is, you don't have to come to my house. You could go to the boarding house instead, if you want. I . . . I won't mind.'

There, clear as daylight now. But even now, she can't seem to think of anything to say. Instead she just looks at me—and begins to blush. Which for some reason—don't ask me why—makes me do the same. Start to blush. Maybe it's because Hilary wouldn't do this, not old Hills-are-alive. Hilary wouldn't make me wait for answer. I even know what Hilary would say. Although the same goes for Lydia. All those messages, remember. All that fun.

Finally, a voice whispers, 'But it's too late. I can't change everything now.'

Meaning she would if she could. Change things.

Oh. Oh, how wrong can you be? She doesn't mind being frightened for me, but give Lydia the smallest chance and she'll be off, still anxious to be one of the gang, a friend of Fiona, with her own seat by the window.

There's nothing like seeing a person in their true colours. I know now what I was trying to do wrong. It's the old mistake I used to make when I was young, thinking I could interfere with the way things are meant to be. Well, I can't. No-one can. And besides, *he's* expecting her. This is the beginning of everything. Lydia Morris is coming to stay with us.

Which is more than she deserves. Despite all her faults and failings, that girl is all set to be the luckiest girl in the world.

ᘺ Chapter Five

WHY SO NERVOUS THOUGH? THIS is the beginning of something and I should be glad.

It's Sunday evening and somebody in Lydia's house phoned to say they were on their way. But that was an hour and a half ago and they should have arrived by now.

That must be the reason I'm nervous. No-one likes to be kept waiting.

I suppose they have got lost. People often lose themselves here. But if they are determined enough, they always manage to find their way. Seek and ye shall find, Dad says. He doesn't mind waiting. He has all the time in the world. The people who want him always seem to find him in the end.

But what if Lydia and her family aren't seeking anyone? What if they have changed their minds?

He gave them final directions over the phone himself. A bend, a dip, and then a church. Our church. He could have told them to look out for cars, too. This is Sunday, remember, and people come from miles, despite the mud, and the twisty lanes, despite having churches of their own, right on their doorsteps, probably.

There are other Services they could come to in the week, but they come today because it's Sunday and because everybody knows he's at his best then, as if all the week has been a build-up to this. Afterwards, in the hall for the Social Hour, there's even more of him to go round than usual. More of the warmth, more of the jokes. No wonder they don't want to go home. They'll hang about by the tea urn long after he's come away, just because it will seem extra specially cold outside, after my father and his warmth.

It's why there'll be cars outside even now—belonging to the fisher folk mostly. They especially like Sunday. They haven't got time to think of their souls during the week, out there, riding the waves miles off Peterhead, and nothing to save them if the weather turns their boats belly up, and the sea swallows them whole, something it seems to do a lot. Especially at this time of the year. No wonder he's popular. They need all the help they can get. They need to know they are already saved, after a fashion.

So if Lydia's father arrives now, the first thing he'll notice is the faint smell of fish hanging in the air. And a lot of rusty old cars. Imagine what he'll think, Lydia's father, I mean.

I know exactly what he'll think. He'll think we are no different from them. And there'll be no way of explaining it so he understands; *we* don't choose *them*. They choose us.

Something to be thankful for then; they've decided to leave in convoy. The last of the cars is pulling away, someone's old banger coughing its way up the lane. They are all old, their cars, older than ours even. It would be nice, for Dad's sake, to see the odd new make, shiny and expensive, just now and then—a sign that he was attracting a better class of person. But it never happens.

And still no sign of headlights from the opposite direction. No light out there at all now, except for the stars, shining hard, and cold, and far away. That's the sort of light I like. Distant and cold. I had the dream again last night, and the light seemed brighter and closer than ever as he carried me through the house. This time, I could feel the heat of it, streaming about us as he walked. Too much light, too much heat—and me like a feather in his arms. A piece of kindling.

Do other people feel as if they could look at the stars forever? So faint and far away.

IT was another three quarters of an hour before they arrived. We were sitting in the kitchen about to have our supper. *She* said he mustn't be made to wait any more. He needed to eat when Nature intended. She can't stand it when anything gets between him and what's meant to be.

So she was about to serve up when there came the knock at the front door. I'd forgotten to tell them, Lydia and her father; the front door is all sealed up—nails to fasten it shut, and tape to block out the draughts. I should have told them to come round the back, despite the time of night and there not being a single lamp to light their way. *She* looks at me, meaning I'll be hearing about this later.

It's my job to hurry round to the front of the house—and there they are, just visible in the darkness. But something's wrong. Although there seem to be two of them, I'd swear neither of them was a man. Maybe it's not them.

Then a woman's voice calls out, making a ringing sound as it bounces off the frosty granite of our house.

'Hello, is someone there?'

It must be Lydia's mother. Silly of me. I never thought of her. Somehow I always thought her dad would be bringing her.

Then comes Lydia's voice. 'Is that you, Kate?' She sounds almost tearful, as if the dark is too much for her.

'Course it's me, goofball.' Notice the lilt in my voice. Lydia's mum—who is still a surprise to me—will hear it, and know what to expect as a result, even in the dark. Someone friendly, someone normal. Not like Lydia at all.

'Is there . . . is there someone else with you?' I feel as if I have to ask. You never know, her dad might be in the shadows, watching, biding his time, the way that . . .

The way that mine would.

Her mother answers. 'Someone else . . . ? Oh, I see, Lydia's father. No, he's not with us. He's driving Lydia's little sister down to her aunt. I would think it's taken him almost less time than us.' Now she's pulling up her sleeve to look at her watch, forgetting she won't be able to make out a thing in the dark. Silly woman.

'Twenty to eight,' she says in a shocked voice. 'We've been two solid hours.'

She must have a luminous dial. I never thought of that.

'Shame,' I say, though it's hardly my fault. And I don't say a word about how we've been *waiting* two solid hours. My voice is still nice and bright. 'Follow me.' Then I lead the way round the back. The way they should have come in the first place.

THE back door was closed again, naturally. Opening a door, any door, is no reason to let precious heat escape. At least that's the way *she* sees it.

There's no fast way of doing this. I push the door open, stand aside, praying they will have the sense to enter quickly. Lydia at least I could give a good hard push without anyone noticing, with the result that she practically barrels over the doorstep, tilting into her mother who's in front. It's untidy but it speeds things up nicely. A second later, we are all inside.

But even that isn't fast enough.

'The cold, what are you doing letting in the cold?'

The voice catches them unawares. Lydia jumps, almost clean out of her skin, although it's not so much because of the words, as the panic (and fury) contained in them. And because she can't see where they've come from, not at first. I've said *she* was making supper. Four bubbling saucepans are there on the stove, each one sending a fat plume of steam towards the ceiling to join the thick blanket that is already there, rolling like a thundercloud overhead. Now, having reached critical mass, the whole thing has begun to sink under its own weight, making half the room invisible. Mr. Jones, the physics teacher, should arrange a field trip to our kitchen just to teach about convection.

So it takes a moment for them to make her out, standing by the stove, the reason for the steam, and the rattling of the pans—and Lydia's panic.

It's Gran, of course. My gran, *his* mother. I had brought them in at the very moment she was adding more salt to one of the saucepans, box tilted for the crystals to pour unimpeded. Now she is standing, back bent, but steady as a rock, holding the box while the salt flows like stone from the stone urn of a statue.

No wonder no-one notices me. Gran seems to have turned our guests to stone themselves, like something out of Greek myth. Something to do with the crackjaw, and the furious glare. Everything makes her glare, the world and every mortal thing in it. Lydia's mum can't take her eyes off her—unless it's not so much Gran as the salt she's watching. It's still pouring of course, a slow, constant, fascinating stream that won't stop until Gran decides it's enough.

Don't they use salt in Lydia's house, then?

Still, it gives me a chance to look at her properly, Lydia's mum. She is small and ever so slightly plump, with dark curly hair and brown eyes. And soft. I don't know that I ever saw anything as soft as her, wrapped up in a coat so downy, so warm, she looks as if she's nestling inside it like some rare, prettily feathered bird.

Poor old Lydia then. Next to her mother, head poking out of the top of her duffle coat, she is all elbows and knees and steamed up spectacles. You'd never guess they were related, not for a moment.

And poor old Gran. She doesn't like other women at the best

of times. And here's one of the worst kind, pretty and well dressed—there's no other way to describe it—standing right in the middle of her kitchen. No wonder the glare has become a concentrated beam that could burn a hole through paper.

But we can't go on like this, staring at each other. Someone has to say something. I clear my throat. Mrs. Morris gives a little start.

'Goodness me, I'm sorry. I think we may have arrived at a bad time.' Gran merely grunts. Mrs. Morris falters. 'I . . . I'm afraid we got ourselves so dreadfully lost. We used a map, when it's obvious now we should have just followed your directions. Poor Lyddie, so clever at everything, yet all at sea when she tries to navigate.'

Lydia opens her mouth as if to protest, then closes it again abruptly. And she's right. Her mother isn't criticising her. No-one criticises anyone in that tone of voice. It's as soft as it can be, just like the rest of her. And if you wanted further proof that no criticism is intended, there's this; suddenly Mrs. Morris turns and touches her daughter's ear. 'Lyddie love, you and I. We're a terrible pair aren't we?'

And it's a shock; the gentleness. And the words that went with it. Telling everyone they were *a pair*. Not even trying to hide that they were connected. Suddenly you find yourself thinking the virtually impossible: maybe Lydia's mother *loves* her.

Well. You can't blame me for being surprised. Every day, Lydia has come to school wearing the same old look. Of someone unwanted, unloved. The one no-one would miss. That's the impression she gives, the reason she's so *easy*. And now here's her mother touching her ear and telling the world they are a matching pair.

No-one's ever fooled me like that. No-one. It's enough to make a person start doubting that she has *It*, suspecting her own judgement.

But now will someone explain Lydia to me? Her mother strokes her ear and Lydia just stands there. Worse, she begins to scowl, shrugging off the touch, pretending the only thing that matters is wiping the steam off her glasses.

Mrs. Morris sighs. Then she glances at me. 'So you're Kate.' And tries to smile.

She's not happy. But it's not because of Lydia. You only have to watch them to see she's used to her. It's Gran, who even now hasn't put away the glare—or said a word.

Still, I can put that right. A smile can make up for anything, even Gran. A special one this time, warm and bright as could possibly be—and as different from her sulky daughter as she would ever see. Smile then.

But for some reason, I get it wrong. It's too much. I smile and Mrs. Morris blinks, as if I had taken a torch and beamed it unexpectedly in her face. There's a noticeable pause.

'Well, it's lovely that Lydia has managed to make such a good friend and so quickly. I'm sure she's going to have a lot of fun.'

The words are all right, but what about her eyes and the way they are drifting over Lydia and beyond, avoiding Gran, avoiding me for that matter? She's taking in the kitchen instead, with all its steam and general damp; the sodden drawers that refuse to close, and tongues of lino peeling off the floor as if to lick the walls.

All at once, *It* comes into play and I know exactly what she's thinking. She's asking herself if she really wants to leave her daughter here, if she shouldn't just walk out and take her beloved Lydia with her, and never mind the upset. In fact, it's *going* to happen, I can tell. Everything is about to go terribly wrong. And there will be only one person left to take the blame. Me.

But thankfully, someone is here to put a stop to all that. Someone they haven't even realised is present, watching, listening to everything. It's the steam of course, clouds of it, getting in the way, keeping him from view. And not even a sound to let them know he's here.

Then again, there's no-one as quiet as Dad when he wants to be.

But finally, as they always would, the clouds part, and a voice booms clear through all the awkwardness and doubt, sending shreds of steam scurrying uselessly into the far corners where they belong.

'No need to look so serious, missus. This little girl is in for the time of her life.'

This time, it's not just Lydia who jumps. Watching their faces, eyes suddenly wider than you would have thought possible, you could believe they were mother and daughter after all. Surprise seems to have brought out the similarities in them.

'Take it from me. A few days here, and you won't know our Lydia. Isn't that right, love?'

He winks at Lydia, puts out his hand towards her mother. 'Carr,' he says. 'Keith Carr at your service.'

It's the way he always introduces himself. The same words as lots of people use. But Dad is different because Dad means them. It must be the reason that, as he takes Mrs. Morris's hand in his, she changes colour, ever so faintly. At the same time, his eyes lock onto hers, and that's the moment when you know she's lost.

Blue where you would expect them to be brown, the centres of my dad's eyes are ringed with a light all of their own. It's the light that shocks people, light where it's least expected, the same light that allows him to fix another person's gaze and hold it, as if he will never let it go. Promising the earth while the world dissolves around them. And all in a single stare. No there's not a soul alive with eyes like my dad.

Now he's looking at Lydia's mother, and here we are again, watching the same old miracle, the miracle of someone falling, never to be the same again.

Or are we? She returns the gaze for a moment, then quietly, without a word, takes her hand out of his. Even more surprising, having freed herself, she takes one, two steps back to look at him, up and down, as if she needs the distance between them in order to make up her mind.

I don't understand it. She's not behaving the way she ought. She's not falling. Oh, there's the faintest suggestion of feathers shivering, a hint of ruffling, but no falling.

And Dad, what about him? Oddly enough, he doesn't seem in the least put out. If anything, his smile grows that little bit wider as if to bridge the gap she's put between them. Not just wider, but warmer. You can feel the heat from him, reaching out to her, ready to wrap itself around her . . .

. . . And she just takes another step back, pulling her coat around her, as if all she could feel was cold.

Maybe it's the look of him, putting her off somehow. But she should remember; don't judge a book by a cover. He may not be tall, but show me a tall man with an ounce of his presence, or a thin man with anything like the power that comes with bulk. Not that he's fat. My dad would never let himself grow fat, because what would that say about him? But he fills a room, this room, as easily as he fills the tweed jacket he always likes to wear. That's what she should be impressed by, if nothing else. The way this room is full of him.

But then, she *is* impressed, isn't she? Why else would she have to force herself to smile the way she's doing now? It takes a moment to understand, but then it becomes as clear as daylight. It's really quite simple. She may be impressed, but she doesn't like him. Lydia's mother doesn't like my dad. Not one little bit.

So it's no surprise to see her hand stretching out to Lydia. No surprise either to see the words already forming on her lips. You can see what she has in mind, something she thinks is going to be, not exactly easy perhaps, but possible. In which case it's going to come as a shock, to Mrs. Morris, when finally she gets round to noticing Lydia.

It was the wink of his that did it. That's all it took. One eye deliberately closing. Because you know what it told Lydia, that single wink. It showed her that he would turn a blind eye. That when he looked at her, he would close his mind to the fact that she was small and ugly, and of absolutely no consequence, which is all that anyone else noticed in her.

Now look at her as a result. Eyes lit up, cheeks pink, Lydia is transfigured. Why, she's almost pretty. That's more like it. That's what we're used to.

Then at last, Mrs. Morris does catch sight of her, and it's almost comical. 'Lydia,' she murmurs. 'Lyddie love.'

But she'll have to do better than that. Lydia hasn't even heard her.

'Darling . . .' Mrs. Morris tries again. That faint colour in her own cheeks is deepening rapidly to a becoming pink, prettier even than her daughter's. 'Darling, I know this is absurd—but I've been thinking how very upset Aunty Jane is going to be, about you going somewhere else to stay. I don't know if she'll ever get over it. But it isn't too late, and I'm sure Mr. Carr and everyone would understand if . . .'

If . . . what? If she dragged her daughter away from us now, after it's been arranged? I don't think Lydia will be going any-where, not this time. Dad has put his arm around Lydia's shoul-ders. She's shrinking into the space he's made for her, growing small enough to put into his pocket if he so minded. As for her mother, I don't believe Lydia has listened to a word she's said even now.

In fact no-one has. Not so it counts. Dad's talking to Lydia.

At least, she *thinks* he's talking to her, but it's her mother he wants to hear him. So she knows how it's going to be. He's caught Lydia round the waist, tickling her a little so she wriggles and giggles, though not too much. 'What's this?' he's saying. 'There's nothing of you, Lyddie-love. What do they feed you on at home? String beans? We'll have to do something about that, won't we, Mother? Fatten the old kid up a little.'

Here he winks at Gran, who stands unsmiling. She has picked up the ladle with one hand and has a saucepan lid in the other, in readiness, Mrs. Morris or no Mrs. Morris. She looks as if she could batter someone as easily as feed them.

All the same she's ready to do exactly as he says. We all are, Lydia included. Especially Lydia.

So you see, there's nothing for Lydia's mother to do now but go. She brought her daughter here, and now she's going to have to leave her. It's what everyone wants. Even Gran. It only took *her* a moment to understand that Lydia was no threat. No-one was going to miss any meals because of Lydia.

'Lydia,' Mrs. Morris tries one last time, emphasising the full breadth of her daughter's name—for others to take note, no doubt. She hadn't reckoned on my Dad, picking up on that '*Lyddie*' the way he did.

But all she wins by it is a brief colliding of heads as Lydia allows herself to be kissed goodbye. A moment later Mrs. Morris has found herself standing by the door, probably wondering how she got there. Still she hangs on, though, refusing to leave, hoping that Lydia will change her mind.

But it doesn't happen. Instead, my father sends Mrs. Morris another one of his special smiles, the sort that could pacify nations, and send old ladies fluttering like pigeons back to their own homes. But, for one of those strange reasons that I can't fathom, it has no effect on her. Mrs. Morris doesn't move. In the end it has to be Lydia, suddenly looking across at her from under his arm and frowning, mouthing that one little word.

Go.

So what can she do except just that?

What's more, she'll probably end up lost again. She doesn't even have Lydia now to help look for signs. Lydia is staying with us.

❧ Chapter Six

NOW IT'S JUST THE FOUR of us, the way it was meant to be, the way it would appear to someone on the outside—a mother, say—stealing a glance through the window, to see what has happened to the daughter she has given up.

We know exactly how it would look on the outside. Dad and me, it's a knack we both have—of knowing—a God-given talent you might say.

But now here's Gran, elbowing her way between us with a steaming saucepan which she bangs upon the table with a thump. But even then, wonderful things continue to happen—wonderful if you were Lydia. Dad leads her to a chair and, with infinite pains, sits her down, right next to him—where normally I would sit. And still Lydia can't take her eyes off him, watching from behind the dazed sheen of her spectacles as if afraid he might disappear.

It's the attention of course, going to her head, putting her in a spin. Don't they pay her any attention at home, then? This morning, I'd have said, of course not. But I'm not sure now.

Unless it's Laura, always getting more, no matter what Lydia does. Curly little Laura who will never need braces, the apple of her daddy's eye.

Well there's no question of Lydia having to share the attention here. Dad hasn't so much as looked at me in fifteen minutes. He's been busy, naturally. But it's the strangest feeling in the world. It's like . . . it's like being invisible.

Is this what Lydia complains about at home? Having people look away, forget she's there? If that's the case, then all I can say is silly Lyddie, stupid old Lyddie-love.

And that's when I catch Gran's eye. I'm not invisible after all. There's always Gran, isn't there? Gran and her nose, forever sniffing in my direction. Gran is there to keep an eye on me. Gran never forgets. She's his mother, so she's bound to have talents, too.

But for once I'm not doing a thing wrong. There'll be nothing for her to report. She won't even be able to say I was jealous, watching the two of them, Lydia and him, getting on like a house on fire. She's talking nineteen to the dozen about Greek, and *he's* making her a promise that one day soon they will go to his study, just the two of them, and read Greek together. The New Testament to be exact. The very thing he had in mind for me.

Oh, this is better than I ever dreamed. Gran may be watching me, but *he's* not. Lydia's there, taking up all his time, chattering away about Greek verbs, about Miss Jamieson, about the books she likes to read. Books you would never catch me reading. In the meantime, Gran has turned off the gas, and the steam clouds are vanishing like mist on a summer's day. Lydia must feel as if she's sitting in purest sunshine. Everybody's happy. Even him.

But then, all good things have to come to an end. Slowly his head turns, and the light that's bathed us all fades—just a little. Suddenly I know what's coming.

'Kate love. I've never heard you talk about Greek once, not even once.'

See? I was right. But no need to panic. There's a correct answer to everything. All I have to do is take a moment to think.

But then, before I know what's happening, there's Lydia, suddenly answering for me. 'Oh, I don't believe Kate likes Greek, Mr. Carr. I think she'd rather be doing something quite different.'

What? *What*? Doesn't she realise what she's just said? Apparently not. She's smiling at me, thinking everything is the same as it was five seconds ago. She doesn't know. She can't see Dad's eyes, for a start. And if she could, she wouldn't understand. All she'll see is the smile. But I know. While Lydia beams, the light in Dad's eyes is telling me that we will be talking about this later, when we're by ourselves. He thinks that I've forgotten what's expected, that I have to be reminded. His daughter, you see.

He doesn't even have to use words. Dad and me, we're that close.

And it's all her fault, Lydia's that is. So you won't catch me feeling sorry for what happens next. In the gap she's made in the conversation, Lydia decides it must be time to eat. She scoops up a forkful of Gran's dinner and pops it in her mouth. And then it happens. Her face changes, as it must when her tongue shrivels and the salt seeps into her cheeks. The only sound is what comes from the back of her throat, tiny, like a bat's squeak.

'Something the matter, love?' says Dad. He has begun to frown. Ingratitude, the worst sin. Then he gives an exclamation, and hits his forehead with the ball of his hand. The frown has disappeared.

'Of course, Lydia love. What a girl you are. And too polite to say a word.'

'What is it, Keith?' Already Gran is halfway to her feet, all that skin and bone bunched for action. If it's something to do with her food, then she would gather up every bit and throw it away without another word. Start over again. That's the way she is. Not for anyone else though. Only for him, only for Dad.

'The Blessing, Mother. I clean forgot the Blessing. And here's young Lydia, reminding me.'

And he grins at Lydia who, still shaken, uncomprehending, does her best to smile back. The food stays sitting in her cheeks, scorching her.

And even now she doesn't understand, even when he closes his eyes and clasps his hands together. I have to push her head down for her. Show a bit of respect.

'Dear Father, bless this food which you have set before us. . . .' At this point, Gran mutters into her fists, as she always does '. . . Bless the people who eat of it. And Father . . . ' here he stops '. . . Bless the new child in our midst. Help us to love her and keep her as one of our own. Help her to love us and become part of your Family of Love.'

And with the Amen, he raises his head—and winks at Lydia, one last time. But look, he's done it again, caused Lydia to stare back at him, incapable of speech. Surely nothing compares to this, not if you're Lydia. No-one has ever prayed for her before, you can tell. I don't suppose God gets so much as a mention in her house, not from one week's end to the next.

The consequence is, there's not a peep out of her after that, not about Greek or anything. Cheeks burning, she concentrates on swallowing Gran's food instead. After all, she's seen us doing it. Maybe knowing it has been blessed makes all the difference.

And now that Lydia's been sorted, it's all clear for Dad. You see, he was just being kind, allowing Lydia to have her say, letting her think she had something to contribute. But now it's his turn. It always is, in the end. Maybe that's why Miss Jamieson and he don't get on. She's used to holding the floor herself, isn't she, so certain she has something to say. About the Greeks and such. And then along comes Dad to make her see; some people have more important things the world will have to hear.

It's what Lydia thinks anyhow. If she was all ears for Miss Jamieson, it's nothing compared to the way she is now. I reckon that if you waited until it was all over, and then asked her what he'd said, she would be able to repeat it, every sentence, word for word.

Or would she?

Because here's something I only started to notice very recently.

The way that Dad talks. Lately, when I've tried to remember what it is he's actually said, there's . . . nothing. Simply nothing. Dad talks, yet it's only his face I remember, and the sound of his voice. And I can't help thinking I'm not the only one. Stand in church and look around you. Do folk actually remember what he's said? Do they? They reel out at the end as if they're drunk. As if they would find it hard to remember their own names, let alone what he's taken the trouble to tell them.

Maybe it's just as well, because it's not all good news, is it? He preaches the Bible, in other words, what is true, and the Bible doesn't say anything about us being put in this world to be happy. Or in the next world either, come to that. Not unless you're Chosen.

Maybe somebody should write it down for them. Jesus had the same problem, when you think about it. Someone had to write it all up for others to digest. People wouldn't have remembered a word He said otherwise. A case of the messenger outshining the message.

So, no reason to think any the less of him. Of either of them. What's more, Dad has a secret weapon. Dad tells the best jokes in the world. No fear of anyone forgetting those. If you want proof, just look at Lydia now. Laughing? The girl is practically falling off her chair. It's all a revelation to her. I don't suppose anyone's taught her to see the joke in being a nun, or a fat lady, or a foreigner. Until now.

No, there's no-one like my Dad to make people see the funny side. Unless you've heard the jokes before, more times than you can remember. Then it can be difficult, laughing the way you should.

And now Lydia may be about to learn something else. Suddenly, the jokes stop. Dad gets to his feet. 'Well, ladies, time to be getting on. Old Keith Carr has work to do.'

'Work, Mr. Carr?' Lydia looks startled, and steals a look at the clock.

Does that mean he's going to explain to her then, about Time and Tide, how it waits for no man? How God's work needs no clocks, because it is never done? No, there's no time. I've just sneaked a glance at the clock myself. It's twenty-seven minutes past eight, only a few seconds to go . . .

. . . And there it is, the sound of the telephone. Bang on time. It never misses. Yet even now, Lydia stares up at him, eyes full of hope, as if she half expects him to ignore it. But of course it's not going to happen. That's what she is going to learn tonight. Some things are always going to take precedence.

'Duty calls,' says Dad, with a sigh. Yet Lydia must see that he's tired just from the way he walks, from the table to the door, closing it behind him. It's twenty-eight minutes past eight, the time Duty always calls, every single evening without fail.

So what's left for her? Only Gran and me. Lydia turns her eyes from the door and gives a little start. You'd swear she was seeing us both for the first time.

'Kate,' she says. '*Kate?*'

Good grief, next she'll be asking me what she's doing here. Blinking and confused as if it's only now that she's waking up from a dream.

Fortunately, Gran's having none of it, starts snatching at saucepans and glaring at us to do the same. A moment later, Lydia finds herself holding a tea towel, damp even before it has touched a plate. And no-one says a word. You'd think we were worn out with talking. And maybe we are, in a manner of speaking.

Just the same, right in the middle of it all, of the wiping and scraping, and the sound of Gran tutting and mumbling, Lydia stops what she is doing and looks at me. Her mouth is open, as if something shocking has just occurred to her.

'Kate?' she says. 'What's wrong with me? I completely forgot to ask. Where on earth is your mother?'

Beside me comes the sound of old bones snapping. Gran, who until now has been bent over the sink, has sprung back into shape, suddenly straight as a young girl. Even Lydia notices and glances at her nervously.

Yet you'd think Gran would be used to it. People are always going to ask. It's only Dad, driving everything else out of their head, that stops them. Then they remember, and notice that something—*someone*—is missing. And that's when they speak up. So why does it have to be my fault when they do?

Better still, why couldn't Lydia have asked me while we were at school, where there is no Gran, listening to every word I say so she can pass it on. Something else she can tell him I've done wrong. You can see why there's the temptation to say nothing, pretend I didn't hear.

But I can't keep them waiting. Not Gran. Not Lydia even. So out it comes, the same old answer.

'Gone.'

The wrong answer. Gran glares and shakes her head. Because there is no right answer.

And now it's Lydia causing problems. 'Gone?' she says. 'Gone?' she says again. Then something unexpected happens. That little voice of hers suddenly raises itself up into a wail that sounds, well, grief-stricken. 'Oh, Kate, poor Kate. Your mother died, and I never even knew. I'm so sorry.'

For a moment all I can do is stare at her. There are tears—real tears—starting in her eyes. And that's what is so shocking. She must be thinking about her own mother suddenly, and imagining.

It's an effort to find the words to put her back on track. 'Not dead, goofball, just . . . I don't know.'

And it's true. I don't know. I don't know anything. Only that's not what I should have said, not with Gran listening. We don't talk about her, we don't even think about her, my mother. That's the rule, the one that is never broken. Yet Lydia has shaken me, because she thinks the worst and is sorry about it. Sorry for me.

You can see how she would get me all muddled, cause me to forget the rules. When people ask, the thing to do is look sad and turn away. But don't say anything, not a word, because even the mention of her. . . .

But still the words come out. Anything to stop Lydia crying. 'She left us, you see. When I was very young . . .'

Gran begins to growl. But she can't say anything. And maybe even she is shocked, at the sight of someone so ready to cry.

'Now she could be . . .'

Anywhere. She could be anywhere. And there I stop. Someone had to get a grip.

Lydia blinks. For some reason she looks down. It's my leg. She is looking at my leg. And it's then I feel the blood come rushing into my face. Is *that* what she's thinking? A daughter with a leg like mine, no wonder she left. No wonder she couldn't bear to stay, my mother. Is that what Lydia's thinking?

And I thought she was a friend.

It makes me want to tell her. I wasn't born like this. I was perfect until it happened, until my leg was hurt. I was like anybody else. Better even. And what is a leg anyway? Someone should remind her of what I've got. A father who loves me. Which is more than she has. Even though I'm less than perfect, less than I should have been, he thinks the world of me. Can she say that about hers? Still lucky, then. The luckiest girl alive.

Actually, I don't have to say anything. She's clammed right up. There'll be no more questions from Lydia. She can't go talking about mothers now. Or about one mother in particular, the one who stole away and left her own child behind, left her damaged beyond repair. She can't ask about what kind of mother would do that. Or why. Or where she is now. That's not a question anyone can ask.

Not even me.

IT'S time Lydia was in bed. No more questions of any sort.

In the passage, though, I see her start to shiver. It's our house of course. Nobody had thought to warn her about the rest of the house. Cold. Darker than dark.

Well, everybody knows that ministers don't earn much. Men like him don't preach the Word of God for money. And they earn even less if they don't actually belong to the Church any more.

It's been a journey, he says, moving through the body of the Kirk to where he is now. Other ministers, the ones who were so high up, they didn't like him because he preached the truth, and because his congregations were bigger than theirs, leaving empty pews all over the place. They wanted him to change his tune but he wouldn't. Now he has his own church and they say that the numbers in the Church of Scotland are falling every week. Well, we know why. We know where they end up.

But the truth is, it's not a question of money, the reason the house is dark. And cold. Or that we have linoleum on the floor and tape around the windows. It's a reminder, he says. We pass from life into death the way we pass from room to room. Cold rooms help us to understand, just as the dark helps us to understand. Unless we are chosen, we will pass from the light and warmth of the world into the dark that comes after, and nothing will change it. And that's what the cold does, and the dark. They remind us.

Maybe that's why Gran can't stand the cold.

In the meantime, I should warn Lydia, about the noise she's making. She doesn't have to bump into things, bouncing off walls, pretending it's even darker than it is. All she has to do is stop shivering and start thinking about where she's going and she'll get along fine. We're right outside the study now. His study. This is where we have to be most careful.

So why does she have to trip and fall just here? Maybe she meant to. I wouldn't put it past her.

Because now look what she's done. There's a silence then the study door bursts open, and here he is, surrounded by light pouring out around him. Now, suddenly, thanks to that golden light, we can see.

But Lydia hasn't noticed. 'Oh, Mr. Carr,' breathes Lydia. At the sight of him, she has begun to glow herself, ever so faintly. But though she gets a smile, there's nothing more for her. Not tonight. It's me he wants.

So he winks at Lydia. 'Up to bed with you, little lass. Old Keith Carr needs a word with his one and only.'

She sighs, but naturally she does as she is told, carries on along the corridor, around the pillar at the bottom of the stairs. But there, suddenly, she stops. You can see her problem. She's frightened, having to climb strange stairs in an old cold house, alone.

Then Dad smiles and everything is all right again. 'Now up you go, Lyddie my love. Nothing to be frightened of in this house. You'll never sleep in a safer place.'

And of course, she believes him. A flash of her braces and she's off again, skipping up the stairs as if every step was bathed in light, and every tread was clothed in soft thick wool. As if there was nothing to worry about at all.

And when we hear the bedroom door close behind her, Dad nods me into his study, where Gran is already waiting. Silly Lyddie, stupid Lyddie if she thinks that lessons stop at school.

❧ Chapter Seven

THE TASTE OF CHOCOLATE IS still in my mouth when I come to bed, coating my tongue, trickling down my throat when I swallow. If I can swallow.

Gran gets chocolate too, every time, although she won't have done anything except watch. Chocolate is the reward for a lesson well learned, but it's a reminder too, the reason she gets some, a taste of things to come. After the bitterness, the sweetness. A taste of heaven.

Rather like his room, with its warmth, and its carpet, its picture by Trompetto, showing the Golden Calf and the dancing girls, and Moses glowing with discontent; and the faint smell of polish and the record player with all the music that appeals to him. It's all there when you step into his study. From the dark into the light. From the cold into the warm. His room reminds you that better things are waiting. If you're Chosen.

But it means I have to clean my teeth twice, to get all that taste of heaven out of my mouth. Sometimes I have to clean them three times. And still I can't get rid of it.

Meanwhile Lydia is unconscious, curled up on top of the other bed without even a single blanket over her. She's wearing a bright pink nightie covered in hearts which doesn't suit her at all, *and* she's fallen asleep with her glasses on. The things you see when you don't have a camera! Another time

I'd want to laugh out loud but not tonight. It would hurt if I laughed now.

Another lesson well learned. Where would I be if he didn't care?

Why didn't she get under the covers to sleep? It's freezing in this room. Even in the summer it seems to be cold, and it's definitely not summer now. There's frost forming on the window, on the *inside*.

Actually, I don't have to wonder why she didn't go under. She was waiting for me. All girls together, remember, giggling far into the night. Those messages under Hilary's nose. That's what I promised her. Now she's fallen asleep waiting, with the result that, if I don't do something about it, she'll catch her death of cold. Is it my imagination or is she already faintly blue around the mouth?

But if I wake her, she might ask questions, and how would I explain; about the odour of chocolate on my breath, and the lateness? What sort of difficulties will I be making for myself?

Her bare arm is icy when I touch it.

She wakes up instantly as I shake her, starts shivering uncontrollably. But she climbs under the blankets without too much help, begins talking to someone who isn't there. Something about Laura, she's complaining about Laura. She thinks I'm her mother! I take her glasses off for her and put them beside the bed. Pull the blankets up around her chin.

Silly Lyddie, stupid Lyddie. She didn't have to wait for me. Hilary wouldn't have. Hilary would have been tucked up and snoring long before I got myself up the stairs.

But then, Lydia shouldn't have told him I didn't like Greek. There wouldn't have been any lesson in the first place. And *she* wouldn't have nearly caught her death curled up on the bed, never dreaming she'd have to wait so long. Look at it that way and you can see. It's all her fault.

And still I can't get rid of the taste of chocolate in my mouth. A sweet reminder that refuses to go away.

I suppose I should have warned her. About mornings in this house.

Actually, I don't think a warning would have been enough. It has to come as a shock then, the tramp of feet on the landing, the crash of the door, and above all the sudden explosion of the wireless, a huge box weighed down by knobs that only he could be powerful enough to carry around at shoulder height from room to room.

Waking up to that, you might think the house was falling down around you. You might think the world was coming to an end. If you didn't know better.

Lydia doesn't know. And so wakes with a jolt that lifts her clean out of bed and onto her feet.

'Morning, Lydia love,' he says, and turns down the wireless, but not by much.

Lydia stands, eyes staring blindly without her specs, teeth chattering, knees knocking. Good grief, she looks so *rickety!* As if one more blare of trumpets would blast her off her feet.

But then, incredibly, her lips move. 'W-w-w-' she stammers. Only it sounds like *V-v-v*. Tries again, keeps at it, until: 'W-wagner.' She manages it at last. Then blushes, still blinking, still shocked, but unmistakeably pleased with herself.

But *pleased* is nothing, not compared with Dad. His eyes, full of the morning, fairly blaze with good things. 'Well, Lyddie love. What do you know? Wagner, absolutely right.'

What does she know? Absolutely everything it seems. And that must have been the culprit—Wagner, every morning all these years. Dad seems to have the only wireless that is tuned to nothing else.

But I should have been concentrating more. Dad has turned to me.

'What do you think of that, Kate? Our Lyddie recognises Wagner. And you've never even asked.'

Here Lydia blushes still further and grins. She really does think it's a game, her doing better than me.

Yet I'd tell him if I thought it would help, how I never needed to ask about the music for the simple reason that it's always there. You might as well ask who made the air you breathe.

Now look at him, smiling at Lydia again. But it's me he's thinking about. You can tell just from the way he snaps off the wireless, snaps off the smile, and marches out of the room.

I should have let her freeze in the night. That way she wouldn't have been able to open her mouth in the morning.

GRAN bangs bowls of porridge down on the table, then pretends to ignore us to carry on with the the sausages and bacon she's getting ready for Dad. But she hisses in my ear while she's about it and that's how I know. How it's only half past seven in the morning, but already I've ruined his day.

The only bright spot is Lydia, and watching her with her first spoonful of Gran's porridge. Now she's sitting there, rigid, lips puckered up with salt, incapable of swallowing.

'I-I,' she stammers. 'I 'm sorry, I can't . . . '

What was the name of Lot's wife? The one who should never have looked back?

But she needn't worry. Gran doesn't care. The sausages are nearly ready. All she's worried about now is that they'll be too brown when he comes downstairs, not quite the way he likes them.

IN the car, Dad knocks a tape into the ancient cassette player. Music blasts—Wagner again—guaranteed to shake the rust off our poor old car. You wouldn't think anyone could drive like that, with music bursting out of his ears. But Dad can, straight into the sun. He's making sure I don't forget next time. That if anyone asks, I'll be the one who answers. Wagner, every time.

And Lydia, she thinks it's wonderful, driving into the rising sun with a full orchestra for accompaniment.

LATER she watches the car pull away. Only when it has completely disappeared does she turn to me. 'Kate,' she says on a ragged breath. 'Oh, Kate!' We walk into school and she never stops talking about him, how wonderful he is, how lucky I am. As if I didn't already know.

She was still at it when we arrived in the cloakroom. Hilary, who was busy hanging up her duffle coat and had her back to us, stiffened. I'll say this for her, however, she turned round almost straightaway, to give a fairly good impression of a smile. 'Having a nice time, then?'

And it's almost touching, the look of surprise and delight when, as Lydia turns to hang up her coat, I grab Hilary's arm. By the time Lydia has turned back again, we've already fled the cloakroom and are racing along the corridor.

But even then, it doesn't sink in, not with Lydia. A moment later we hear her, calling out happily that we have to slow down, that we are leaving her behind. Which of course, just makes us go faster still. By the time she arrives at the classroom, Hilary and I are already sitting at our desks.

'Hey,' says Lydia huffing and puffing, on the very edge of being upset. 'Hey.'

But we are busy, aren't we? Hilary and I have things to discuss, things that no-one else is allowed to hear. There's no room for her today, not with us. She'll have to go and sit next to Moira MacMurray.

And discuss Wagner with her.

You'd think she'd have got the message then, but you'd be wrong. It was almost sad, the first few hours, the way she kept watching us, expecting that any moment it was all going to change, that we were going to have time for her.

But by lunchtime, even she can tell it's not going to happen. Hilary and I have better things to do. And anyway, she has Moira. If it's attention she wants, she can try getting it from her.

Oh, but almost I forgot. Moira, as usual, is busy. Moira is watching me, the way she always does. As if she has nothing else to do. As if it is the only reason she is here. One day, that girl's eyes are going to fall right out of her head from staring too much.

'Oh, Kate, whatever's the matter with you?' This is Hilary talking, and there's a strange look on her face. It must be because I've gone very still suddenly.

Because it's a horrible thought, the idea of Moira's eyes, falling out from all that staring. Now I have a vision of them on the desk, rolling around like two fat marbles, free of Moira, and still watching me.

The thing to do, then, is to watch Lydia, just to take my mind off things, the way you watch kittens at play, to pass the time. Lydia's easy. Half a day at school and she's so miserable she's almost forgotten about him. Now she just wishes she was going home—to her home, that is.

That's the benefit in having It. People are more transparent than plate glass windows. You can watch them to your heart's content. See every little thing that's going on behind.

At the end of the afternoon, when the bell goes, she doesn't know what to do with herself. Hilary and I are busier than ever. Hilary is making me promise to phone her tonight as soon as we get home, and I'm agreeing, naturally. And naturally I'll do no such thing. You have to leave the phone free in our house. Otherwise how would people ever get through when they want him? I mean the needy, the ones who know they can't do without him.

Anyway, Lydia can see it's no use and starts to make her own way outside—at the exact moment that every other person in the school does the same. Yet haven't I said already? That's the way to become invisible. One little ant among five hundred. And this time the effect is instantaneous. I never saw a person disappear so fast. Even the other girls can't see her, jostling past her as if she wasn't there.

In fact, it's impressive, how very invisible Lydia has become. Just inside the school gate, Mrs. Chatto ploughs right into her and draws back startled. *Gracious, child, I never even saw you* . . . Then carries on as if it never happened. Ask her later and I bet she'll have no memory of ever meeting Lydia there, let alone nearly grinding the poor girl into the school gravel.

But help is at hand. Just as Lydia steps out onto the pavement, a car door opens. Lydia judders to a halt. Watching her from a distance, the shape of her, skinny arms, skinny legs flailing, is like watching the letters of the alphabet, spelling out a series of words. Surprise, disbelief, realisation. And finally, relief.

It's Dad in the car. It will be coming back to her, everything she's forgotten.

A moment later, I'm right there beside her. Well, we don't want him thinking I haven't been taking care of her. And then it's smiles and hugs all round. Yet only for the three of us. Hilary has to stay where she is. Wait until she's invited to step into the magic circle.

But it doesn't happen. Even though she's standing not three

feet away, Dad is acting as if he doesn't see her. Hilary might as well not be there. He is well and truly ignoring her.

I don't know how he does it. Somehow he always knows. He knows about all the work Hilary has put in to today, making sure Lydia is ignored, making Lydia miserable. Now she's getting what she deserves.

And so we leave her, still standing on the pavement, forgotten and not that far away from tears. It's Hilary's turn to disappear. And as if to prove the point, here's Mrs. Chatto again, striding along the same pavement, giving every impression of looking where she's going—and yet a moment later, ploughing straight into *her*, Hilary. Resounding clash of bodies. But read Chatto's lips an instant later. *Gracious, child, I never even saw you . . .*

As we drive off, the music starts up again in the cassette machine, the same as this morning's. Ignoring the traffic, he turns round to look at me. *Well?* he's saying, though not out loud. Dad and me, we don't need words.

I bawl the answer right back at him.

'Wagner.'

And he beams. As a result the car is full of sunshine, even though it's growing dark outside, and the light from people's headlamps as they flash us seems unfriendly and lacking in warmth, as if there wasn't enough road for everybody. It doesn't matter though, because there's all the warmth you could want right here in this car.

Eventually, though, even Lydia begins to notice, the way the other cars keep wanting to flash at us. Which doesn't happen, I bet, when *her* father drives. Her father is probably content just to go with the flow. But then my Dad is different. He drives in accordance with his beliefs; whilst her father, unless

I am very much mistaken, has no beliefs to drive in accordance with.

And talking of beliefs, the interesting thing now is to watch Lydia. You'd almost think it was a test, the way, just occasionally, he glances at her before the brow of a hill or approaching car.

If it is a test, I would say she passes. As we slide into yet another bend, or clip the rim of a kerb, as lightly as an angel might graze your bedroom window with its wing, Lydia doesn't turn a hair. Not even once. She believes in *him*, in my dad.

Who after a while turns round to her and says: 'Lydia love, did you have a good time with our Kate today? Is she looking after you the way she should.?'

Now comes a silence that even the music can't fill. Lydia looks out of the window, at the countryside sinking so quickly into darkness. If she says a wrong word now, the warmth in our car will vanish and it will be colder than if we were outside.

And yet Lydia understands. I believe she actually has been learning. 'She's been wonderful, Mr. Carr. The best friend a girl could ever have.'

Not a word about Hilary or Moira MacMurray, or having to sit by herself, ignored, invisible. As a result, the temperature in the car rises by yet another degree. Dad turns the music down, and begins to tell us about *his* day. About the cups of tea drunk, dogs stroked and problems solved. Lydia listens and knows that thanks to him the world has become a better place. She shakes her head and forgets every minute of her day.

She's a touch unsteady getting out of the car. In fact, she's beginning to remind me of the old ladies at the close of Service, teetering from the threshold, unable to keep a straight line. Dad has gone straight to her head.

Inside the house, the kitchen is dark, the gas rings shut down. No sign of Gran. Fortunately, it never occurs to Lydia to ask where she might be, otherwise I might be tempted to tell her. Blame it on the old ladies, forever bringing tokens of their good-will—chocolates, tins of biscuits, bottles of brown sherry. Generous to a fault, he lets her have the sherry, and that's the last we'll see of her for the day.

Yet he never complains. Perhaps it's because he doesn't have any use for sherry. It's the chocolates he keeps, for the study. He finds a use for the chocolates almost every day. Education, it all comes down to education. Sticks and carrots—isn't that what people say? Bitter and sweet.

But with no Gran, we have to fend for ourselves. Tinned ham, tinned salmon, tinned pears. Lydia, who for some reason had no appetite at lunch time, gobbles everything up as if she has never seen food before. Dad winks and smiles, and promises that she'll get so fat no man will ever want to marry her. He says it won't matter, though, so long as she's quiet with it, because a woman's silence is better than beauty anyway. And she thinks that is funny, the idea of being fat and suitably silent. Oh yes, Lydia just laughs and laughs. Almost chokes on her tinned salmon sandwich.

Twenty-eight minutes past eight, and the telephone rings, catches her by surprise.

'Oh, Mr. Carr, don't go,' she says as he gets up, which you might think was terribly forward of her. But he's made her feel so at home, so happy she never thinks of watching her tongue. Not yet.

It took my breath away, though. The recklessness of it. The idea that she could *order* him to do something else. But my dad, all he does is smile. He's letting her get away with everything. Because she's special, I suppose, and because she's new. And because he doesn't want her running home to her mother, telling all sorts of stories, ruffling feathers he wants to keep smooth.

It's funny that she doesn't ask, though, about the phone calls. *I'd* ask if I were her, if everything about him interested me, the way she's making it out to be. I'd want to know who was on the phone every evening at precisely twenty-eight minutes past eight.

Chapter Eight &

I SAID SHE WAS LEARNING though.

This morning, I watched Lydia's eyes open long before any movement on the landing. That's the trick, isn't it. Be awake before he wakes you. Now she'll have time to prepare, compose herself—and in this case, to smooth all that stringy brown hair into some kind of shape. Lydia is trying to make the best of herself, just for him.

And quite right, too. He says you can tell everything about a female just from the way she wears her hair. Shoulder length is best. Not too long and not too short. Short is what makes him think of Miss Jamieson, not caring what people think. Long is caring too much.

Shoulder length is just right. Like mine. My best feature, he says. Sometimes he strokes it, tells me I should be proud, that a woman's beauty is the one of the greatest gifts God gives to men. My hair is different from his, lighter—honey coloured, according to Hilary, who must have got *that* from a magazine. Different from his, then. Yet it's only lying here now, watching Lydia that I've ever thought about it. Lydia's hair is stringy, but the same colour as her mother's. If my hair is different, it can't have come from him. So where did it come from? Who gave me the colour of my hair?

Did *she* have hair this colour? The person we don't mention?

Don't. Don't ask, don't even let it cross your mind. More

important, don't let it cross *his* mind. Because if I have *her* hair then it would be a reminder, like my leg; only worse, much worse. You can hide the sight of a leg, the damage that's been done. But a head of hair? What can you do with that? You can tell everything about someone by looking at their hair, he says. And what would happen if one day he looked at my hair, looked at me, and saw somebody else instead? What would he . . . ?

It's seven o'clock. The room explodes. But this time it's me that jumps. While Lydia stays calm, I'm the one whose hair is standing up on end, arms, legs flying in all directions. I'm the one in shock.

LATER, at breakfast, Lydia applies herself to Gran's porridge, forces herself to eat every scrap. But it rebounds on her. Later still, in the back of the car, she begins to look distinctly ill. It's the porridge of course, thudding against the walls of her stomach as we veer into the bends, reminding her that she has a way to go before she can become one of us.

But once again, you have to admit she's learning. Outside the school she mumbles something and disappears. The next time I see her it's in the classroom, already slotted in beside Moira, careful not to look at either Hilary or me.

It's just a pity Hilary couldn't take a leaf from her book, try to show a bit of restraint. Hilary was a complete nuisance today. It's gone to her head, thinking she's got me all to herself, as if she hadn't learned a thing from Dad, teaching her a lesson last night. The worst was having to sit next to her in Latin while she fired off notes right under Jamieson's nose, just so Lydia could see them—and know none of them were for her.

It's childish, that sort of thing. And tiring, having to pretend to be enjoying every second of it.

It was a relief to get into Greek—especially as Lydia had done all the homework for both of us. As usual though, Miss Jamieson gives me no credit, not even for a job this well done, and concentrates on Lydia. Maybe she's worried I'm going to smile at her again, the way I did before.

Promises, promises.

But after Greek, it's the same old story. Hilary acting as if she's Queen for the day, and Lydia sitting closer and closer to Moira as though there was comfort to be got there, of all places.

Just before the bell rings, though, I squeeze her arm and smile, to show there are no hard feelings.

But would you believe it, Lydia just sniffed and looked the other way. Yet the car will already be outside. Someone is waiting to hear all about everything, every minute of our day.

What if Lydia has decided not to behave?

And it gets worse. The bell goes but Miss Grumpy never even bothers to wait for me and marches off on her own, straight into the crowd but with a surer line this time. I have to run to keep up with her, just so that we arrive together to make it look the way it should.

'Good day at school, girls?'

Horns blare, lights flash. We are moving out into the traffic.

'Yes,' I cry from the back seat. 'Oh yes.' But Lydia, what is Lydia going to say?

The answer is—nothing. Lydia says precisely nothing. And silence of course is the ultimate give away. He turns around in his seat, ignores the road, ignores everything just to stare at her. 'Lydia?' He says again, eyebrows rising. 'No word from Lydia?'

And still Lydia just keeps quiet, staring out of the window. There's a cold feeling, spreading in the pit of my stomach. Because this is how things go wrong, isn't it? When people suddenly realise they have power.

Stupid of me, stupid. Allowing Hilary to go too far. Allowing Lydia to get cross. Allowing Lydia to get even.

And still she doesn't say a word. Instead we have to listen to it, the sound of silence, telling all sorts of tales. Making sure he thinks the worst. Even the car seems to have grown more quiet as we carry on, waiting for Lydia to say something.

Finally an answer. Lydia breaks the silence. Opens her mouth and says: 'I had a lovely day, Mr. Carr. An absolutely lovely day.'

I have to stop my breath, or else the sigh of relief would be too loud. Dad grins at both of us, then turns back to pay attention to the road, and just in time. A lorry is bearing down on us, horn booming, with the face of the driver flat against the windscreen, mouth wide open.

A flick of the wheel to the left and the lorry disappears behind us. But the danger isn't over yet. Not by a long chalk. The fact is, I started breathing again too soon.

Dad hasn't finished, you see.

'And what did you like best about today?' He has to know everything. He has to feel that he was actually there.

But what is Lydia's reply? Nothing about Greek. Or getting top marks in French spelling. Or having her maths homework held up for everyone to observe. Instead she says, 'Latin, Mr. Carr. Latin was the best thing about today.'

And that means she's lying. Because Latin must have been the very worst thing about today—if you were Lydia. Notes flying and Hilary sniggering. Being left out of everything.

But here she is, carrying on and looking as if she means every word. 'We're doing *Caesar's History of the War*, and it's really interesting, isn't it, Kate?'

Is it? Sometimes I just give up. Half the time Lydia is completely see-through, and half the time you don't what on earth she's up to. Maybe she's telling the truth now. Who knows?

But here comes the real trouble. In the front seat, behind the wheel, Dad is thinking hard. 'What's the famous quotation from that? Something Caesar himself says?'

He's showing that he knows, of course. That he may not have had the education we're having, but he still knows. Everything. The car drifts towards a line of hedges as he wrestles with the problem. Angels alone correct our course. Then he smacks the wheel. 'Got it. *Iacta alea est.*'

Which is when Lydia sits bolt upright in her seat. 'Oh, Mr. Carr, that's *exactly* the bit we did today. *Iacta alea est.* Fancy you remembering that.'

Well, fancy indeed. I don't remember any such thing. Blame Hilary, and her messages, making sure the entire lesson was nothing but a blur. And now look where it leaves us. Dad has remembered me.

'Kate, my love. Haven't heard much from you recently.'

I want to close my eyes. But I can't, because he's got them, caught in his rear view mirror. Suddenly I know what's coming.

'*Iacta alea est,*' he's saying. 'Famous last words, eh?'

'Oh no, Mr. Carr!' This is Lydia. 'Those weren't his last words at all. They . . .'

But he ignores her. This is between us. Father and daughter.

'*Iacta alea est,* Kate. Now tell your old dad what they mean.'

What they mean is another silence. Because I don't know. How could I, when there was Hilary and her messages? You can't be thinking of so many things at once. Something has to get lost. Surely he would understand that. People have to be kept on board. Hilary has to be kept on board. What about Fiona McPherson?

But it's no use. Something has ended up lost and I have nothing to say.

'Ah, Kate. Kate love.' And he sighs, turns his eyes back to the road, as if that was the end of it.

As if.

Then something touches my hand. I look down and Lydia is tickling my wrist with a piece of screwed-up paper. I take it, unscrew it—and read the tiny, neatly printed words. '*Iacta alea est* = the die is cast.' Whatever that means.

The fact is, it doesn't matter what it means. I needed to clear my throat first, but out it comes, as loud as he could wish. '*Iacta alea est*. The die is cast.'

In the front of the car, Dad goes still, then throws up his hands. Once again he's turning round, but this time to smile at me, to catch my knee and squeeze it tight. 'That's my Kate, that's my clever Kate. Knew it all along, didn't you, love?'

And I nod, nod like anything. But when it's over, and the car is back on a straight line, I slip my own hand across the seat to find Lydia's. Snatch it and hold it tight. She looks at me in surprise, but then smiles. Not that she knows. Lydia has no idea what's happened. Which just shows. People can achieve immeasurable good and never even guess what they have done.

When we get out of the car, Dad is still smiling. Puts his arm right around me. I can smell the wool in his tweed jacket, and the ever present scent of something else, something always there. Sweetish. Perfumed.

But inside the house, I grab Lydia's hand again, and together we run past Gran, who stares at us, open mouthed, as we race through her kitchen, into the hall, and upstairs to the bedroom. Lydia is laughing out loud, but with no idea of what she's laughing about. Gran's voice rises to complain about the din, but *he's* not listening to her. *Leave it, Mother.* His voice reaches up the stairs, making sure we can hear him. *There's nothing like the sound of innocent young voices. Good girls are God's gift to all men.* Lydia listens, lips parted, and blushes like the good girl she is.

And the wonderful thing is, he's talking about both of us, Lydia and me in the same breath, using one word to describe two. You

could say that is what Lydia has done. She's made him think double. Made him see double. It's not just me any more. Attention
shared is attention halved.

It's the sort of thing that makes you wish she was staying a
month. No, not a month. A whole year.

SUPPERTIME, and I'd bet Lydia would say exactly the same thing.
She couldn't wish for more. She is sitting next to Dad, she is the
absolute centre of attention. It must feel as if she's turned into
Laura overnight, everybody's favourite girl.

And Dad is being so funny. At first Lydia was shocked when
she heard his impression of Miss Jamieson, all manly and com-
manding. Half a minute later however, and she was laughing, too.

One thing is for sure, she won't be seeing Jamieson in the same
light again.

'Ooh, Mr. Carr,' she says, over and over. 'You should be on the
stage.' But she doesn't realise. That's exactly where he is, every
minute of the day, on the stage.

And it's only just occurred to me, watching him doing his
impression. Dad must have known all along, about Miss
Jamieson, how she's no different from the Games teacher. It
explains why he leaves her alone, never tries to get on the right
side of her. He has all the other teachers blushing like young girls
when he meets them, leaves them all heated and confused. But
that stops with Miss Jamieson. He never even goes near her, not
unless he has to.

That's what it means to have *It*. You know when to leave well
alone. My Dad has *It* in spades. More than me, even.

At eight o'clock precisely, though, he stands up. 'Time for a
stroll down to the church, girls. Someone there's been waiting all
this time to have a word with Old Keith Carr.'

Lydia opens her mouth, and you can guess what she's about to
say. Who could be waiting for him at this time of night, in a

lonely church? Then she sees the light in his eyes, the way his hands lie still in his pockets. She sees the bulk of him, the power of him—and the penny drops. A look of awe comes over her face. It is the idea of God, waiting, hoping against hope that *he'll* turn up, my dad.

But he'll have to hurry. By my reckoning Dad has twenty-seven and a half minutes before the phone goes.

The back door closes and we get on with the dishes. In the middle of it, however, Lydia turns to me. And not just to me, but Gran. It's funny how even now she hasn't noticed the difference between Gran and other old ladies. She thinks she can say anything in front of her, that there's not a jot of harm in her. And all because she's old, like her Aunty Jane who wouldn't hurt a fly.

It's the only thing that could explain how she could have done what she did next, which is to blurt out, suddenly, as if it's been building up and she can't keep it back a moment longer: 'I love it here. Everything's right as it is. You're so happy the three of you. You don't even *need* a mother, Kate.'

And there, it's happened again, that mention of *her*. Now Gran is standing stock still, staring at her, we both are. *Why* can't Lydia understand the rules? Gran is going to have a field day, when he gets back. When they're alone.

My leg aches. Other times, worse than this, not remembered.

But what's this? There's something wrong with Gran suddenly, something changing the shape of her face, making it so you would hardly recognise her. So different from herself that if I'd walked in now, I wouldn't know who she was.

Gran is *smiling*. Looking at Lydia and smiling. And you know why? It's because of Lydia, telling us we're happy, that we don't need anyone else—especially not *her*, the one who went away. We are perfect just the way we are.

And at that very moment, the door opens.

'Oh, Mr. Carr. You're back.'

Then she stops, because even Lydia, *stupid* Lydia, can see that he's not the same man who left us earlier. Slowly he makes his way to the table and sits down, heavily, as if he was exhausted. Doesn't look at us. Lydia sees the weight of him and thinks he's tired, that's all, and this is the reason he continues to sit, his hands bunched into fists, staring at the table. But I know that look, the jutting of the lower jaw. I know when power is concentrated in his hands. I know the sound even, of his breathing grown heavy. This isn't tiredness. This is something far worse.

But still Lydia hasn't understood. 'Oh, Mr. Carr, whatever is the . . .'

But a look from him silences her. Just a single glance. Her mouth falls open, her face a picture of confusion.

Then, without a word, Dad raises one fist from the table. Opens it. From high out of his palm falls a tiny ball of paper which hits the table with a minuscule thud and rolls toward his other hand.

He gives it a poke.

'I found *this* in the car, down behind the front seat.'

And of course we recognise it straightaway, even though the words are invisible. *Iacta alea est.*

'Well?' He says to me, only me. 'What have you got to say. Who wrote this?'

But the only sound is from Gran over by the stove, standing with an old damp tea towel pressed against her mouth. These are the times she lives for, but she's afraid of making too much noise in her excitement, thereby distracting him. She shouldn't worry. He's deaf to her, the way he is blind to her when he so chooses, and he doesn't hear a thing. There's only me here, saying nothing. Dad and me, by ourselves.

Suddenly though, Gran makes a tutting noise. It's then I realise that, for some reason, I'm touching my hair. She'll see it as fiddling, frivolous. I make my hand stay still, but it's too late. Slowly, his eyes move from my face to my head, to the light that must be shining on my hair. Hair the colour of honey, not like his, and his eyes narrow. It is as if he is on the edge of noticing, of seeing something that was hidden from him. Until now.

Then a voice answers. '*I wrote it.*'

The voice belongs to Lydia. Speaking as if she were surprised, as if she thinks there's been nothing more than a small mistake. Not a thing to be upset about.

Silly Lyddie. Stupid Lyddie. She doesn't know. Now she's brought herself into the frame. Now she's not safe, not any more.

But he blinks. His eyes leave my hair and move on, searching, until they find Lydia. A second later, we hear a tiny sound. It came from Lydia, who has just discovered, for the first time in her life, that sometimes it is better to be forgotten, best not to be thought of at all.

She should have done what Hilary would have done. Leave the room, leave me to it, to him. His one and only.

But attention shared is attention halved. Now he's signalling to both of us. We've to sit down and hear what he has to say, Lydia and me, in it together.

He picks up the ball, flattens it, then smoothes his hands on his hanky to wipe away what can only be filth. Stranded, the scrap of paper trembles on the table.

'*Iacta alea est.* The die is cast.' He looks at Lydia. 'You wrote this? Why?'

He knows why, of course. But he wants to hear her say it. That she wrote it because I didn't know, and because she wanted him to think I did. In other words, that we both lied. Cheated and lied to him. He wants to hear her say just that.

But sometimes folk don't always do what you expect. Lydia stirs then sighs, and with the sigh her entire body shivers as if, with that one breath gone, there's nothing left of her. But despite that, she doesn't say a word. Not a single word. And the silence continues, all because of her, Lydia.

It's strange to be watching this. To see it happening to someone else, to see both sides. I can even see his problem. He says that Truth is everything, and until we hold the Truth in our mouths, and pronounce it for all to hear, then we can never be saved. But he can't force the Truth into her mouth. He can't act on Lydia. Lydia has a mother. She would go home and tell her everything.

But this is my father, and there are other ways. He sighs, brings his hand to cover his eyes, and lowers his head.

'I don't know what to say. As God is my witness, I don't know what to say.'

And the bewilderment is clear. How can Good understand Bad? A moment later though he lifts his head from his hands and makes a movement, almost hopeful, towards Lydia. But at the last, he turns away, as if the sight of her is more than he could bear, cries out as if in pain. 'I thought you were a *good* girl.'

And that's all. Because what else is necessary? Look at Lydia now.

Lydia has stopped breathing because of him, because of his disappointment. Yet she should breathe. Lydia should breathe. She should tell him the truth about the note, how she wrote it for me. She could turn all this around. For herself anyway.

But she doesn't say a word. Not a single word.

'Kate?' Dad looks at me. It's a dangerous moment, the one I've been waiting for. But attention shared is attention halved, and the danger is nothing like it could be.

'Kate,' he says again. 'Take . . . take Lydia with you upstairs. And tomorrow . . .' But he can't find it in him to say another word. Besides, he doesn't have to. 'Tomorrow . . .'

'Mr. Carr,' Lydia whispers, interrupting. 'Oh, Mr. Carr, I . . .'

But no matter what she has to say, it's too late, because there goes the phone.

Which is a mite surprising, because even now, I can't seem to stop myself glancing at the clock, and it's only twenty-seven and a half minutes past eight.

But he hasn't noticed the difference. Another sigh and he heaves himself up from the table. And that's when suddenly we see him reel, as if he's lost his sense of balance. He steadies himself, but it shows what we have done to him. Or, to be exact, what Lydia has done to him.

Out in the hall the ringing stops. Not that Lydia cares. She is staring at the table, at the little scrap of paper that started all this. She seems to be in a state of shock, lips moving as if she were reciting a prayer, one that is forbidden to be said out loud.

But then, the unexpected. The door opens and here is Dad again. He looks at Lydia, and says simply, 'It's for you.'

At the same time, he looks at me. Go with her, he's saying. Not in words of course. It must be clear enough by now. We don't need words half the time, Dad and me.

So when at first I don't move, it's not because I haven't understood him. It's because of the shock. Why is Lydia having to take Dad's phone call? Gran has to dig me in the ribs to make me do as I've been told.

In the hall, Lydia has picked up the phone, but even though she has it cradled in both hands, she can't stop it shaking as she brings it to her ear. There's a pause as she listens, then from high in her throat, one little word escapes.

'Daddy!'

It must be a terrible sound to hear, that word, all the way down the other end of the line, across the sea and under the Alps to the farthest side of Italy. One little word. How would they ever know it came from their daughter? Maybe they are not sure even now. It sounded more like a bird than anything else, something fallen out of the nest.

And then of course, she begins to cry. But even this must be better than that one word escaping the way it did. Huge great sobs, but all the better because there's no mistaking who they belong to. Not making an iota of sense, though. Whatever must they be thinking?

The answer is, what ever they think, it's not bad enough. Not unless they remember the sound of that *Daddy*.

But just when I think I'm going to have to put an end to it, take the phone off her, Dad arrives from the kitchen, steps quietly up from behind to touch Lydia lightly on the shoulder. To me, it seems impossible that she will feel it, not with the force of her sobs shaking her entire body.

But I was wrong, the moment he touches her, she whirls around, very nearly drops the phone. But he steadies her, reaches out to brush her cheek—oh so gently—with one hand, then takes the phone away.

After that, it's all him. The words he murmurs into the phone are quiet, but clear enough to carry across the miles, regardless of mountains and seas. After what Lydia has just put them through, they must sound like the still small voice of calm.

And what is he saying?

He's telling them everything is fine. That there's been a misunderstanding. That girls will be girls, but no great damage has been done. That there may be something they might need to discuss with Lydia when they return, something that can only help her. But not to worry. Lydia is in good hands. Lydia is safe.

I'm curious to know exactly who is holding the phone at the other end. I have a feeling it must still be her father. Because of the silence, because no-one is arguing with him, I have a feeling that it cannot be her mother.

But his words have had the desired effect—on Lydia at least. She is staring up at him, listening, eyes damp, spectacles hopelessly steamed up. But she's not crying any more. Soon it's safe to hand the phone back to her.

Not that the conversation is what you could call normal, even now. She sounds wooden, almost surly, telling them everything is fine, that nothing at all is wrong. But then, I don't suppose Lydia has ever been any great shakes on the telephone. The important thing is what comes at the close. She is having difficulty convincing them, you see. Or one of them. I'd say it was her mother talking to her now, not willing to let it lie, going on and on till finally, Lydia says—or rather shouts, 'Look, I'm telling you once and for all, it was all my fault.'

And slams down the phone. Just like that.

Did I say a while ago that she was a fast learner? Maybe that's not putting it strongly enough. If you ask me, Lydia is learning as if she is forgetting everything else she ever knew.

But will it make any difference? Everything is quiet now. Dad is staring down at her, and you know what he is doing; he's wondering whether to give her a second chance, trying to make up his mind, trying to decide what is best. No good attempting to hurry him. And no good trying to hope. We can only wait. Meanwhile, behind us, the kitchen door has opened, and here's Gran. So now we're all here, waiting, and not one of us knowing what is going to happen.

Then suddenly Dad is smiling, beaming at us, filling the hall with such warmth and light it's never seen the like. He opens up his arms.

'Come here, both of you.' And we go to him.

No-one, *no-one*, knows how to hug so well as him. Lydia must feel as if she's been taken up into heaven. Look at her, snuffling happily against his waistcoat, breathing in the same scent of wool and sweetness that I've known for years. It's a moment to savour, something for her to remember for ever.

Still with his arms around us, we are turning to go back to the kitchen, when the phone goes once more. The sound makes Lydia jump, and begin to look anxious all over again. But she doesn't have to worry. It's not for her, not this time. Gran and I, we know exactly who it is, trying again after failing before. Dad looks at us, rolls his eyes, then pulls his arms away to answer it.

But she has a cheek, has Lydia, if I hadn't dragged her away, she would have stopped just where she was, ears flapping, listening in on things that had nothing to do with her.

And still too caught up with herself to think to ask who it is at the other end.

❧ Chapter Nine

SO NOW NOTHING'S QUITE THE way it was. Not for Lydia. You can see it most clearly at school. At school she's in a world of her own, dreaming about what comes after, when we go home. School being nothing more than an interruption.

Tell that to Miss Jamieson. This isn't what she's used to, not from her star pupil. Half way through the lesson and it becomes too much, even for her.

'Lydia Morris,' she booms. 'Will you please sit up straight and listen.'

Lydia jumps, awake again at last, and stares wide-eyed at Miss Jamieson. It's the old frightened-rabbit look we know and love. But then the seconds on the classroom clock tick by and, little by little, a change comes over her. Lydia's mouth begins to quiver, and then her shoulders to shake, something not even her school blazer can conceal. Because, would you believe it, she's *laughing*. Doing her best to hide it, but laughing nonetheless.

You know what's happened of course. It's Dad with his impressions, more like Miss Jamieson than Miss Jamieson herself. Now, thanks to Dad she can't help but see the funny side.

And Miss Jamieson? She purses her lips in annoyance. But also she's confused, maybe even shocked. This isn't the Lydia she knows. And she's right. Because although Lydia settles down, something has changed, never to be the same. She can't stop fidgeting for one thing, completely unable to sit still. Forever shifting in her seat and looking out of the window, looking for something that won't be there for a long time yet. Or someone.

No, this isn't the Lydia we know. She's long gone, I'd say.

It's almost a relief to go down for lunch. We'll have the dinner hall to ourselves and Lydia can day dream to her heart's content. And Miss Jamieson can find a quiet spot and ask herself what's happened to Lydia.

But as it turns out, I'm wrong about having the hall to ourselves. Another person is still there, as late as we are, sitting at a table all by herself, having her lunch. Moira MacMurray looks up as we walk through the door, then carries on eating her Spam fritter.

Lydia stops, then gives herself a little shake—and heads straight for her, pulls up a chair. Perhaps sitting next to Moira has become second nature to her these last few days. But even that doesn't explain why she then chose to sit the way she did, bringing her chair so close she's practically leaning up against her. Watching her, you'd almost think she *likes* sitting next to Moira.

I suppose there might be a reason. If we were on a mountain or a beach, you might even call it natural. Moira would make the world's best windbreak, so huge she would shelter you from anything. But Lydia doesn't need shelter. For goodness sakes, we're in school, in a dining hall. There's only me here. There's nothing to be protected from.

And Moira? She doesn't say a word. It never seems to occur to her that a little conversation at lunch would be desirable, not to say normal. This is probably how they eat at home, Moira and her granny, neither of them saying a word, happy the way they are. Two old ladies content just to sit and eat and stare. The way Moira is staring at me now. . . .

'*Stop* it, will you just stop looking at me!'

Lydia, silly Lydia, jumps. Nearly hits the ceiling. She thinks it's her I'm shouting at. And of course, it's Moira. Who else but Moira?

But maybe she has a point. She wasn't expecting it. *I* wasn't expecting it. The words seemed to shoot out of my mouth of their own accord. Nothing to do with me. Why should *I* shout? Moira can stare all she likes. It's not a problem.

Besides, it hasn't made a blind bit of difference, to the staring. True, Moira's jaws may have stopped moving, just for a second or so. And, did I imagine it, or did Moira blink? The trouble is, Moira doesn't even blink like other people. Moira blinking makes you think of a shutter closing on a camera. Another picture for the collection. Something for the record.

I push my plate away. 'I'm off to find Hilary.'

And that's where Lydia truly lets me down. A proper friend would have been on her feet before the words were out of my mouth. But not Lydia. Lydia didn't move. No-one would believe this, but she was actually *snuggled up* against Moira now. And showing no signs of wanting to budge.

Yet who's meant to be looking after her, me or Moira?

If you ask me, Lydia needs to be taught another lesson.

WHICH brings me to this afternoon, and what happens after school.

Hilary is waiting outside, huffing and puffing with excitement. And fretful with it. Today's the day I catch a bus. In other words, it's the highlight, the very best part of her week, and she's afraid of missing a second of it.

So when we move off, Hilary sets the pace, neck stretched out like a racing camel, picking up speed as she goes. Lydia is left behind from the very start, mostly because no-one had told her. She was expecting the car. Now she can't keep up, not with the pavement full of people and that great satchel of hers wedging her between sections of the crowd.

It would help her if she knew where we were going, but she has no idea. Somehow I never got round to telling her.

She made me wait, you know, at lunchtime. I had to stop

while she sat tight, claiming she wanted to finish off her banana sponge pudding. Making me have to sit another five minutes while Moira . . .

. . . While Moira just did what she always does.

But there's no waiting for Lydia now. She'll have to concentrate, take care not to lose us in the backstreets. Otherwise how will she ever find her way home?

There's no sign of her when we arrive at the arch, the one that leads into the bus station. But then, it would be hard to see anyone in that mob. First there are the girls, the ones who also have to catch the buses, but secondly, and far more importantly, there are the boys. Hilary stops and sighs, the way she always does, overcome by the moment, lifting up her head as if to sniff the air, air that is thick with bodies completely different from our own. She can practically smell them. Browning School Boys.

Not a very nice smell, actually. Too much sweat, too many unchanged underpants, unwashed hair and skin. Boys smell so very different from girls. I'm surprised Hilary seems to like it so much, when you think of all the frills and freshly ironed blouses and even her own bathroom at home. There's no accounting for Hilary. Here she is, more alert than she's been all day, eyes twitching this way and that. She honestly thinks if she keeps looking, she'll catch someone looking at her, one day. But she won't of course. It's me they are looking at.

Oh yes.

It's what they never have understood, Fiona and Jackie and the rest. They know that if they came and stood under the arch in the bus station, the way we are standing now, nobody would give them a second glance. Not if I was there, too. And they simply can't work out why, not with everyone telling them the important thing is to be blond, or nicely developed, or just plain sweet. They don't get it. You don't need to be any of those things. All you need is to have *It*.

Not that I'm interested, in boys, that is, not properly, for their own sake. *He* would have something to say about that. But I'll admit this much. I like Thursdays almost as much as Hilary does. Just to see *It* at work. Proof if I ever needed it.

And here comes Mark, as I always knew he would.

Now there's something for Fiona to think about; Mark, head of the sixth year, head of rugby, head of everything apparently. And *eighteen* years old. You wouldn't think a person his age would be interested, not in someone from the third year. But Mark is. He's so interested he doesn't know what to do with himself. And I'll say this much for him; he smells better than most. Maybe it's the aftershave, covering a multitude of sins.

But what does he see in me? I know the answer, but he doesn't, and that's half his problem. He's been told the same things as Fiona and the rest, about what's important. And he believes it. Which explains why he always looks so shifty when he's with me. He can't even explain himself to himself.

Poor thing, someone should tell him about what it means to have *It*. Maybe he would feel better then, knowing he can't help it. That I have something no-one else has, something he couldn't even name, the only thing he sees in me.

Oh, but I've forgotten, haven't I. There *is* something else he sees in me. He likes my hair. He said so once, said he liked the colour of it. But I hardly paid any attention then. Now, today, it's making me blush. Suddenly thinking about the colour of my hair.

Don't think about it, then. Don't think about *her*. Remember the rule.

But today, I don't even say hello. Something else has cropped up. It's Lydia of course. She's made it to the station, but she has-n't seen us. Instead she's carried on, past our group—straight into a crowd of boys playing football with somebody's duffle bag. Next thing she's getting jostled right and left, yet they haven't even noticed she's in the way. That's Lydia again. Invisible.

Now if I were to walk into that crowd, there'd be a silence. Complete absence of play. No more jostling. It's what I would do for her now—if she were the right kind of friend. Stop the scuffling and lead her out before she does herself an injury. But why should I? The right kind of friend would never have kept me waiting at lunchtime.

Besides, there's too much going on. Mark's brought a friend of his own, exactly as I told him to do.

Not much of one, I'll admit. He looks about twelve. In fact, it's only the physics text books under his arm that show he's in the same year as Mark. But he'll do, despite being small and wearing the kind of spectacles that make him look like a cartoon character. Come to think of it, he reminds me of someone.

But now Hilary has noticed that there are two of them, and has grabbed hold of my arm, each ounce of excitement translating into a ton of grip, making it difficult to think. She'll have to stop that. I need to concentrate. *It* only works when you remember to use it. It's like a light you have to keep switched on. You can't just forget.

And you can't be distracted—the way I am now.

It's Lydia, making me forget what I'm here for; watching her try to cope, turning this way and that, looking for a way out of a game that is fast turning into a scrum.

How can anyone be so invisible? It almost makes you want to laugh.

'Lydia.'

But it doesn't carry, my voice. We're not in a dining hall now. In fact, it only makes things worse. Typical Lydia, she jerks her head round to find out who is calling, then trots off through the crowd of boys—in completely the wrong direction.

Well, that's it. I did what I could. She can't expect me to be watching out for her the whole time. I've more important things to think about.

Five minutes later, here she is again, plodding towards us. Her satchel looks even heavier now, pulling her shoulders in, making the rest of her sag. Her face lights up, however, when she catches sight of us, only to fall again as she takes another look.

You can hardly blame her. Everything has changed. Just before she lost us, there were only the two of us, Hilary and me. Now we are four. Two boys and two girls. And one of them she can hardly dare to look at. It's too much to take in. Boys like Mark aren't supposed to exist outside *Just Seventeen*.

She could always steal another peep at his small friend instead. Well, actually, she can't. It's too late. Hilary has already moved in to stake her claim. And just to make sure there is no mistake, Hilary is glaring at her, daring her to so much as look at him.

So here we are. Two matching pairs and one left over. And to think it could have been so different. The little boy for instance, I hadn't actually planned him for Hilary at all. Didn't I say he reminded me of someone? Pipe-cleaner Girl meets Owl Boy. Lydia could have been having the time of her life.

She should have thought about that at lunchtime, when she made me wait, forcing me to spend those extra five minutes being stared at by Moira MacMurray. Now Hilary and I are just fine as we are, thank you. In the mean time, everyone is looking at me, waiting for me. It's turning into one of those rare moments when, just for once, everything seems to be going like clockwork, letting a person stand there feeling as if she's the one with the key, the one who's in control . . .

. . . Until something comes along and ruins it all. Or rather, someone.

Do I even have to mention the name? It has to be me that sees her first, heaving her way through the crowd. Not looking in our direction even, yet apparently drawn to us like a huge moving magnet. As if there was no getting away from her. No escape.

Moira MacMurray.

Look away then. There's just the chance she might not see us, might not see me.

But I was forgetting Lydia. 'Moira.' A tiny little cry of relief you wouldn't think anyone would hear.

But Moira does. Moira stops, turns—and through all the different heads in the crowd, looks directly at me, eyes mild, not even curious. Eyes that are just . . . there. And that make everything else disappear like so many objects sinking into milk.

Mark is saying something now, is touching me, but I can't hear him. I've decided we should go home. Mark will have to understand. There's nothing for him today. He'll just have to keep on hoping and waiting for the things he thinks I've promised.

AT home there's no sign of Dad. He won't be back till late. Thursday night, remember. Pastoral visits.

But you should have seen Lydia's face when she discovers it. Coming home was the whole point of her day. Tonight is her last night, her last chance to read Greek with him, show him how much she knows.

Instead she's just got us, Gran and me. Or rather, she just has Gran. Thursday night is bath night, when he's out of the house, and there's no danger of an accident. No danger of a towel falling or covering less than it ought. No danger of his coming into the bathroom and catching me staring at my leg through water, watching the water smooth all that stippled skin.

As for Gran and Lydia, they'll be good company for each other. They'll get on like a house on fire. Like Moira and *her* gran.

❧ Chapter Ten

THIS MORNING, LYDIA IS VERY quiet. It's Friday and she doesn't want to go home. She wants to stay with us, with Gran and me—and him. Just one of the family. And even more so because she missed him last night, and because she never did get to read Greek with him all by herself.

Does anyone remember the old Lydia now? The Lydia who didn't want to come, who wanted to go the boarding house? The Lydia who was ready to cry her eyes out because she thought I didn't have a mother? Of course not. We have a new Lydia, who has seen us, seen how happy we are. Now nothing's going to be the same.

In short, you could say we've done her a power of good.

Dad carries her bag for her to the car, which, rightly enough, she considers a great honour. But her eyes only light up at the very last moment, when he takes her by the shoulders and promises faithfully; next time they really will read Greek together, just the two of them, in his study.

But then, sensible Lydia, she's looking over at me, eyes suddenly anxious. She's wondering what I think of it, all this talk about the two of them, in his study, and no mention of me.

I could tell her and put her mind at rest; attention shared is attention halved, and I don't mind. But she wouldn't understand. She couldn't think why anyone would want to share his attention.

She should cheer up all round, stop looking so tragic. We don't let go of people, not so easily. And as Dad himself said to her as she was getting out of the car, *This isn't goodbye, Lyddie love, simply au revoir.*

Meanwhile, at the end of the day someone else is waiting patiently, just for her; it's Mrs. Morris, hovering right outside the gate. I could see her clearly when I looked out of the window during French. I didn't say a word to Lydia though. She was too busy doodling names on her jotter, not taking an ounce of notice of anything. So it was only me that knew she was there, Lydia's mother. Almost like a secret between ourselves.

She looks softer than ever. Perhaps a little plumper even. All that pasta and ice cream—just a shade too much of it maybe—having their effect while her daughter was struggling to force down Gran's porridge every morning.

It suits her though, all that softness, and some more besides. A person who has just returned from the most romantic city on earth should be all smiles. Instead she's staring into the school, trying to find our window, biting her lip as if something was bothering her, as if she was worried about what lay ahead.

Finally the bell goes and we all pile out, with Lydia looking ever so slightly surprised because I've slipped my arm through hers, while Hilary has to follow as best she can. Today it seems important to go slowly, keep a dignified pace.

But then she sees her mother, and for a moment it's as if she's going to forget about dignity and pace. Yet I've got her arm, remember. And she can't expect me to run, not with my leg the way it is. And anyway, that's what friends are for, sticking together no matter what. So Mrs. Morris has to wait, and watch us coming at no great rate. But it's not a bad thing. It gives her plenty of time to see the new Lydia, a more dignified Lydia. A Lydia who doesn't run even when she catches sight of her own mother.

But the very best thing about being arm in arm is that when at last we do arrive, she has to throw her arms around us both.

Lydia's mother has to give us both a hug. We are so locked together she can't avoid it.

Attention shared is attention halved. But Lydia is hardly going to complain. She's seen me set an example.

'Hello, Kate,' says Mrs. Morris.

Odd, don't you think, her greeting me first? I thought so, too, for a moment, especially when it was clear as daylight that all she wanted was her own daughter. But you know what's happened, of course; It is at work, making sure it's me she looks at, whether she wants to or not.

'Have you had a nice time?'

Again, it's me she's addressing. Poor thing, it must be confusing, wanting to concentrate on Lydia and not being able to. She can't work it out. She doesn't know about It, that nothing will change until I switch it off or turn away. And why should I do that? She's the softest thing I ever saw.

'Lydia's had an outstanding time, Mrs. Morris.'

This time when I smile, I remember to keep it down, not too wide, not too bright. Just right.

Hilary drifts past. Out of the corner of my eye, I see her, taking a sideways peek at us, trying not to look interested. But folk are always going to be interested in Lydia's mother, aren't they, just for the softness of her.

But blow Hilary, it's had its effect. She's distracted me, catching my eye for just that instant. Suddenly free, Mrs. Morris blinks and turns straight to her daughter. Starts talking hurriedly as if afraid that something else will stop her. 'Is that true, darling? Did you really enjoy yourself?'

Lydia looks at her and says, straight faced, 'I had the best time of my entire life.'

At which Mrs. Morris blinks again. As if somehow, this wasn't what she wanted to hear. So then you have to ask yourself what it is she had hoped Lydia was going to say. I mean, what sort of mother actually *wants* her daughter to be unhappy?

No time to think about it however. 'Look,' I say, bright and breezy. 'Here's Dad.'

And sure enough, here is Dad. Lydia's face changes. Her mother puts a hand on Lydia's shoulder. But Lydia shakes it off and runs straight for him, my dad—who throws both his arms around her and fairly lifts her off the ground. Beams over her head at Mrs. Morris. As if to say, Look what I've got.

But what he actually says is, 'That's a lovely girl you've got there. Truly lovely.'

Lovely? *Lydia?* Lydia hears the words and blushes, right to the roots of her mousy hair. She blushes deeper still when he adds, 'We're going to miss her, you know. Are you sure you want her back?'

He's joking of course, making it sound as if she is some precious jewel left in his care, and doesn't want to return. But hearing it, Lydia's face has lit up as never before, so her mother can see there's no mistake. Lydia would rather stay with us.

But nothing is said. Instead they just stare at each other, Mrs. Morris and my dad. And is it only me, or do all the sounds of school seem to die away around us, as if just for these few seconds everything has stopped, waiting to see what will happen next? In that silence—real or imagined—Dad's eyes seem to grow lighter, his smile warmer. His arms around Lydia that little bit closer.

Then Mrs. Morris puts out her hand again and gently—and this time effectively—pulls Lydia towards her. She smiles at him, suddenly prettier than ever. But not soft, suddenly not soft any more.

'Oh, we want her back, Mr. Carr. Let there be no mistake, we want our Lydia.' Now she has both hands on Lydia's shoulders, stroking them as if she could smooth away all the difficulty that has temporarily entered her daughter. 'And now I'm afraid we have to go. Lydia's father can't wait to see her.'

She turns. But then, at the last moment, she walks back towards us, towards me.

'Kate, my dear. I almost forgot. Give me your hand.'

It's a moment before I realise what she is doing. She is pressing a tiny box into my hand, all done up with gold paper, and gold ribbon streaming off the sides.

'Don't open it here,' she says. 'It's fragile.' This time she really is smiling, properly and sincerely. 'This little thing came all the way back from Venice with us. I do hope you like it.'

Then she was gone, and Lydia with her, leaving me standing with my hand still held out, and sitting on top of that, the tiny golden box. Dad is staring at it. I know just what he's thinking.

But *Don't open it here.* That's what she said. And something else beside, I'd swear it. Other words not spoken, but clear as a bell—if you knew how to listen. *'Don't open it in front of him.'*

How could she have managed that without words? The only answer must be that Lydia's mother has *It* too. After a fashion.

Well then, he says later, in the car. *Aren't you going to open it?*

Answering is easy; Not here, it's fragile. And somehow, he can't say anything. Don't ask me why. Mrs. Morris seems to have impressed him more than anyone would have thought possible. What she says, goes. For the moment.

And the very second we walk into the house, the phone begins to ring in the hall. Which means he has to answer it, leaving me to walk right past him, and Gran, to my bedroom.

Whatever is in the box, I'll get to see it first.

AND what is inside the box is a horse, a tiny crystal horse with a long neck and legs that look as if they have been spun out of sugar. A perfect thing. When I hold it in my hand, its hooves prick my palm, but the rest of its body is smooth, with a coolness that becomes warm the very moment it touches my skin. It's almost impossible to remember it's only glass. It looks more like a sweet, something you could suck.

In a way that makes it easier. To put one barley sugar leg in my mouth and feel its hoof pricking my tongue the way it pricked my hand. And bite.

After that, I put them both back in the box, the horse and its broken leg. It was the only way, you see. He'd never have let me keep it otherwise, not if it had been perfect. Now he won't mind so much. Now it can stay mine.

MONDAY, and Lydia must have spent the whole weekend doing homework. In Greek she seems to know twice what she did last week. Miss Jamieson listens to her translate with a nod and a smile—and ignores me. She thinks Lydia is doing it for her, or for the love of Greek. She doesn't realise. This is all for *him*. For when she next comes to stay.

Which serves Jamieson right, for forgetting she has two pupils not one. It makes her think she can go easy now, spend a little of the lesson having 'a chat.'

But yet again, it's only Lydia she's interested in. Miss Jamieson wants to know what her father has been up to in Italy all this week. (Note that she never asks similar questions about Dad. Remember Scarborough? Not so much as a query about that.)

Consequently Lydia tells her all about Trompetto and Venice, and Miss Jamieson looks impressed, goes on to say how much she has always liked his treatment of grand classical themes. In return Lydia looks faintly bored. I suppose she has to hear too much of this at home. She would rather we were banging our heads learning still more Greek! Lydia is the funniest girl in the world.

'He did the Bible as well, you know. He painted things from that.'

Both heads turn. They hadn't expected this. But I had to let them know that if there's an expert on Trompetto in this room, it would have to be me.

'He did that picture of the Golden Calf, remember? With Moses coming down from the mountain. That's not classical, that's from the Bible.'

And that is why we have it at home.

But I might as well not have bothered. Both of them look blank. Lydia has never been to Sunday School, and Miss Jamieson only cares about the Greeks. They don't know anything about false gods and dancing girls lining up to give their gifts, or Moses coming off the mountain to make them pay. There's a yawning gap in their knowledge, and they haven't even noticed.

NEVER mind, as Dad would say, there's always something to look forward to. Going to stay with Lydia, at Lydia's house, for example. It's only a question of time. That's the logic of things, one of the laws of friendship. If someone asks you to stay at their house, the next thing to happen is that you ask them back.

Only tell that to Lydia. Who doesn't seem to know the first thing about friendship.

Because first one week goes by, and then another week, and Lydia doesn't say a word. Too busy concentrating on her Greek, if you ask me, getting ready for him, for when she comes to stay the next time. Forgetting I've got to come to her house first. It's just the law.

Besides, I want to see them at home, Lydia's mother and Laura. And her dad. I want to see how different he is from mine. Natural curiosity, that's all.

But I don't know what's wrong with Lydia. I'd swear she was getting stupider in the things that count. It must be all that sitting next to Moira, having its effect. Because here is almost the oddest thing of all, about Lydia, I mean. She sits by Moira every time now, out of choice. Hilary thinks it's wonderful.

And Moira? Who knows what Moira thinks—or if she thinks at all. Sometimes you'd swear someone else was doing her thinking for her, turning her head, turning her eyes, using them to focus as if through a pair of binoculars. Someone who has no eyes to call her own, someone who is watching me. Nothing to do with Moira.

ONE thing is for sure. A person can only be prepared to wait so long for an invitation. With Lydia not up to the mark, I have to take matters into my own hands.

I do it right at the beginning of break, with half the classroom empty and no-one likely to interfere this time. In other words, no Fiona McPherson.

'I know, why don't we all do something together this weekend?'

Lydia's eyes widen and a smile spreads over her face. She actually thinks I mean doing that *something* at my house.

Hilary in the meantime has caught hold of the opposite end of the stick.

'Oh *yes*,' she cries. 'Let's do something.' And she carries on. 'I tell you what, Kate. You could stay with me. I could ask my mother. You could sleep in the spare room, and . . .'

. . . And there she stops. Hilary has said something rash and she knows it. It's no good her asking anyone to stay. The carpet wouldn't stand it, a weekend of girls tramping in and out, bringing all that dirt into the house. Hilary goes bright red, claps her hand over her mouth and doesn't say another word. Whatever happens this weekend, it won't be happening at her house.

But suddenly, out of the blue, comes another voice. Quite unexpected, the voice of someone who wasn't even meant to be part of the conversation.

'Kate could come to my house. We've got room. My gran, she likes girls.'

It's Moira MacMurray of all people, a reminder that when she speaks, her voice is thick, somehow clotted, as if there was too much flesh in her throat. And naturally we stare at her, speechless, the way you might if your wardrobe suddenly started to talk.

As so often happens, Hilary is the first to recover. 'Moira

MacMurray, what are you sticking your nose in for? Mind your own business, why don't you.'

Which would have been all very well—if that had been the end of it. But it's not, because now, despite it being none of her business, and despite Hilary giving all the answer that was necessary, somehow everybody now seems to be waiting for me to add something. As if such an offer could be serious, requiring a serious response. And then, as if that wasn't enough, suddenly Hilary has to go and giggle, as though it's not just Moira that's amusing, but both of us, Moira and me, together.

Amusing, but *altogether possible*.

So what do you do when people act like that? The only thing you can do. Pretend it never happened, that Moira never opened her mouth, that Hilary never giggled. Instead I turn to Lydia and say quite casually—only now not as casually as I would have managed if Moira had kept her mouth shut—'I'm *really* surprised you're not saying anything, Lydia. I mean it was nearly a whole week, remember.'

Lydia simply frowns. Even now, it hasn't seemed to occur to her that—forget Hilary and Moira—*she* was the one who should be asking.

So I have to put it another way, make sure she understands. 'I mean, really, Lyd, if I stay with anyone, it should be with you, I mean, surely.'

Finally, the penny drops. Lydia goes beetroot, perhaps the reddest I've ever seen her. At long last there's a light shining through all the clutter of her schoolgirl brain. But even now, believe it or not, despite the blushes, not a word passes her lips.

So again it's me that has to do the work. 'Why don't you ask your mother? Make it for next weekend. I can meet your dad then, and won't that be nice?'

Which means at long last, even Lydia has to say something. England expects. Slowly, you might almost be tempted to say *reluctantly*, she nods. 'Oh, I see. Of course. I'll ask Mummy. I . . . I suppose it will be all right.'

Of course it will. Mrs. Morris is nothing like Hilary's mother. This is the woman who went all the way to Venice but didn't forget to bring home a present for someone she doesn't even like. Not yet.

So there we are. At long last I'm off to stay with Lydia. And her mother. And her father. And the only question remaining is how Moira ever got the idea that *I* would ever want to stay with *her*. And her gran.

☙ Chapter Eleven

AND DAD? HE APPROVES NO end, thinks it's a wonderful idea. He doesn't even seem to mind that I'll be visiting a house where they never go to Church. On the Friday morning, before we leave home, he tells me to wait, disappears into his study. He comes out with a box of chocolates.

It's lucky that he doesn't see the look on my face. I've already said, Gran gets the sweet sherry and the fruit jellies and whatever else the old ladies bring by way of burnt offerings. But the chocolates he keeps. For us. They go with the study, the boxes of chocolates, like the Trompetto and the dancing girls and the warmth. *A little taste of Heaven and things to come.* A strawberry cream between my lips.

He knows that chocolate is the best thing sometimes. The only thing. It sits on your tongue, sweet and solid, before it melts, taking its sweetness to other parts, to where sweetness is needed.

But today the chocolates are for her, Lydia's mother. I have to take care to tell her they are from him. A way of saying thank you for having me. Yet I wish I could say they were from me. She would eat them, and think of me.

Now she'll eat them, and be thinking of him instead.

AT the end of the lesson, Miss Jamieson asks what we'll be doing this weekend. Quick as a flash, I tell her. 'I'm staying with Lydia,

Miss Jamieson. Her folks can't wait to have me. I expect it's a way of saying thank you. They couldn't have gone to Venice you see, not if Lydia hadn't stayed with us that time.'

Miss Jamieson gives one of her tight smiles, and nods. Then when she thinks I'm not looking, glances swiftly down at Lydia. And there, I've caught them at it, Lydia and Miss Jamieson exchanging looks, Lydia *telling* her she doesn't want me to come. It's right there in her eyes.

Something I hadn't expected. You'd think Lydia would be over the moon, and yet she's not. She's happy enough to come to my house, but she doesn't want me to come to hers. She doesn't want me in her home.

'Kate, whatever is the matter?' Miss Jamieson is staring at me in surprise.

Something must have happened to my face. Something I couldn't stop. It's never happened before, not that I can remember. It's Lydia's fault, exchanging looks like that, making Jamieson think she doesn't want me to come, giving her the wrong idea. Making her think she doesn't like me.

Some people just don't know when they're lucky. I *was* going to make sure Lydia gets almost as much fun out of this weekend as I will. But she can think again now. Silly Lyddie, stupid Lyddie, she's gone and ruined everything.

In the end it's a battle just getting out of the cloakroom. That was thanks to Hilary, hanging on to me till the last minute, wanting to make sure she wasn't going to be left out of a single thing. She only let go when I whispered into her ear exactly what I have in mind for us over the weekend. Now she's gone home with a great big smile on her face. Hilary can't wait for tomorrow.

But where is Lydia?

Not far away. Plodding across the front court from the direction of the Lower School to be precise. But she's not alone. Dancing ahead of her, leading the way, complete with rosy cheeks and curly hair, is someone else, a proper little Shirley Temple.

I had forgotten about Laura, forgotten that we would be going home together. They stop when they see me, though. In fact, the little one not only stops, she stares. Starts off with my feet and keeps going till she gets to my head—and makes a face, wrinkling up her nose as if she had smelt something gone bad. As if she could see something Lydia couldn't.

Not very attractive in a child. I give Lydia a look that says, *Let's ignore the kid.* But Lydia is no use. She just smiles in an embarrassed kind of way, and whispers something to Laura, which is not what I'd call ignoring anyone.

And to think that all this time I had expected to approve of Laura! She had sounded like a person who knows how to get what she wants. I'd thought we would have something in common, but I was wrong. Children like her just make things difficult for everyone.

Worse is to come. When we get on the bus, she makes sure to sit herself between us, spreads herself out, not worried about using her elbows. You know what she's doing of course. She's trying to keep us apart. Lydia probably hasn't even noticed, but I do. With people like Laura, it's important not to miss a thing.

Nasty child, acting as if she could see right through me. Trying to get between her sister and the only friend she's likely to have.

But she's not the one who counts. That person is in the garden when we arrive, hanging over the gate, halfway into the street, as if on the lookout. Lydia's mother is waiting for us. The three of us.

And the first thing she does is run out on to the pavement

and hug them, the other two, Laura and Lydia. For a moment I even thought she might be about to hug me, too. But no. There's none of that. Not for me.

'Kate,' she says instead. 'How nice to see you,' and gives a smile meant for no-one else but me, a really lovely smile. 'And it's like a slap across the face.' You see, this isn't how she smiled at Lydia. This is a smile to keep you at arm's length. Milkmen, travelling salesmen, even bank managers would be perfectly happy to be smiled at like that. But they don't have It. They don't have to know when they are being held at bay, like something nasty, barely allowed to come in.

Just for a second I feel like doing something about it. Something to make her regret that smile. Then I remember the horse, still prancing away in its tiny box, hobbled a little now, but safe enough, and believe it or not, the feeling melts away. She doesn't know me yet, that's all.

'This way, Kate.' And she smiles again.

I follow her up a path and somehow it's no surprise to see roses growing on either side, even at this time of year with winter already upon us. Roses all the way to the house. The door is standing open.

'Are you all right, Kate?'

Again this is her mother speaking, but now she's sounding half anxious. It must be the look on my face. I felt it arrive the moment I stepped inside, and looked around me for the first time. The roses were no surprise, but this is too much; Lydia's house is light. Late afternoon in early winter, and somehow the house is chock full of light. And not only is it light, but warm.

Her mother's doing I suppose. In fact, I know it's her doing. It's like having her all around you just in the colour and the shape of things. Curtains the colour of her lipstick, walls the exact shade of her skin. Wooden floors shiny as expensive shoes. Of course, Gran would want to know why there aren't more carpets, instead of all these rugs, thick and warm looking as her coat, never quite meeting the wall. Carpets are a sign of something with Gran. But she should realise. You don't need carpets if a house is already warm. Where even the floor is warm.

Then we come to the kitchen, and there's more light here than where else. White walls, green tiles. Lydia's mother turns away to lay chocolate eclairs on a bright blue plate. Time to glance at the others. But Laura is pretending I don't exist and Lydia is looking as if she is somewhere else, a cold dark cave, perhaps, with a fire that went out long ago. Neither of them knowing what they have. Much nicer to look at their mother, then, arranging the eclairs, watch her as she licks the cream off her fingers. You can see straightaway why she's not a thin woman.

That makes me remember and I bring out the box of chocolates.

'These are for you, Mrs. Morris.'

'Kate dear,' she says. 'You shouldn't have.' And she smiles. A better smile than last time.

'My father sent them.'

There is a pause and then she takes them from me. The smile stays where it is, but now something has gone out of it. She turns and quickly puts the chocolates away, and not just anywhere, but up in the highest cupboard—right out of sight. There will be no way of remembering they are there, not unless she looks. And somehow I don't think she will be doing that.

LYDIA'S bedroom is tiny, absolutely minuscule, as if she had deliberately chosen the worst room in the house. And the books only make it worse. Books on the bed, books on the floor, books lying with their pages split open as if to let all the words escape. And this is where she manages to sleep. No wonder she knows it all. You can almost imagine the words crawling across her pillow in the dead of night, like a line of ants, marching in one ear and out the other. I wouldn't like it.

But Mrs. Morris doesn't seem to notice the mess, or the fact that the books are taking up so much space. She says I could either have a camp bed here with Lydia, or instead, sleep in the room next door *where she is sure I will be more comfortable*. And it's obvious, isn't it? If she'd wanted me to stay in the same room, she would have made Lydia tidy away the books.

And Lydia doesn't say a word, not about the books or where she wants me to sleep.

So I don't say a word either. Because, frankly, I'm shocked. When you have a friend to stay, you're supposed to share a room, all girls together. What sort of friend is one who would make you sleep in the room next door instead?

But then her mother opens another door, and everything changes.

This bedroom is three times the size of Lydia's, and ten times better. Here are walls the colour of lemons, and a carpet the colour of green apples. Green curtains. There's a lemon-painted fireplace and above it a picture of a tree. It has its own wash hand basin with a bar of soap you can smell from here, and even that is lemon scented. A single bed with lacy covers spread out like a layer of foam. I have never seen a room quite like it. Not even in my dreams. And that's the reason everything changes.

It doesn't do to bear a grudge. Lydia can keep her messy little cupboard. I'll hang my clothes in the wardrobe, sleep in the lemon-painted bed under the frothy cover and forget every little thing.

ALL the same, you mustn't let people off *too* lightly. When we are by ourselves, sitting in the muddle of Lydia's room, I ask what she has in mind for the weekend. And of course, she goes bright red because she hasn't a thing lined up, not unless you count a pile of homework.

But then, when it's almost too late to answer, she stumps up with a reply—of sorts.

'Daddy's giving a lecture tomorrow morning at the art gallery. We could go to that. He might even let us change the slides.'

A lecture. At an art gallery. I give her a look which I can only hope just says it all. Strangely, she doesn't seem to see it. I notice she has gone very still, however. Then I realise; it's because she's listening. And I bet I know what for. It must almost be time for her dad to come home. Lydia wants to get to the door before Laura.

Everything goes quiet after that. Well, I have to listen too, now. Wouldn't it be funny if I beat them, arrived at the front door before any of them, Laura, Lydia and their mother?

But all we hear is her mother, calling to us to help lay the table. Lydia makes a face, but I don't mind at all. It's a chance to show how helpful I can be.

And I was right. Downstairs, Laura and Lydia are worse than useless, standing in the kitchen with empty hands and sulky mouths, deliberately getting in each other's way, ready to bite each other's head off for no reason. Except they do have a reason of sorts. Time's getting on. Who'll get to the door first?

Makes you wonder how she puts up with them.

What a difference to have me, then, all sweetness and light, nothing like her daughters, running back and forth into the dining room with plates and cutlery, *candles* even. She says the candles are just for fun, it being Friday night, that they always have them.

Not that Lydia or Laura seem to be having much by way of fun. They'll be slapping each other in a minute, two daughters wh just don't know how to share.

Maybe that's why she sends them both upstairs, Laura to get undressed, and Lydia to supervise.

Or did she send them away for another reason, altogether? With Laura and Lydia gone there's only the two of us left. And at least I know how to be cheerful.

Lydia's mother asks me if I know the way to toss a salad.

A moment later, she is showing me how, helping me measure out vinegar and oil and little bits of sugar. When I told her the salad oil is the exact same stuff Gran uses to get rid of the wax in her ears she burst out laughing, as if she'd never heard anything so funny. It would have been nice to ask her why, but I was afraid it would spoil the joke. Spoil everything.

If anyone walked in now, you could see just things would look—as though there was another daughter in the family, one who knew how to share, and how not to sulk. And not to make faces.

Even Mrs. Morris seems to have fallen into the swing of it. Laughing at every little thing, holding up the spoon for me to taste, making sure I hold the knife the right way to cut up cucumber. This isn't how Gran makes dinner. This is almost like having fun, a way of losing track of the time. . . .

Then comes the faint sound of a key in the lock, followed a split second later by another sound, much louder. Footsteps on the stairs, frantic, uneven, so you can imagine the scuffling involved, the elbowing and pushing. At the bottom something goes crash and something else begins to squeal, louder than a stuck pig.

Mrs. Morris sighs, and forgets to wipe her hands, pushes a streak of olive oil right through her hair.

A moment later, everyone's piling into the kitchen, ruining what's left of our peace. First Lydia, red faced and panting, then Laura, smiling now and looking like the cat—or rather the kitten—that's got the cream. And behind them, the person everyone's been waiting for, the reason for it all, Lydia's dad. At long last.

And doesn't he look pleased? Here's someone who likes to be the centre of attention, no matter who gets hurt. No mistaking the signs.

Not that he's seen me yet. That's because you won't catch me pushing myself forward before I'm invited, unlike some folk. Besides, he's not in any state to pay proper attention, not with Laura and Lydia hanging round him, and his wife stepping forward with that smile of hers—the good smile, not the poor one. A smile you'd think she'd want to keep for someone who spends his days doing something worthwhile—and not just messing round with a lot of old pictures.

But most importantly, hanging back means you get to have a good look, make up your mind, and decide the best way to go about things. Learn about a man from the way he lets his family quarrel over him.

Although now Lydia's father seems to have eyes only for Lydia's mother. He is pulling her towards him so as to give her a kiss, a long one, right on the mouth. It's almost enough to make a person blush. And as if that's not enough, next he puts his lips to her ear, whispering something no-one else can hear, words that make her laugh and turn away.

And still he hasn't noticed me. After his wife, he turns to the table, towards the salad that I've just tossed, picks up a fistful of leaves and folds them into his mouth. Big hands, he has, with long thin fingers, shaking the salt and drops of oil into the air. Hands that look as if they could paint a picture, but never a fence. He's been at work all day, but he's not even wearing a tie. Curly black hair, sleepy black eyes. He looks like a husband. He looks like the father of daughters, the male of the family, the sort that half-grown ugly girls moon over—unless they meet someone better. He'd die if he ever had a son.

And even now he doesn't know I'm here. But things are quieter. I would say that he was about ready.

The dinner plate makes an awful crash as it hits the floor. Makes them jump, even him.

'Oh, Mrs. Morris,' I cry. 'I'm so sorry. It just slipped out of my hands.' Right away I drop to the ground to pick up the pieces, which means he has to lean across the table to see where I've got to.

And of course, a moment later, *she's* down there with me, urging me to my feet, telling me she'll take care of it. Only when she's crouched right down, busy with dustpan and brush do I stand up. And smile at Lydia's father.

My very best smile.

Mark, the Games teacher, Miss Jamieson, and now Lydia's dad. It never fails. Not if they are the right sort, the ones who are looking for something they never even know they wanted. Until they meet me. Whatever it was he whispered into his wife's ear, it's as if I've whispered it back to him, and more besides.

All with a single smile.

His eyes aren't sleepy any more. They are wide awake, and startled. Sometimes even I forget how easy it is.

'John?' Lydia's mother's voice reaches from behind, on her way to standing up. 'John, can you help me?'

He gives a little start. Next thing, he's sneaking glances to right and left, checking that no-one saw what just took place. But there's no problem, at least not with Lydia. All those books, yet she doesn't know the first thing about people, least of all her own father. She's staring at him with that half baked look on her face—and can't actually see a thing. But he should take a better look at Laura, who is staring at both of us with an expression I doubt she has ever worn before.

My, she's quick, that one. Maybe we have those things in common after all.

'Oh look,' I say very softly. 'My finger is bleeding.'

And so it is, blood trickling from the very tip as I hold it up, running in a thin red ribbon down the centre of my palm. I lick the blood from my wrist, salty as Gran's cooking, never take my eyes off him.

Mr. Morris swallows and looks away. 'Elizabeth,' he mutters, gesturing towards me, 'Do something, won't you.' At once Mrs. Morris stands up.

'Oh, Kate,' she exclaims. 'Poor little thing. I'll take care of that for you.'

She's *so* nice, her hands infinitely gentle with sponge and cream and plasters. I almost regret that it had to happen, the smile, I mean. But it's like Dad always says. If you are blessed with a gift, then it's a sin not to use it. You have no choice. It's up to other people what they do about it. So there it is. I had to smile.

But he could have looked away.

Yet it seems almost unkind to her, Lydia's mother, who is busy wrapping a plaster round my finger. Her touch seems so familiar, it's as if someone has been doing this for me all my life. Which isn't true of course. If I hurt myself, there's only Gran, scything strips of adhesive bandage for me to stick on myself. Old fashioned stuff that rips your skin when you try to take it off, does more harm than good. There only ever has been Gran.

Or has there? Someone must have put plasters on me when I was little. Someone I can't remember. Using such a gentle touch that *her* touch feels familiar to me now. Makes me wish I could make all my fingers bleed, one after the other, just so it could go on, and never stop.

I won't smile at him again, Lydia's father. Even if it's a God-given gift. I won't smile. *She* wouldn't like it.

AT dinner I ate my salad but I can't say I was impressed. Not enough salt, not enough vinegar. We use salad cream at home which disguises the taste of the lettuce nicely. Yet nobody else seemed to think so. Everyone eats it up and says that it tastes fine. Meanwhile, Lydia's father has begun to let himself believe he imagined it, that smile. Too many hours looking at works of art, at the smiles painted out of people's imaginations. He'll be telling himself that's what caused it. Everything goes swimmingly. Everybody talks, even Lydia. You'd think we were one big happy family, really you would.

Until you look at Laura, that is. She hasn't taken her eyes off me, not since that first smile. And she's hardly touched her dinner, wasting food. Yet no-one says a word about that. Her mother just tells her she must be tired, that she should be in bed. Says it to her twice. Time for bed. Yet Laura doesn't move a muscle.

I never saw such a thing. A child wastes food, is told to go to bed, yet she stays just where she is. *And nothing happens*. No-one seems put out even. I don't understand it—unless it's the wine they are drinking, dulling their sense of right and wrong. That's one thing I won't be able to tell *him* when I go home, about the wine. Or the candles either, I especially won't tell him about the candles. The only people I know who light candles willy nilly are the Catholics, and what would that say about them?

And still Laura just sits there, refusing to budge, making her parents look like a pair of fools. Why? Then the reason hits me. Laura's staying where she is because she's afraid something is going to happen if she goes. Something to do with me.

In the end it's easier for me to be the one to move. Lydia comes, too, the way you'd expect.

Outside her room she turns to me.' Would you like to come in for a chat or something?'

Or something. It would take a detective to discover an ounce of enthusiasm in that. But who's to mind? What would I want to talk about anyway when my room is waiting?

So I give a great big yawn, the sort actors do on stage, that don't look remotely real. 'Sorry,' I say to her. 'Really I am. I'm just too tired. Can't stay awake another minute. I'll have to go to bed.'

Which is a good answer because just for a moment Lydia looks put out. As we both know, real friends stay up till all hours no matter how tired they are—unless they have school the next morning. And tomorrow is Saturday.

Finally I get to open my door—and close it behind me. Someone has been in and pulled the covers down the bed, making it ready just for me.

But before I climb in, before I wash my face and dry it with the embroidered towel, before I get undressed even, I go and stand in front of the mirror, and practise smiles. Good smiles, not bad ones.

And last of all, after undressing, I sit on the edge of the bed and let my feet curl into the green carpet, both of them. One pink and smooth, the other brown and streaked with other colours, with its own slight sheen as of something polished. I can look at it to my heart's content. It's safe. No-one will come in. No-one will stop me.

I don't even think it's so very bad, my leg. If I touch the skin, it may not be exactly smooth, but it is soft, softer than anything else I know. Except perhaps her coat.

Damaged goods though. A falling away from perfect.

WHAT would *she* have to say if she saw it, Lydia's mother? I know the answer to that. She would ask me how it happened. And there'd be nothing I could tell her. You can't talk about what you don't know. But in a way I'd like her to see it. Because I might have a question for her. If this happened to Lydia, would she leave and never come back?

Then again, I don't have to. You only have to look at her to know. Lydia's mother would never leave. Lydia's mother would stay no matter what. Lydia could be twice as ugly as she is already and her mother would still be there. You don't even need to have *it* to understand. Lydia's mother would die before she would abandon her daughters. Either of them.

If she had to leave, Lydia's mother would take her with her. It would take an act of God to stop her doing that.

❧ Chapter Twelve

IT MUST BE BECAUSE I'M in someone else's house, having its effect, making me dream. A different dream this time. It began the same way, with the light and the heat. But then it stopped, quite suddenly, and everything went dark—as if to begin again, become something altogether new.

Now for the first time, I was alone. Alone and in a different part of the house. Instead of the light and the groaning walls, there was only his room. Here was his desk, and here was the picture of the Golden Calf and the dancing girls. I should have been frightened, seeing them. There was only ever the one reason for being in his room.

But not this time. This time I was only waiting, patient as could be, because, after all, Patience is my middle name. Someone had told me to wait. Wait and not to worry. Wait and stare at my feet, count ten rosy little toes. Wait and listen.

Listen for what? For the sound of footsteps, what else? Footsteps would be the sign that the waiting was over, footsteps belonging to the person I was waiting for. Footsteps that are right there, outside the door, coming closer, and then stopping. . . .

Outside, on Lydia's landing, real footsteps are walking past my door. Nothing to do with my dream, though, nothing to show who it was outside my father's door, or who I had been waiting for. And nothing to explain the strangest thing of all—the feeling that comes with waking.

I mean the feeling you have when something lovely has been

snatched away. Like dreaming it's Christmas only to find that it's a day like any other. Disappointment, no other word for it.

Did I just say this was a new dream? It's not. It's a very old dream. So old I had forgotten that I ever used to dream it. I had to sleep in someone else's bed, in someone else's house, to dream it again, as though it was something against the rules at home.

There are more sounds on the landing; the creak of a floorboard, the flip of someone's slippers. But no-one stops at my door. Instead, someone makes their way downstairs as if the last thing they want to do is wake anyone.

Minutes pass. In the room next to mine, something goes thud. A book probably, sliding off the bed. Presently that door opens and someone plods to the bathroom. It can only be Lydia. No-one else is that flat footed. And while she's in the bathroom, still other footsteps make themselves heard, heavier, running downstairs as if in a hurry.

Everybody's up then. I'm the only person still in her bed.

And yet, no-one comes near me. No-one bursts into my room telling me it's late, that Time and Tide wait for no man. The light shines on in peace, through the green curtains and it's like watching the morning slowly filtering through a sliver of green apple. *Yet nobody minds.* This isn't what I'm used to. Time wasted is time thrown away. But nobody seems to care. Away in the distance, a phone rings, muffled by doors that I would swear had been kept shut so as not to disturb.

If *he* ever found out I had stayed in bed, I would have to say I was only lying here to test them, seeing how long it would be before anyone came to get me. In a way, that's just what I am doing.

But it doesn't happen. No-one comes. I only get up when I remember there are things I have to do.

THE kitchen is empty except for Lydia who looks up from the book she has propped against a milk jug.

'Your father phoned.'

Next thing, she's looking astonished because she can't understand why I have to sit down so suddenly, as if she had kicked the backs of my knees, the way we do to the girls in front of us during assembly.

Stupid, stupid of me. They don't care, but *he* does. I should have remembered. Time wasted is time thrown away. He'll have rung to check, and now he knows.

Mrs. Morris walks into the room, Laura right behind her.

'Kate, you're up. Did you sleep well? Lyddie love, pop some toast in for her.'

She has her back to me now, pouring water from the kettle into a coffee cup. 'Oh, I nearly forgot, Kate, your father phoned. He wanted to know if you were up yet. I spoke to him and I'm afraid . . .' suddenly her voice sounds careful '. . . I'm afraid I gave him the idea we'd *all* been up since the crack of dawn. Totally wrong of course. You can phone him back, if you like.'

And then she turns, cup of coffee in her hand. Her eyes meet mine. And it's a shock. She knows. About time wasted. Time I'll have to pay for.

Except I won't have to pay for it, not this time, thanks to Mrs. Morris, who doesn't seem to care that we should hold only the truth in our mouths.

'It's all right,' I say. 'I won't phone.' Lydia looks disappointed. She was probably hoping to speak to him.

'Well,' she says. 'We've missed going to the gallery with Daddy. You shouldn't have slept so late. He went ages ago.'

Oh. Then someone else did mind, after all, about me staying in bed. But it *would* be her. It would be Lydia. But listen to her mother.

'Lydia!' She cries. 'You weren't going to drag poor Kate off to one of Daddy's lectures. Tell me you weren't.'

Lydia stares at her book, face leaden. Mrs. Morris sighs. Sometimes she must wonder, surely, what it would be like having an elder daughter who wasn't difficult. A daughter who knew how to behave the way a daughter should.

Maybe that's why she has to leave the room.

'We're late,' I say, jumping to my feet.

Lydia scowls. 'That's what *I* said.'

She thinks I'm talking about the art gallery and a load of old slides. Silly Lyddie, stupid Lyddie. Did she really think I was going to leave it to her to make sure we had fun this weekend? Now it will all have to come as a surprise.

WE are terribly late in getting there, but Hilary doesn't mind. When we arrive at the Dairy Maid she is sitting bolt upright on one of the red plastic seats. Cheeks almost the same colour. She's staring straight ahead of her, doesn't move her head even when we walk in. Judging by the skin on her coffee, she's been here for ages.

But we won't hear her complaining. Hilary is keeping very very still, as if any sudden movement might make her explode. Well, she has company, hasn't she. Sitting in the seat right next to her is Mark's friend, also staring straight ahead. And he hasn't touched his coffee either.

The only person to show relief is Mark, who has it written all over his face. He must have begun to think I wasn't coming, that he was sitting here for nothing.

It's a magic moment really. What you could call a major triumph. He's not supposed to be here, you see. Somewhere, miles away from here—is it Kirkcaldy this week?—there are a bunch of people shivering on a rugby pitch, asking what could have happened to their star player.

He deserves the best smile I can deliver, the one that promises more than he could dare to imagine. Besides, Mark likes the colour of my hair. Honey coloured—he said so. Hair no-one else seems to have noticed, not even . . .

. . . Not even Dad.

It must be why, when I sit down in the seat next to him, I let my hand fall along the top of his leg—just for a second. Just long enough for him to feel it, and for it to have an effect. Then I take it away again.

'Oh, poor Lyd,' I say, looking up. 'That's all four seats taken. You'll have to find somewhere else to sit.'

It's true, but there's no need for her to look so tragic. There's a place just across the way, opposite two old ladies in felt hats. She won't be able to hear half of what we have to say, but then I don't suppose we'll be talking much.

She goes bright red, but a moment later she turns and walks over to the old ladies. And even they don't want her. It seems whatever they are talking about is not for young ears. They scowl as she sits down, then bang their heads together and carry on in whispers. Good grief, it's just like school.

But what's this? Without even looking at me, Mark has taken my hand, put it back on the very top of his leg, where his . . . I can't say it. Call it his you-know-what. Yet it makes for an interesting problem. Namely, what I should do next.

Maybe I don't actually have to *do* anything. He is staring at the table as if Formica has become a special interest of his, whilst I, I can sit here and wait for matters to take their course, cool as something straight off the cold counter. The difficulties are all his.

In the meantime, I can always consider Hilary and Owl Boy— his name's Nicholas, by the way—wedged in beside her, and no hope of escape. I never saw anyone look as miserable as he does now, pinned there by the sheer force of her will. Of course, you know who would make him more cheerful, willing to stay put. Someone almost identical to him. Someone like Lydia.

Talking of which. A quick glance just to check.

And would you believe it, she's gone. Lydia has gone. The old ladies are still sitting there, but talking out loud again now, because Lydia has disappeared. And it must have been the shock, making me jump, making my hand contract, because next to me, Mark, who has been sitting absolutely still, suddenly jerks and goes rigid, then slumps down in his seat, with a peculiar (and I have to say, not very attractive) groaning sound.

Honestly, some people.

I kick Hilary under the table. 'Lydia's gone.'

It takes a good few seconds for the words to sink in. 'So?' She says at last. She has just noticed that something is up with Mark, and she's staring at him, pop eyed, never having seen anyone in his state, not in a café. Or anywhere else for that matter. Hilary has no idea.

But that's Hilary all over, ready to be distracted by the least thing. She doesn't understand, does she? Because, what if Lydia has simply gone home? They'll want to know why, and she will say it's because of me, making her sit by herself with a couple of old ladies. Because I didn't include her in the arithmetic.

But Hilary doesn't see any of that. And, as if things weren't bad enough, she's started talking suddenly. It must be Mark, still slumped over the table, making her nervous.

'Lydia's the one who was here just now, a friend of ours. Actually I don't even know that I *would* call her a friend. I mean she's all right, but she's so odd half the time. Isn't she, Kate? Isn't she odd? Probably about the oddest girl in the whole class.' Then she stops and giggles suddenly. 'Unless you count Moira, of course.'

Moira. Moira MacMurray. At the mention of the name, a light goes on in my head. Lydia's not the sort to move, not of her own accord, not when she's been told to go somewhere and stay there. That's the thing about Lydia. She does what she is told. So something else must have made Lydia move. Some*one* else. And Hilary had mentioned Moira.

Next thing you know, I'm on my feet, and heading for the door. And it's a fight. A real struggle. The café seemed to have filled up since we came in. It must have started to rain, because there were crowds of folk in steaming coats everywhere, standing about, getting in the way, wanting to know why I needed to push. But finally, I make it to the outside. And sure enough, far in the distance Lydia and *Moira* are walking away together in the wet.

Back into the café. 'Come on,' I say to Hilary. 'Get up.' She stares at me. Stays where she is. 'Come *on*.'

But still she doesn't move, not till Owl Boy mumbles something in her ear. Hilary goes bright red, then stands to let him out. There's no explaining it, but somehow having Lydia go has given him permission to do the same.

Now the only problem is Mark. 'Hey,' he says weakly. 'Hey.' And that's all he can manage. Hardly what you would expect from the star of the Sixth Form Moot.

Ignore him. We have to go, Hilary and I. We have to keep together. And anyway, it doesn't matter about him. That thing that happened just now, he thinks I did it deliberately, letting my hand go tight, having its effect. As if I would. It was a complete accident. But he doesn't know that. We can leave him. He'll come again.

No the only thing to slow us down is Hilary, still fumbling with her duffle coat as the rain hits us. And thanks to her, it's too late. Now there's no sign of them.

Then Hilary clutches my arm. She's seen them, Moira and Lydia, standing at a bus-stop about a hundred yards off. I was right then, Lydia *was* on her way home, ready to tell tales, ready to ruin everything. But then something else occurs to me. She's waiting on the *wrong* side of the road. She should be on this side. If she were to catch a bus from where she's standing, it would take her in the very opposite direction.

Unless. Unless Lydia isn't going to her own house; unless she's planning on going home with Moira, to Moira's house. Suddenly

I know exactly what Moira is doing. She's taking Lydia home to meet her gran.

That's when I start running. Because what about me? What could I say to explain it, having to go home all by myself? What would her mother think? And something else. If Lydia actually prefers to go off with Moira MacMurray—*Moira MacMurray*—then what does that say about me?

Silly me, I put that all wrong. What I meant to say was of course; what does it say about her, Lydia?

Just for once, Hilary does the right thing. The moment we arrive at the bus-stop, she goes to the other side of Lydia and catches her by the arm. Lydia, who didn't even see us coming, jumps and then squirms with pain.

I always knew Hilary could be vicious.

Moira stays at the bus-stop as we move away, yet I can feel her eyes on my back long after we've left her behind. It's like having a piece of elastic stretching all the way down the street between us. Stop walking and I might snap right back beside her. Then it would be me going home with Moira, instead of Lydia. Home to meet her gran.

And what about Lydia? I don't think that girl has stopped being a problem from the day she was born. Here she is, newly rescued, and is she grateful? Not a bit of it. Lydia is sulky and silent, doesn't want to be with us one little bit. And simply because the arithmetic didn't add up.

Which is awkward. We have to go back to her house in a short while. Somehow I've got to get on the right side of her, and quickly. But how? Then, inspiration. Because away in the distance, lit up in the rain, shining like a beacon to folk who are lost and troubled, is a bookshop.

Now I know exactly what to do.

IT'S almost as crowded here as in the café. People are shoving up against the shelves, pretending they all want a book, pretending the rain has nothing to do with it. But even with the crowds, I have no difficulty in putting my hand on it, the one thing guaranteed to bring Lydia round.

In fact, you might even say the crowds are a Godsend. They make it easier—although they had thinned out in the space next to the religious section. Apparently it takes more than rain to drive some folk closer to God. But there are still enough people around to make what I have to do an absolute cinch. The only problem really is Hilary. The look on Hilary's face would give me away better than any store detective.

But here's another Godsend. This time in the shape of the Horror Section. Hilary catches sight of the severed heads and crawling hands, and forgets all about me. By the time she's had enough of amputation and eyeballs, it's more than time to take them both outside again.

'Hey, Lydia,' I say. 'Stop a moment.' You see, she was already about to charge on ahead, still sulky, still thinking she can take offence. But she can't resist a direct command, and she stops.

'Look,' I say. 'Look what I've just bought for you.'

It had still been there on the shelves, thank goodness. Hadn't moved in a twelve month. Well, Dad's audiences aren't the sort of folk to land up in bookshops as a rule. So here it was, the only copy I've ever seen outside his study. His face is on the cover, the face everybody sees, eyes alight with the loving kindness of the Lord. They are directed straight at Lydia now as she holds the book in her hands. In fact, so far as she is concerned, it might be his head she is holding, like a bookwormy Salome.

And in a way, she's right. This *is* his head. These are his thoughts, aren't they, gathered up at source and written down in stone. Well, not stone admittedly. They don't make books out of stone tablets any more. But, stone or paper, what's the difference? His thoughts, his opinions. His face. Look at *her* face though, and see what I've done for her. I've given her a little bit of him, just for herself.

'Kate,' she whispers. 'Oh, Kate. I never knew he'd written a book.' She stares down at the cover, but can't seem to take it in. '*For the Love of God*.' She has to read the title aloud, just to hear herself sounding the words.

There's another sound beside me, tiny, hardly worth the mention. It's Hilary sniffing, a sign that she's confused. She thought she hadn't taken her eyes off me all the time we were in the shop. She's forgotten about the Horror Section. Now she's wondering when it was I bought the book, how I could have done it without her noticing. Hilary just can't work it out.

TIME to go home. Lydia sits on the bus hugging the book to her chest, does her best to ask questions, but somehow can't seem to finish any of her sentences. The result is that I hardly need take any notice of her after that, even when she finally manages to squeeze out a single complete string of words. She wants to know if there's any mention of me.

Which has to be the stupidest question of all. When her dad writes his papers on Art, does he go mentioning Lydia on every other page? Of course not. This is about the two of them, him and God. As she will discover for herself.

Besides, if he mentioned me, he would have had to mention *her*, the reason I'm here, the person we're not supposed to talk about. No getting round that one.

I should have realised there would be problems though. That's the trouble with Lydia, she has no *tact*. She runs through the front door meaning to carry on up the stairs straight to her bedroom. But there's her mother, getting in the way, wanting to know the reason for the hurry.

And like an idiot Lydia shows it to her, shows her the book, says, *Look, look what Kate has bought for me*.

Her mother takes the book, glances at it, then quickly hands it back to Lydia as if she can hardly bear to touch it. 'How very kind of you, Kate,' she says automatically. But she doesn't mean it. It's like the chocolates all over again. Only worse.

I'd like to tell her, it's no good blaming me. If anyone's responsible, it's Lydia, not behaving the way she should. There wouldn't be any need to have the book in the house if it weren't for her, if she would only learn to act like other people, and recognise what's good for her.

AFTER lunch, Mrs. Morris gets embarrassed because there's no sign of Lydia. She's disappeared, although we all know where she is. She's upstairs on her bed, turning the pages of his book, drinking it all in, every word of it. Her mother goes up a couple of times, but there's nothing she can do.

Yet I don't mind, not in the least. In Lydia's house they have a room that's simply there for watching television. *Television!* We don't have TV at home. Dad says it's a distraction, a reason for not talking. Or listening to him.

The only trouble was, Laura was already there. She was on the floor, busy with a sort of house she was making for her dolls with a shoebox and bits of cardboard. It was quite clever really, the way she had fashioned teeny tiny chairs and tables out of little more than paper. When I sat down on the sofa behind her, however, she froze, actually gave a little shiver the way grown-ups do when a goose walks over their grave. But she didn't turn round, not once. Instead she just carried on, folding and glueing, trying to pretend I wasn't there. Only now nothing seemed to work any more. Things she had glued came unstuck. Things she had folded came apart. She was wasting her time really.

Poor Laura, she may have *It*, but she hasn't got the foggiest idea of how to make it work. She can't make me go away, not even in her mind. I can stay here for just as long as I want, enjoying the peace.

• • •

LYDIA looks up when I open the door to her room. Her eyes are full of tears, her spectacles watery, like miniature aquariums—just the thing for Laura and her shoebox sitting rooms. 'Oh, Kate,' she says. 'Your poor father, having *his* father die like that.'

She must have got to the bit about the pit-roof falling in, and about Gran being left alone, and about how she never gave in, how she battled to give her son the best of everything. Gran this, Gran that, making sure they were never like the ordinary folk.

Forty other men died in the same disaster. I saw it in a newspaper clipping I found stuck between the pages of another book nobody ever reads. It doesn't say a thing about them in *his* book, or what happened to their families. Then again, why should it? This isn't their story. You can only tell a tale the way you see it, even I know that.

IN the middle of dinner Lydia's mother asks again if I want to give Dad a ring. I shake my head, then explain that Saturday is his busiest night. A fork supper with the Friends in the City, followed by work on his sermon for the next day.

The result is exactly what you would want. Lydia's mother stretches right across the table to touch my hand. 'Poor Kate. Such a *busy* person, your father.'

It's almost comical. Lydia's mother thinks I'm not getting enough attention. It's so difficult keeping the smile off my face that in the end I give up, and let her see it—see how brave I can be.

'I don't mind, Mrs. Morris. He can't help it. And there's always Gran.'

At the mention of Gran, she frowns and bites her lip. Well, she's met her, hasn't she. Which means there's nothing she can say. For the moment, there's a silence as we all consider Gran. Silence except from Lydia, that is.

'Oh, Kate, she's such a wonderful person.'

That's the book talking. But she sounds wistful, because as he says, they broke the mould when they made his mother. Mrs. Morris though gives my hand another squeeze. And you can see what she is thinking. What a shame it is, having a grandmother like mine, and a father who . . .

A father who does what? This is where I don't understand Lydia's mother. Why doesn't she like my father? Why doesn't she see him the way others see him? It's almost enough to make you worry about her, ask yourself if there may not be something wrong with her.

Then I catch her looking at her husband, and any worry I might have had on her behalf just disappears. She's smiling at him, Mr. Morris, bending towards him and the wine I had almost forgotten she was drinking. And you can see what is happening. She has stopped thinking about me. She's only got eyes for him, Lydia's father. She doesn't care about anything else.

Serve her right then when it slips away from me, a little flash of It. As she goes to sip her wine, I turn and catch his eye—and smile, just the way I did yesterday. For a second he stares back at me, mouth half open, sleepy eyes waking. Wouldn't it be interesting to know what is going through his mind right now? Then again, there's no need to guess. He's just like Mark, only older. They all are if you ask me, except for him. My dad.

Finding that she's lost him suddenly, Lydia's mother turns to look down the table, mystified. But there's nothing there for her to see. And he's hardly going to tell her, not after what's been passing through his mind, coming to him from out of the blue, as he would say. As he would *like* to say. So she's none the wiser, and already I'm almost sorry it happened.

Still, it's taught Laura a lesson. Seven year olds should be in bed at this time of night. That way she wouldn't be sitting there, staring first at him and then at me as if she had seen something infinitely more shocking than a simple smile.

At nine o' clock precisely I yawn. Golly, I say to everyone.

Golly, having so much fun has tired me out. I'll have to go to bed.

Suddenly it seems that everyone is looking relieved—except for Lydia, who hasn't even heard me, who has a head full of pit disasters.

You'd almost think they didn't want me around. But I don't mind. It means I can go to the room that is all mine, the room I would never have left if it had been up to me. Given half a chance, I would have stayed here all day, and let them muddle through the best they could.

But now I'm back, I can lie on the bed and let it all open up around me; wardrobe, curtains, greens and lemons. Tree above the fireplace, green-painted table. Play a little game with myself, planning what I would change and what I would keep the same if it all belonged to me.

The fact is, if this room were ever to become mine, I wouldn't change a thing. It's perfect just the way it is.

❧ Chapter Thirteen

NEXT MORNING AND I'M OUT of bed the moment I wake up, before the phone can even think of ringing. It's Sunday, remember. No-one sleeps through a Sunday.

At least that's what I thought. But downstairs their newspapers are lying untouched on the mat under the front door and the curtains are still drawn. The kitchen is warm, but empty. Lydia's family haven't even begun to get out of bed. And it's *Sunday*.

I knew they didn't go to church in this house, but somehow I never thought they would begin the day like this, by doing nothing. Just sleeping. As if they had all the time in the world.

Let's hope he doesn't phone now, for their sake. He'd never let me come again. Because I'd have to tell him; how they are all in bed on a Sunday, how even *she* hasn't appeared yet.

Although of course, she'll be the first one to do just that. Mothers generally are. The day can't start without them. Not unless you have Gran instead, ruining it all before it's begun. So Lydia's mother will be the one to come down, yawning and rubbing her eyes. A little ruffled perhaps, not quite herself, not yet.

What a surprise for her, then, if she walks into her kitchen and finds someone is already up, happy to keep her company. While the rest of her family stay wallowing in their beds.

It will be just the two of us, the way it was the first night, like mother and daughter. And this time, no-one to interrupt.

I wonder where she keeps the teapot?

• • •

FIVE minutes later, and it's all ready. Plates, cups, saucers, a table set for two. Bowls and spoons. Jam and marmalade and honey. Milk in a jug. Everything she could possibly want. A treat for someone everyone else seems to take for granted. And all I have to do is wait.

And then at long last, here it comes, the sound of footsteps on the stairs. The very lightest of sounds. That will be her bedroom slippers. I noticed them yesterday, fluffy things with kitten heels that go tap tap tap like a dancer's on the polished floors. You'd almost think it was a child walking.

What is she going to say when she sees breakfast all ready and waiting? That Lydia has never done this for her. That Lydia would never dream. Not Lydia.

The door opens, and in walks . . .

. . . Laura.

Laura, carrying a doll that is almost as big as she is, so big it's a struggle just getting it through the door. It's the reason she doesn't see me, not at first. When she does, she stops, looking suddenly quite drawn. For a moment I thought that she might turn right around and go back the way she came. But the moment passes and she looks away, carries on past me, into the kitchen, as if to pretend I wasn't there. Before I realise what she is up to, she is putting the doll in one seat and taking the other seat herself. Then she fills both the bowls with cereal and begins to eat.

You know what's happened of course. She's put herself in my place. And as if that wasn't bad enough, she's made sure there are two of them, that it's like seeing double.

And there's nothing I can do. Because now there are other footsteps, heavier, and this time, unmistakeable. Lydia's mother appears, yawning and rubbing her eyes. Soft in her dressing gown, a little ruffled. The way I knew she would be.

But she doesn't notice me. Seeing Laura and her doll, both with their bowls of cereal, she begins to smile, goes positively misty eyed.

'Having a quiet breakfast with Angelina, darling?'

And would you believe it, she kisses Laura, and *kisses the doll*.

Only then does she look up and give a start. 'Why, Kate,' she says. 'Kate, you're up too.' But she isn't pleased to see me, not the way she was pleased to see Laura. She doesn't even ask who laid the table. And you know why. She thinks her precious Laura did it. With the help of a doll no doubt.

I really wasn't going to do this. I was going to let Lydia decide what to do today. But that was before her mother came down-stairs and didn't even notice I was there. So now I'm going to do it anyway.

Lydia looks suspicious when I tell her I have an idea for this morning. She's remembering yesterday. So just in case she has it in her mind to say no, I ask her where she has got to in the book, and that draws her up short. Then, just to clinch it, I say:

'I was thinking we might go to church,' and sit back to watch her face light up. It's the book again, isn't it, having its effect.

FOR a second time, Lydia's mother doesn't ask us where we are going. Another sign that she's different. *He'd* want to know where we were going, so he could be with us, every step of the way—in spirit, that is. Some people care about their children.

But it's just as well she doesn't ask. Lydia's mother wouldn't like it if she knew, not one little bit. Yesterday I wouldn't have done this. But I'm going to do it now.

ON the bus, Lydia keeps spotting churches, and every time thinks this must be where we get off. But I stay put, don't even bother looking out of the window. After a while, I can feel her becoming suspicious again, wondering if religion is really what I had in mind. Silly Lyddie, all too quick to think there's only one kind of church.

So, when finally I do stand up and ring the bell, she's not ready and almost gets left on the bus. It would have served her right too, letting her suspicious mind run away with her like that. I told her we were going to church, didn't I? Why think otherwise?

The trouble is, standing on the pavement and staring round her, she just can't see it, not a church, or anything remotely like one. She doesn't even know where we are. And why should she? You can't see her mother ever bringing her to this part of town. There's nothing here they could possibly want. Over there is the harbour, and the wind is blowing straight in from the sea, leaving traces of salt and dead fish on our lips, pushing old bits of paper against our knees. The street itself is empty, the shops not just closed, but boarded up—except for the bingo hall behind us. I *could* mention to Lydia that her good friend Moira lives with her gran only a street or so away from here. But I won't. We're not here to think about Moira MacMurray. Or her gran.

'Come on,' I say, and push open one of the big swing doors to the bingo hall. For several moments she's too surprised to follow, with the result that the door swings right back behind me. When I turn around Lydia is still outside, face up against the glass, like a baby owl looking in.

Poor Lyddie, silly Lyddie, thinking there's only one kind of church.

Yet all she she had to do was take a look at the posters on the doors. It's there in big letters, unmissable. *A meeting for Friends in the City*. And in even bigger letters, his name, my dad's. She should learn to notice things better, should Lydia. That way she would be more prepared.

'Come on,' I say again, forgetting she can't hear me through the glass. It's a forgivable mistake. Bingo halls are my second home, but I have to remember this is all new to her. Lydia still thinks that God lives in those churches that we passed, like something kept in a museum you have to visit specially. Something that never sees the light of day. But she should know by now. She's read *his* book after all. God gets about. And for some reason He really seems to like bingo halls.

With Lydia safely behind me now, I push on another door, the one that used to lead to the big screen when the bingo hall was still a cinema. 'Stick close,' I say. Well, I wouldn't want to lose her, would I? I'd never find her again, not in this crowd.

Because behind the door is a solid wall of people. It's standing room only. But then, it always is.

And still Lydia doesn't understand. She doesn't know where all these people have come from, or what they are doing here. Or even why the smell of the harbour seems to have followed us indoors with its tastes of fish and salt. Lydia's parents don't move in these sort of circles. Lydia's parents don't even go to church.

She should have read the posters, though. Because most of all, she doesn't understand the silence. The silence of the led. Lydia hears it and stops, then looks at me, wide eyed with alarm. Some people can't take silence. They expect crowds to be noisy, not quiet like this, making you think that anything could happen. She begins to edge back towards the door, making it clear she wants to leave. But we can't do that. We've only just arrived. There's no escape now.

And anyway, who said anything about the silence lasting?

At first it's just a groan. Lydia hears it and stares sharply round, looking for who's making it, for where it comes from—only to find the sound is coming from everywhere. *Then* look at her face when she realises that, instead of dying away, the sound is growing, gathering strength like something with a life of its own, filling the spaces of the hall, above and below her. Inside her even. Oh yes, look at Lydia now. A case of pure terror. And all because of a noise. Suddenly it becomes too much, she starts into action, begins to make a dash for the door. Fortunately I'm too fast, and grab her by the arm.

Wait, I say.

Because the noise has reached its peak. And now, little by little, it is falling away, gathering itself in, coiling round itself, to come back to nothing, to the silence that gave birth to it.

Silence again.

For a long moment nothing stirs. Then somewhere in the crowd a woman begins to cry, sobbing as if in fear or grief.

Lydia's body has begun to pulsate.

Perhaps I'd better put her in the picture. So I pinch her arm and point, making sure she looks. First at the giant speakers above our heads, responsible for turning a simple groan into an ear shattering event. Then at the crowd who are no more than ordinary, just a little over-excited, including the woman crying. There's always one. By the end, they'll all be at it, all the usual suspects, heaving and sobbing. You'd be surprised at the number of folk who believe they can speak in tongues, who believe they have something to say.

But there's only one person really, only one man who has something that needs to be heard. But before I can point to him, the speakers come to life again, not just with a groan this time, but with actual words. Lydia yelps and grabs my arm. Then she recognises the voice, magnified a hundred times, and her hand goes limp.

Well, it's *his* voice, isn't it? Didn't I say folk come from miles around? In churches and chapels throughout the land there are empty pews and empty collection bags. He's stolen them away, all these people with their fifty pence pieces. Although, of course, *stolen* is the wrong word. No-one forced them to come. They simply prefer to be here, the fishermen and their wives, listening to the things they want to hear. That God is definitely with them, in wind and high weather, in squalls and in shifting cargoes of ice and fish, in the rusty hulks they call their boats. A word in their ear before they motor away from shore and safe harbour. Something to keep them going—and something else besides for the wives who get left behind.

That's what the other churches aren't giving them. The personal touch. That's why they come to Dad. He knows what they like. He tells them God is everywhere, and they don't seem to notice what he leaves out, the most important bit. That God may be with them, but he's not necessarily going to do anything about it. Only if they are Chosen.

Although really, it's something they should understand better than most. What do *they* do with all the fish that the fish monger won't touch?

Anyway, now Lydia is one of them. Look at her. She can't even see him, not with so many folk standing in the way. But she can *hear* him. The silence was just a pause, an invitation to consider. We've come in half way through his *The Love of God Is a Flaming Spear* sermon. That always gets them. The way it's getting Lydia now. She'll never listen to anything as closely as she is listening at this moment.

. . . For my friends, how can a man—a *man*—describe the love of God? The length, the breadth, the depth of it. The sweetness and the pain of it. How can a *man* put into words a thing that is beyond the power of speech?'

Only a special man. And long last, Lydia, spectacles flashing, leaning and listening with her entire body, is learning just how special he is.

' . . . For the love of God is a hot desire, burning in your belly, melting the most inward, the most tender parts. Feel the heat, my friends, feel the flames of God's desire as they consume you, making you hollow and filling you with His warmth. Feel the fire as it licks the flesh from your bones, sucks the marrow from the very centre. Feel it, my friends, my sisters, my brothers. The sweetness and the pain of it. . . .'

And so on in the usual way. Rise and fall, rise and fall, his voice reminds me of the engine of our car, cutting back then driving forward, changing tempo, changing tone as the road requires. The sermon itself is like a journey we've made so often that I could close my eyes and know, just from the sound of the engine exactly where we are. . . .

But Lydia doesn't hear it that way. And quite right, too. She is beginning to feel the heat, what God wants her to feel. After the confusion, and then the panic, there is this. Already his voice has brought her out in a hot flush, sweat forming in a fine line below the rim of her spectacles. She looks as if the flames of God are busy even now, licking the soul right out of her. In fact, Lydia is beginning to look like every other person here.

And it's him, his voice, making everyone the same. My dad, talking about fire, as usual.

Well, she'd better make the most of it. He's about to reach the end.

'Oh, my friends. The love of God is indeed a hungry flame. It tempers, it consumes. It destroys the evil in your soul leaving the pure metal to shine through, proclaiming a faith as bright as gold. His love will make you suffer. His desire will make you burn. For the love of God is a *flaming spear*, piercing the softest parts and melting every thing . . . every mortal thing it touches . . . '

His voice breaks, tips over into a whisper. Lydia looks as if she may be about to faint. People often do. An old woman broke her hip last year she hit the ground so hard. Her relatives sent a letter threatening to sue. *She* sent a letter with a cheque, saying that the pain had cleansed her soul. She's probably here now, somewhere, ready for another cleansing. Let's hope there's someone to catch her this time.

But Lydia, oh, Lydia. You've fallen straightaway. Somehow I'd thought you might have stood a while to consider. All that education, teaching you to think. You work out maths problems by thinking. The same with Greek. You're a *thinker*. You're supposed to be clever. It's the reason you do so well.

Well she's not thinking now. Lydia is all feeling. And it's funny. In a way, I'm almost disappointed in her. Almost sorry I let her come.

He really is close to the end, though. We were so very late, you see. Didn't I say I hadn't intended to do this? He must have been speaking for an hour already. He does it all the time, when the spirit moves him. He'll do it again at home this evening, in our own church. And of course he knows the words so well.

'This, then, is the love of God. But in the heart of his love lies the greatest miracle of all. A sweetness, a suffering—so gentle, so douce that I . . . ' he stops here. He always stops '. . . that I cannot say another word.' A pause, then a final, a whispered cry magnified a hundred times:

'Take me then, oh Lord.'

And that's it. Silence. This time a proper one. The crowd stirs, but stays where it is, feet rooted to the spot. Sometimes I wonder what would happen if someone set off a fire alarm right at this moment. Or made a pile of coats and lit a match. Would they run, or would they stay? He's told them the flames would taste of honey. Would they still believe him?

But now, after the silence, the usual response. Or to put it another way, Pandemonium. By which I mean the outbreak of cries and sobs, and the lalala of all those women up the front, especially the younger ones, wailing out in tongues, smearing their lipstick not to mention their mascara. Always the same. Never different. The part I hate.

Oh, but don't tell him I said that.

I turn to Lydia. But she's not there. Lydia has taken to her feet. Something must still be at work inside her brain, something still able to think, which has told her to seize the moment while everybody else is incapable. It takes a good few seconds before I discover where she is, but then I spot her, way ahead of me, wriggling like an energetic worm to the front of the crowd.

I almost don't get there in time. Half a minute later and she's nearly arrived at the stage. At the last possible moment I catch her by the arm and hold her. Not that she notices at first, not properly. After a momentary struggle she stops, is content just to stare, up at the stage. And my dad.

She can see it all now, everything the crowd had hidden from her.

He's collapsed onto a chair, legs sprawling in front of him as if he had lost every bit of strength he had. Sweat is pouring off his face, and he is staring straight ahead of him. At what? The fire exit sign perhaps. All that talk about burning.

As usual though, it's the sheer amount of sweat that fascinates me, and the idea that even a fraction could be absorbed by that tiny scrap of wispy lace. *She* stands over him the way she always does, mopping his brow with the same useless piece of cotton. It's pink today, her handkerchief. That's because she is wearing the pink suit, and matching shoes. She looks like a rosy overweight angel, puff pastry hair, bosom rising like leavened bread, a plump and sacred vision. Good enough to eat.

Lydia turns to me, her eyes suddenly sharp behind her spectacles, more focused than you might have expected for someone who had been on the verge of fainting five minutes before.

'Who's *she*?'

And there was me thinking she would only have eyes for him. But so as not to make things too easy, I answer with, 'Who's *who*?'

Lydia points, finger shaking ever so slightly. Up there, on the stage, she's bending even closer now, the outside edges of her bouffante grazing up against his face.

'Oh,' I say as if it's the most natural thing in the world. 'That's Mrs. Forbes White. Didn't you know?' But then of course, how could she? All that interest in Dad, but Lydia has never thought to ask, who exactly are the people in such need—and who it is that phones at twenty-eight minutes past eight. Precisely.

Lydia stares at me and then at the stage. Bites her lip. A

moment ago, I'd thought I'd have to stop her from calling attention to us both. Now there doesn't seem the danger. Already she's
beginning to shrink back. Apparently Lydia has an instinct for
what is right after all. She understands, even when she doesn't
understand.

Still, at least we're safe.

Or are we? It's as I turn away that I see it. A white blur to the
left of me, a familiar face in the crowd. Or thought I did, because
when I look again it isn't there. But that may be because at last
people are beginning to come to their senses, to shift from their
chosen spots, understanding they'll get no more from him today.
He doesn't give encores. Besides, the bag will be going round,
and sometimes that gets people moving too, towards the doors,
even the ones who were foaming and speaking in tongues two
minutes ago.

But Lydia, who seems to be noticing more today than she ever
has, glances at me, catches me looking for something that's probably not even there.

'What?' she says. 'What's the matter?'

The only answer is to shrug my shoulders. There is absolutely
no point in making a fuss. But then, simply to avoid making a fuss
by dint of saying nothing, I add; 'I thought I saw Moira
MacMurray for a moment, that's all.'

Lydia's eyebrows go shooting up. 'Moira? Where?' Now she's
looking all around her. 'Well, I can't see her.' The stupid girl actually sounds disappointed

'Oh, well then,' I say. 'That proves it.' Which even I will admit
was hardly sensible. Because what does it prove? I know what I
saw. Or at least I thought that I did.

I tried to make sure we were out in the first wave, to be standing
somewhere so as to see everyone else as they came out. But it was
impossible. There were three exits and a rush for each one, and
with so many people, the result was a standstill. It took us ten

minutes to reach the nearest door. It really did make you wonder what would happen if there had been a fire.

OUT on the pavement, however, Lydia suddenly seizes up. Delayed reaction. It gets some folk like that, when it's all over, and they are out in the real world. Accordingly, she starts shivering and shaking, blinking as if she hardly knows where she is or how she came there.

'K-Kate,' she says. 'Kate.' Her teeth are chattering so much her braces will end up with metal fatigue if she doesn't watch out.

'What?' I say. '*What?*' There's a funny tone in my voice that surprises even me. And I can't look at her. I don't *want* to look at her for some reason, not when she's like this. I'll say it again. *I never thought she would be so easy.* Not Lydia. If I had dreamt for one minute that she would be, I would never have brought her.

There'll be no going back after this, not for her.

And here she goes, just the way you'd expect now. 'Kate, he's just the most wonderful, wonderful . . .' Her face is still all flushed and she has one hand pushed up under her coat, rubbing her stomach as she speaks. She doesn't know what she's doing. It's freezing out in this street. She should button up or she'll catch a cold to end all colds.

And even the bus driver notices, looks twice at Lydia as I hand over the money for both of us. Looks three times. It's the flush in her cheeks, and the way her hands are still moving up and down her body as if looking for a resting place. I practically have to push her into a seat.

But there, surprisingly, her eyes come into focus again, making her turn to me just when I'm least expecting it, and say: 'I'll say this though. I didn't much like the look of *her*, I didn't like the look of her at all, that Mrs. Forbes White person.'

To tell the truth, I'm too busy looking out of the window to take much notice or even be surprised at how a person can be away with the fairies one minute and as sharp as a pin the next.

Out there on the street people are still walking away from the hall, trying to make headway through the wind and the same dirty scraps of paper, some of which have his name on them. Lots of people out there, walking home, but not one of them is her. Moira MacMurray.

THERE'S trouble at home, too, at Lydia's home, that is.

We had to run up the garden path because Lydia was too excited to walk, thus giving no warning that we were coming. And there, in the sitting room, is her mother, an open book on her lap and Laura curled up at her feet. As we burst through the door, Mrs. Morris's head shoots up, with an expression that is more than just simple surprise. What is it? Guilt? Definitely guilt, I would say. But something else besides, more troublesome than plain old guilt.

'Why, Lydia!' she exclaims, and there, now we've both noticed it, the small half-hearted attempt to close the book before we see what she's been reading.

Lydia gasps and goes pale. She darts forward in a sudden, almost graceful, movement and scoops the book out of her mother's lap. 'This is mine. You must have got it from under my . . .'

She stops, but it's too late. Because now we all know exactly where Lydia's mother got the book. From under Lydia's pillow.

Isn't that funny? Just the place where I keep my horse. There must be something about pillows, something that makes us think they are safe, places too private for anyone else to disturb. But Lydia was wrong, wasn't she? Someone else did come along to disturb, even in this house. Which suddenly makes me wonder. And worry. About who might be disturbing what at home.

But for the moment, the trouble is here and nowhere else.

'How dare you, how dare you,' Lydia is mumbling over and over. 'How dare you.' And that's all she can come up with. No imagination, you see. It's all been used up, back there in the street and on the bus. After a moment, she turns and flings herself out of the room.

A comical sight, I'll grant you. All that heaving and passion on the part of someone who still looks as if she is made out of pipe cleaners. Down on the floor, Laura giggles. Only a tiny sound, and understandable really. But the effect is astounding. Because the second she hears it, Lydia's mother darts forward and cuffs her round the ear. Laura hiccups and stares at her, eyes round, mouth slack, suddenly not pretty any more, not even minutely enchanting. Just profoundly shocked, as if this is something that has never happened before in all her life.

'Mrs. Morris . . .' I start to say, because with Lydia gone and Laura in disgrace, this is my chance. I'll be able to show her that not everyone in this house is behaving badly. That there is someone here she can turn to.

But it's no good. Because when Mrs. Morris turns to look at me, her eyes show it all; she's been reading the book. Reading about him, and the way things are. Reading about how everyone will have to follow *him* otherwise there's no hope, not even for those who have been Chosen. Because this is the truth he writes about. God may choose but it's Dad who delivers. That's the way it is. And it's not fair. She can hardly bear to look at me now. As if it was my fault. As if I was the one to blame.

❧ Chapter Fourteen

LYDIA HAS THE BOOK STRAPPED into her satchel as we set off for school.

And her mother knows it, because when we say goodbye, Mrs. Morris smiles at me exactly the way she did on Friday afternoon. The way she would smile at anyone, the way she would smile at *him*. Nobody in their right minds would take us for mother and daughter now. It's like losing someone after you thought you'd found them. Losing them all over again.

And it's Lydia's fault, not knowing how to act, looking as if she hated everyone in the entire house. All because someone sneaked a little something from under her pillow. If only Lydia would learn to smile when it matters, everything would be fine.

As we walk out of the house, her mother says wearily, 'Don't come straight out today, Lydia. Laura has her ballet lesson, remember. Last week you forgot. Stay in school until you can both come home together.'

If looks could kill, then believe me, Mrs. Morris would be lying stretched out on the pavement right this minute. And why? Because *he* will be coming to pick me up tonight, will be right outside the school for anyone who wants to see him. Now Lydia's been told she has to stay inside and wait.

Looks can't kill, naturally, but I never realised a grown-up could be so visibly upset by a bit of common or garden glaring. Mrs. Morris looks as if she doesn't know whether to shout or burst into tears. But why the fuss for heaven's sake? She's still got Laura.

And there's me of course. If she would only stop blaming me for everything.

IN Greek, Miss Jamieson can't make out what's gone wrong.

Last week she mentioned we were going to be reading Plato and Lydia was positively ecstatic. A girl after Miss Jamieson's own heart. But that's all in the past, absolutely prehistory. That was before Lydia went to church. Now Lydia couldn't care less. She isn't even remotely listening. For nearly the whole of the lesson she just sits there, clutching her satchel and staring into space. Every now and then, her cheeks flicker with sudden flashes of red, and you don't have to have *It* to know what's going through *her* mind.

'Forgive me for asking, but is there something valuable in that bag, Lydia, something that needs to be kept safe?'

The sarcasm is cutting—but it's lost on Lydia. She merely clutches the satchel closer than ever to her chest, and nods. Carries on as before.

So it might as well be just the two of us sitting there, Miss Jamieson and me. Yet she should look at it this way; half a loaf is better than none, and at least *someone* is listening, even if her star pupil is a hundred miles away. Lydia may be not be, but *I'm* taking in every word. I don't know when I last paid such attention.

Maybe it's because, just this once, Jamieson has found a subject that is interesting.

Apparently this Plato person had a teacher, a man called Socrates, who taught him everything he knew, but seems to get only half the credit. And Socrates had all sorts of tricks up his sleeve. Like pretending to be simple when he was with clever folk just to get them to say things they never would have dreamed of saying otherwise. Jamieson called this a philosophical trap. Which is odd, because I'd simply call it having *It*. In the end, though, it got him into all sorts of trouble, because then the young folk went round repeating everything he said, such as not liking the government, and how there should be just a few good men in charge. Their trouble was, they were young, which is the way Socrates liked to catch them, in their teens, the way he caught Plato. An impressionable age.

I might have asked a question here, such as whether Socrates included girls. But what would have been the point? I doubt if Jamieson would have even heard me. She was too busy watching Lydia, looking for signs of life.

Back to Socrates then. And another question. In fact, the only question that really matters. The one we should always ask. If Socrates had been alive today, would he have been Chosen? Would he have been one of us?

And the funny thing is, Jamieson actually manages to answer it.

Because then she goes on to say that one of the most important things he taught was how there is only the one truth about anything. Only one proper way of looking at a thing, ruling out every other way there is. Which doesn't leave much choice. Choice is about exploring the alternatives, which means once you start exercising *choice* you get into all sorts of trouble, upsetting the way things are meant to be. In Socrates' ideal world therefore, no-one tries to choose who he is or what he does. Each man sticks to what he was when he was born. That way, rulers get to rule and poor men do as they are told. A place for everyone and everyone in their place.

No wonder the government didn't like him; Athens was supposed to be the world's first democracy. It's what she was famous for.

Was Socrates one of us, then? I'd say he was. Without a shadow of a doubt in fact. Because I've heard all this before, haven't I, from a completely different quarter. Forget Socrates, it's my dad they should be teaching to children in the schools.

You'd think Lydia would make the connection, but she doesn't. It's lost on her because the truth is that, although she's read his book, she's only understood about a half of it. The rest she has ignored. Miss Jamieson takes a look at her and sighs. Tries one last time to prod the interest of her favourite pupil.

'There you are, Lydia,' she says, handing her a book with a picture on the front. 'That's what he may have looked like, Socrates himself.'

She's talking about a bust, carved out in purest white marble. A powerful head that makes you think he must have had a body to match. A forehead twice the size of anybody else's. Not what you'd call handsome. But it hardly matters. Handsome is as handsome does. Besides, there's something else about it, something that makes me look again, more closely this time. Something familiar. . . .

At the same time, something beside me stirs. It's Lydia waking up at last. One glance at the book and suddenly she's pulling it towards her, and stammering, hardly making any sense, until:

'It's your f-father, Kate. Look at him. It's your f-father.'

There, she's beaten me to it, put a name to what was so familiar. And she's right of course. Ignore the beard, and you could see the resemblance, right down to the shape of his nose.

And it's like a miracle, the effect it has. Suddenly you'd think she was her old self again, more alive than she's been all morning. Lydia puts her head down and starts paying attention to what's in the book, reading what's there, like a little pig truffling about for nuggets of information. Miss Jamieson smiles, convinced everything is back to normal.

But then, little by little, the smile disappears. Because even Jamieson can see it; this isn't the old Lydia after all. The old

Lydia would have been interested in Socrates for his own sake. Now there's a different reason altogether. And it has nothing to do with the love of learning. This is what you might call the result of a one track mind.

Much more of this and Miss Jamieson will be wishing she'd never brought up the subject, not if this is going to be the effect. But there you are. You can't teach Greek without mentioning Socrates. Even I know that. It would be like history without the Spanish Inquisition. Or Attila the Hun.

OR school without Moira MacMurray. By which I mean that you may not think very much of someone, but you notice if they're not there. And Moira wasn't at school today. So I couldn't ask her. I couldn't ask if she had come—uninvited—to the bingo hall yesterday; and if she had come, then what she was doing there; and how it is she always seems to know where I'll be and what I'm doing. As if her only purpose in this whole life is to watch me. Never take her eyes off me.

Come to think of it, it's probably a good thing she's not here to ask. Those questions, suddenly pouring out like that. She'd have got the impression it was important for some reason, that what she did mattered. And nothing could be further from the truth.

On second thought then, it's probably a splendid thing, Moira not being at school today. Even better if she doesn't come tomorrow either.

ON the way home, I told *him* what Lydia had said, about looking just like Socrates. He laughed, but he was pleased, you could see that. Told me he thought the world of Socrates, and Plato, too, for that matter. Then he rubs my knee and tells me it's a proper treat to have me home, that there's nothing in the world like having me to himself.

It's at moments like this when a person knows. What is it to be the luckiest girl alive.

Then suddenly he looks at me again, and the car goes quiet.

Kate love. You're wearing your hair differently.

And he's right of course. I've pulled it back with one of Lydia's bands, into the tightest of ponytails. That way it looks darker, less . . . noticeable. At least that's what I thought.

But I was wrong. All I've done is made him look the harder.

That's when I begin to talk, about Lydia and her family. Or to be more precise, about *her*, Lydia's mother. Because for some reason she's important. What she says goes. And because for some reason he's interested, perhaps because she's a challenge. Or perhaps just because she's so very soft . . .

. . . Oh no, that has to be wrong. That's the reason *I'm* interested.

But it works. His eyes leave my hair, return to the road as I tell him everything about her, every single thing I can remember—and more besides. Such as how much she liked her chocolates. How she popped one into her mouth straightaway, how she closed her eyes and smiled, because of the sweetness perhaps, or maybe another reason besides. Dad listens and drives. Fiddles with the loose change in his pocket and doesn't once look at my hair again.

That's how important she is.

I think he may be trying to make up his mind about her. Usually he can tell straightaway with people simply by looking at them. It's what he does when he's outside the school: watches the big girls go by, spotting souls. Could it be that, just this once, he has to think about it? Because he isn't sure about her yet, about what she is, and where she's going?

And if she's been Chosen.

It's the reason I don't tell him the truth about the chocolates, or the book, or the wine even. Because I know what the answer would be then. I know what he is bound to say. And wouldn't it be a shame, knowing there's no hope for her? Even if she doesn't deserve it.

IT'S strange, but our house seems darker when I walk through the door tonight, our walls damper, our curtains skimpier. And colder. It's cold everywhere. Except the kitchen of course where it's too hot and the steam seems to cling to my hair and the backs of my hands.

But never mind, because there's still a little chink of light, a brightness you can touch. I only have to run upstairs, close my eyes and put a hand under my pillow, fingers tingling. And feel. Feel all over. Open my eyes. Remove the pillow altogether. Throw it across the floor, throw it out of the window if I only could, because underneath there's nothing there.

You see, it's gone, the tiny horse, shining in its tiny box, looking as if someone had taken a portion of pure light, mixed it with sugar crystals and spun it into glass. Just for me.

It's gone.

But why? I broke it. It was broken. No-one could say I had allowed myself to take something without flaw and keep it. A person is *allowed* to keep what isn't perfect. You can't accuse her of anything. She can't take pride in an object that is broken, or get above herself, or boast that she holds perfection in her grasp. I broke it.

I broke it. But it's gone. There's nothing there, not any more. And now I have to go downstairs and remember to smile when it matters.

In other words, smile and smile until I see the approving look come into his face, and know it's safe to come to bed. Smile to make sure there are no more lessons tonight since obviously I've learnt this one so very well already.

• • •

BUT I had the dream again. Or something like it. I mean, the new-old dream where there's only me. No heat or streaming light, or arms carrying me aloft. No Dad. And it's funny because I thought dreams were nothing but a distraction, or something to make a person feel uncomfortable. I didn't know they could make you feel better. That a dream could be the strangest of comforts—at least until you wake up.

I am in his room again. Everything is where it should be—the desk, the warmth in the carpet and, of course, the picture on the wall. Those girls with their trays of fruit and smoky burned offerings. I can see their faces, see their pretty deluded smiles. I can see their bare feet and little toes, perfect, just like mine.

And something else besides. Something I've never noticed before. The handles on the desk drawers glowing, shiny as if someone has spent all the day polishing them, shiny as new pins. So bright they make me want to touch them. They remind me of something, something that has yet to happen, but not here, not in this dream.

But listen, there's no time to stare. Because here's the sound of footsteps, coming closer, footsteps stopping outside the door, the sound of a promise being kept. The reason I've been waiting. Smiling now as the door begins to open and . . .

. . . And I wake up, before I have a chance to see who it is behind the door, the one I've been waiting for. The room has gone, the comfort of the dream has gone. There's nothing here but dark and the shape of my pillow.

My pillow. Before it knows what it is doing, my hand moves under the pillow—as I expect it will for weeks now, until it gets used to it, and learns to remember in time. And there's nothing there. The horse is gone, and there's nothing under the pillow except the sheet, musty and damp from Gran's washing.

All of me remembers now. It's gone. The horse is gone.

GO to sleep, Kate.

Or if you can't sleep, count your blessings, the way other people count sheep.

For example, there are no secrets in this house. In this house, there is a place for everything and everything in its place. Our house is like the whole wide world as it should be. I am lucky to be here. That is a blessing. Birds in the air, pebbles on the beach, me in my bed—and every thing that is precious where it belongs. In his room.

(Even with its broken leg, my horse was precious. Anything she gave me would have been precious. Why didn't I realise that?)

Go to sleep, Kate. Otherwise in the morning they'll look at you and know you stayed awake. And why. Or if you won't sleep, keep counting. Remember that Pride is the worst of the sins. Sins keep a person from God. Pride is what my father has to fight against, wherever he finds it. He takes the source of pride away and saves me from the sin. That is a blessing.

(Yet if I close my eyes, something gleams behind the lids. Not the horse, but something else. It's the gleam I saw in my dream, belonging to the handles on my father's desk. Shiny as a new pin.)

Go to sleep, Kate. The only true gifts are those we get from God. No other gift is real. This is what Dad has done for me. He's taken away the gift that was never really a gift and saved me from myself. Count this also as a blessing.

(But what is real anyway? If she had *really* believed a crystal horse was too precious, she wouldn't have given it to me. But she did. She gave it to me. She wanted me to have it.)

That's what is real. She wanted me to have it, the crystal horse. There are no secrets in this house. In my dream the handles of his desk had flashed and winked like a signal. Like a reminder. His desk is where all the precious things end up. It's where you could find them even now.

No-one need ever know. I only want to see it again. Hold it again, feel its hooves prick my hand, and its sides grow warm against my face. Just for a minute, before I put it back where it belongs. Then I will go to sleep.

OUT on the landing, on the other side of a door, I can hear some-one snoring and the sound is like a person tearing bedsheets into strips, as if for bandages. It's Gran of course, dreaming of things you wouldn't even dare think about.

But nothing from his room, not a sound. My father is sleeping the sleep of the righteous, the only time when he is quiet.

But still not as quiet as me, making so little noise, I could almost believe I was dreaming, even now. Except nothing could make a person shiver like this, not if it was just a dream. The cold comes up through the floor, old lino, damp, sticking to the soles of my feet, but more than anything, cold, sending an chill right through to the bone. Making me wish I'd remembered shoes.

Then again, you could say it serves me right, being cold. A place for everything and everything in its place. My place is in bed, isn't it, not stirring until he wakes me. If I turn back now, it wouldn't be too late. I wouldn't have done a thing wrong.

If I turn back now, I will never see it again. My horse. The one she gave to me and no-one else.

Then it really is too late. Because a moment later I'm standing in his room, and you know what I've done. I've crossed the threshold, gone from being good to being bad in a single step. And it's the worst thing I've ever done. I have fallen away from perfect before today, and kept on falling. But that was always a mistake, the fruit of ignorance. I have never done anything like this in the full knowledge. It's no wonder I need something to hold on to, the door knob, the back of a chair, anything.

Then I see the picture, and below it his desk and, suddenly, falling is the last thing on my mind. Because there are the handles on his desk, gleaming, shiny as new pins. And it's like the dream again, standing here, gazing at the picture, at the silly girls—and the gleaming handles on his drawers.

Then I look down and see my feet, both of them. Only five rosy toes. One good foot, one bad. Not like the dream after all.

Only tell that to the desk. Those handles just keep on winking and gleaming at me as if there was no difference at all. I could be awake or asleep, it's just the same to them, and they only seem to want to tell me the one thing. What I want is in the desk. A place for everything and everything in its place. That way he can look after every precious object, keep it from falling into the wrong hands. My hands.

Suddenly it's my hands that are at work now, moving of their own accord, as if they had a mind of their own. Starting with the topmost drawer, the one that would be closest to him as he sits, writing sermons, working for all our sakes. Inside the drawer is a box of chocolates. Unopened. But then, I've been away. I haven't been here for him to teach me anything.

I wouldn't dream of taking one, though, not even with the scents of sugar and cocoa seeping through the cover with its picture of kittens with bows around their necks. They aren't mine. I'm only here to find something that belongs to me. Or used to. Still, I have to take them out of the drawer, just so that I can see to what's underneath.

But it's as I stand here, box of chocolates in hand, that something happens. I hear a sound. And with the sound, something goes astray, gets lost in the dark behind me. And why? Because this is the very sound I have been waiting for, the sound of footsteps, coming closer, the sound of a promise about to be kept. It's the reason I can't move, not even to put the chocolates back in the drawer. Suddenly, I can't even remember why I'm holding them. I'm in my dream again. I never was awake.

The footsteps have stopped. Someone is behind the door. This time, I am going to see who it was, the person I've been waiting for.

The door opens.

And I don't wake up. Of course not, why should I, when I am awake already? Even so it seems to take a few seconds, with both of us staring, to recognise each other, as if for all the world we had been expecting someone different.

It's Gran. Only Gran.

The long nightdress she is wearing has a frill around her neck that makes it look just like a shroud. You might think you were seeing a ghost—the nasty kind, the kind that hates the living and can't find a moment's rest for thinking about it.

But she doesn't cross the threshold. This is his study. Even she doesn't come in without an invitation. Which only makes it worse, what I've done, standing here with a drawer open and a box of chocolates in my hands. Instead she lifts up her head, and screams out his name. Tells him to come down and see what she has found.

Odd what you remember, though, in times of trouble. In the silence between his waking and the slow beat of his feet upon the stairs, I find myself thinking of just one thing: the look on Gran's face when she opened the door. As if she had been expecting to find someone else completely. It took several whole seconds for her to make the switch, and realise it was only me. Then you should have seen the relief. As if she was the one who thought she had seen a ghost.

But there's no time to think about it now. Dad is here, wanting to know what's happened, and why he's been called from the sleep of the just. Wanting to know what has gone wrong. And what needs to be put right.

❧ Chapter Fifteen

NEXT DAY, HILARY CATCHES ME unawares.

'I've got something here you'll like,' she whispers. And pushes a bar of Cadbury's right under my nose.

I should have seen it coming, been alive to the rustle of silver paper. But I didn't. Now it's too late. The scent of chocolate catches the back of my throat, and I can't help myself. Before I know what I'm doing, I've slapped the entire bar out of her hand, sent it flying like a missile across the room.

It falls with a thud on the floor—right at the feet of Moira MacMurray. Hilary, naturally a little shocked, yet never missing a beat when it comes to food, screams at her:

'Moira MacMurray, just you give me back my chocolate.'

Slowly, Moira bends and picks it up, weighs it in her hand. Hilary opens her mouth to bawl at her once more, then closes it because now Moira has started to do what she's told, is bringing it back to her. But instead of simply passing it under my nose, she is lumbering round the far side of the desks, right away from me. It's as if she's knows, as if somehow she realises what chocolate would do to me today. Even the smell of it.

Last night Gran was all set to tell him the whole story. But really there was no need. All he had to do was look at me, standing in my bare feet by his desk, holding the box of chocolates. Take one look and sigh.

Now I don't think the taste of chocolate will ever go away. It's still there, coating my tongue, clogging up my throat. Every breath feels heavy with it. So you see, even the scent of it now, the faintest suggestion . . .

Only the one cure for gluttony, that's what he said. And with Gran's help, he set about to administer the cure.

But how could Moira MacMurray know any of that? How did she know to come the long way round with Hilary's chocolate? Just so I didn't have to catch the smell of it, not again, not today.

How did she know I needed help?

HILARY stayed on her high horse nearly the whole time after. Well, she's not used to having her confectionary smacked across a room. I could have tried harder with her I suppose, come up with an explanation that would have brought her round, but I'm so tired. I'm too tired for anything.

It would almost be nice to be Lydia at times like this. Look at her, she's tired too, absolutely run ragged. All that heat and light, twenty minutes in a church, endless time with a book; now she looks as if she hasn't had a wink of sleep since. Too much heated day dreaming keeping her awake.

But what does she do about it?

She heads for Moira MacMurray, that's what Lydia does. Not to talk. She and Moira never talk, not to each other. In point of fact, they don't *do* anything at all. I have half a belief that this is how Moira and her gran behave at home, and you could almost see how they could be happy, how *anyone* could be happy, content just to let the person beside them exist, never interfere. But it makes Hilary snigger watching the two of them drift through the day, side by side.

Yet I know exactly what Lydia is doing. She's relaxing, something that could only happen next to Moira. She's getting her energy back. Keeping close to Moira, who wants nothing, asks for nothing, says nothing. Who is just there, like a great soft cushion. Like that giant windbreak, protecting you from anything.

So you see, you could almost envy Lydia, tired out, but able to disappear next to something so large, and that hardly seems to know she's there. It nearly makes me wish I could do the same thing. But I can't relax, not for a moment, and especially not with Moira, even if she did help me just now. Because if she knew about the chocolate, what else might she know about me?

And anyway, who wants to be connected with a laughing stock? I haven't mentioned what happened at the end of today.

It was final period, geography, with the bell about to go any moment. Everyone was busy drawing contour lines on maps, but listening at the same time, ready to throw down her pencil the very second it rang. Meanwhile, young Mr. Harris is at his desk, studying the topless native girls in the *National Geographic*, trying not to breathe too hard. We know all about him.

Then it comes—but not the bell, not the interruption we were expecting. A different sound altogether. It begins as a tiny, high pitched whine, as though a gnat has just this second entered the classroom, then grows, both in pitch and volume to a peak where it could shatter glass, stays there, shivering, for an unbelievably long space of seconds—before finally falling away, back to the sound of the gnat's song.

And in its wake, silence. At least at first, just for those few incredulous seconds. Then just as you'd expect, someone begins to giggle.

'Moira MacMurray, you absolute piggy!'

And that sets off the rest of them. Next thing you know, the entire class is in fits, row after row of girls howling as if it's the funniest thing they have ever heard. Mr. Harris stares this way and that, looking almost frightened. He claps his hands a few times, raises his voice, even raps the rolled up *National Geographic* against the front of the desk. But it's no good, he's no Miss Jamieson or Mrs. Chatto. When the bell goes, it hardly makes any difference. Class was already dismissed; Moira had seen to that.

Yet not everyone was laughing. Not me for instance. What makes people think that breaking wind is a laughing matter? It's a sign of weakness, a reminder that the body is beyond control, dragging you down. Sometimes Gran will let out a squeak at the table, and we have to sit in the aftermath, pretending it never happened, that she is still up there, fit to be with the angels.

And another thing, stopping me laughing. It reminded me of something, the small sound that grows to a crescendo and fills a room—an entire bingo hall, even—before it dies away, leaving a silence which in turn gives way to chaos. Just so much hot air.

It's that that makes me blush suddenly, so hard I can feel the heat rising in my face. Some thoughts should be banished before they have the chance to see the light of day.

And would you believe it? They are *still* at it, the entire class, laughing their heads off. Some people here have already turned fifteen. You'd think they'd know better. But they don't. There's only the one other person who's not laughing, and guess who that is.

Moira. She is sitting just a little way from my desk, perfectly relaxed, perfectly comfortable—and staring at me. But now—or is it my imagination?—it's with the faintest hint of a question in her eyes, as if she expected me, of all people, to tell her what it's about, why everyone is laughing. As if she doesn't even know what she's done.

EVEN Lydia is careful to keep her distance from Moira after. Instead she tags along with us, Hilary and me. Hilary, meanwhile, is still insisting on laughing hysterically. But at least she's forgotten about this morning and the flying chocolate. Something else I suppose you could thank Moira for.

So with Hilary laughing and Lydia smiling, we look the very picture of schoolgirl fun, the three of us—not exactly arm in arm, but close enough. Even Hilary couldn't ask for more. They could write a book about us, call it *Schoolgirl Chums at the Abbey*, something like that.

And as if this wasn't enough, as if fun is the sole order of the day, there's another treat in store—if you were Hilary or Lydia. Right outside the gate, where nobody else would dare to park (headmistress's orders) the car is waiting. Lydia spots it first and goes rigid, fingers pinching stiffly at my elbow. Hilary merely squeals.

He's seen us coming. I daresay he watched us walk out of school. He's winding down the window now, and beaming. You can see he has a special twinkle in his eye for everybody. Even me. Especially for me. He's a great man for forgiveness, is my dad. Later, on the way home, he will say it's behind us, last night I mean. Forgive and forget. It's what he always says.

But now of course, he has to concentrate on Lydia and Hilary. Make sure nothing slips away.

'That's a very heavy looking satchel you have there, Lyddie love. It must be full of books.'

One book in particular, but he knows all about that. Yet still she thinks she has to explain, blushing and stammering, tell him it's *his* book weighing down her satchel, let him know that she's read every word, that she'll never be parted from it, and so on and so forth—until Hilary begins to get jealous and starts clearing her throat as if suddenly it's full of frogs. Much more of this and she might even walk away.

But he's not going to let that happen, not my dad. 'And Hilary, my *lovely* girl. How are you?'

Hilary goes bright red, snickers and stares at the floor, tells him she's fine, all the better for seeing him. And waits for him to ask more questions, the way he did with Lydia. Yet nothing happens. Dad doesn't say another word. Hilary's smile begins to dim. But she shouldn't fret. It's just that, suddenly, he's busy thinking. Dad is planning something, I can tell. . . .

A moment later, he bangs both hands down on the steering wheel, making them jump.

'I've got it. You know what should happen, don't you. Why didn't I think of it before? We need to have the three of you to stay, first possible opportunity. You can be all girls together, having a whale of a time. Making a mess, clattering about, keeping old Keith Carr from his beauty sleep, chattering the whole night long. What do you think, eh? What do you think?'

What do they think? Hilary and Lydia are speechless, hardly daring to believe their ears.

And of course he hasn't finished, running pictures through their minds no-one could resist '. . . Midnight feasts, secret gossips, no end of fun. Terrible girls, the lot of you, fit to turn a man's hair grey . . .'

Oh, he's a wonder to watch. Something to be proud of. No-one can hear him and feel the same. Hilary and Lydia were happy enough before. Now they are fit to burst. All they can do is smile, smile so hard you'd think their faces are going to break into little pieces.

So I smile, too. What else is there to do? Attention shared is attention halved. And besides, he is watching me.

Then something goes wrong. I can feel it before I even know what's happened. Suddenly Dad's eyes dart past us, attracted by something moving behind our backs, claiming his attention. And somehow I know, before I have even turned round, what that Something is.

Moira is standing behind us, filling up the pavement with the combined bulk of her, her old lady's coat, and the carrier bag which passes for a satchel. But the first thing I notice about her is this: I'm standing here but, for once, it's not me she's looking at.

Dad blinks, so quickly you would hardly notice. But I did. Time slows when I'm watching Dad. I see a hundred expressions come and go in the time it takes others simply to spot the smile. He's felt the gaze, Moira's gaze.

And this time, it's turned on him.

'Moira love. I didn't see you standing there.'

Moira says nothing, merely shifts whatever's bulging in one cheek into the other cheek. But she continues to stare at

Dad—*exactly the way she stares at me.* Except it doesn't seem to matter. If he notices, it doesn't show. Dad smiles at her again, before turning back to Hilary and Lydia.

But moment later, almost reluctantly, his eyes return to Moira. Who continues to stare at him.

And suddenly, it hits me. Like a bolt of lightning, like a flash from Heaven, like a message from above it hits me. I thought I'd picked the right person to bring home, but I hadn't. I'd picked the *wrong* person. Lydia seemed to be just up his street, but she's too easy, isn't she. There's no real challenge in Lydia. All those brains have just made her stupid. In a little while, there'll be nothing else about her to hold him. Not even the Greek.

No, the person to hold his attention, really hold it, is someone completely different. Someone altogether unexpected. Someone he can't forget is there.

Because look at him now. We're all standing here, but who is he staring at? Moira. He's trying to look away, but he can't. In fact, he's worse than I am. I can turn my back on her any time I like. I can forget Moira if I really put my mind to it. But I'm not sure that he could.

Though I'd like to see him try. I would.

Is that why, before I even know what it's going to say, I can hear my own voice speak up, clear as a bell, so that not even a crowd of fifth formers suddenly spilling out of the gates behind us can drown me out?

'Moira has to come, too. Moira's got to come and stay. It wouldn't be the same without Moira.'

And you should see the look on everyone's face. Hilary is practically pop-eyed, staring at me as if I have lost my mind. Even Lydia looks taken aback.

But Dad is the one to watch. He's trying out expressions, one after the other, faster than even I can follow—until he hits on the final one, the one that seems to have escaped him for just these few split seconds.

A smile.

But what a smile it is. Tender and understanding. A smile that tells you words are quite unnecessary, that he sees everything, knows everything. 'Kate love,' he murmurs. 'That's a lovely idea, a really fine idea. But I'd say that Moira here has better things to do.'

He is talking to me, but looking at her. Letting that smile rest on her. It must feel as if the sun is shining, for her and no-one else.

'You're forgetting an important thing, you see. Moira lives with her grandmother. And old ladies need their young folk. Last thing they want is for the apple of their eyes to be gallivanting off without them for nights on end. Isn't that right, Moira love?'

By way of reply, Hilary, who is standing next to Moira, nods her head. She's listening so hard, she probably thinks she *is* Moira. The same thing has happened to Lydia, who is also nodding. That's what he does to people; he makes them forget who they are. He makes them all the same, breaks down the barriers, reducing them to one happy blob of feeling centred only on him. It's a miracle to see, really. It's what he does so well.

And now we know. Moira won't be going anywhere, because it's impossible, something that was never meant to be, for reasons I've already begun to forget. It's only his smile I remember. The singlemost surprise is how the question cropped up in the first place.

And Moira? She says nothing. Well, no-one would expect her to, would they, not after that. But it's strange, I feel almost let down. I had nearly begun to believe the impossible there; that there was something about Moira, something working through her, almost separate from her. Something to explain the way she stares, the things she knows. Something bigger than Dad even. I had, I had nearly begun to believe that. But now I know. She's just Moira. And nothing is bigger than Dad.

Meanwhile, he's winding up the window, signalling for me to

get into the car. He wants to get away, soon. Before anything else happens.

But then, at the last possible moment, Moira speaks. And what Moira says is: 'No, it's not right. My gran says never to mind her. She says I should get out more. She says it all the time. I'll come to Kate's house.'

Dad's hand comes to a complete stop on the handle. The window stays where it is, half up and half down. For a long moment he looks straight at Moira, stares right into the eyes that are fixed on him. But it has to be said; he looks away first.

Then suddenly it's smiles, smiles all round. 'Rightie ho,' he sings out. 'Four of you it is. You tell your mums and dads. What a treat, what a riot eh?' And he winks at each one of us. Even Moira. Especially Moira.

HE was quiet on the drive home, though. Or he was at first. He seemed to be chewing on something, as if he had a problem that needed to be worked out, that required more than a modicum of thought.

Not far from the house, however, he came right back to life. Started asking questions about Moira and schoolwork, about Moira and school, about Moira and how she got on with other girls. In turn, he listened carefully to every word I told him— except for what I had to say about her gran. He didn't seem to think her gran was important. Apart from that, he never interrupted, not even once.

And by the time we reached home, he was blazingly cheerful. A different man, you might say. Or rather the same man, the old dad, the one we are used to.

Naturally, there was a reason for the change. But strange to say, I'm not sure he would have recognised it, not even Dad. It was to do with Moira not actually being there in front of him, meaning he could begin to see her in a different light, let his imagination do the remembering. And that alters everything. Since then he has been turning her this way and that, working out the problems, giving her the benefit of the doubt. Now he thinks he can see the way ahead. Moira has become a challenge. And there's nothing my dad likes so much as a challenge.

I know this is true because it's the way it used to be with me. At the beginning when I first noticed she was staring.

And that is exactly what he's forgotten. With Moira not actually here to remind him, he's forgotten that Moira stares. He won't remember that until she's in front of him and it begins again.

AND now I have a problem of my own. It comes to me as I lie in bed, trying to go to sleep, and failing. It's a simple problem, but I can't seem to get it out of my head.

What if I'm wrong about her and Dad?

What if they don't look at each other once in all the time she comes to stay? Moira will be here, in our house, right through the weekend. And so will I. Which means two days of having Moira watch me instead, never looking away. And not just in the daytime. We'll sleep in this room and even in the dark, I'll know she's there. Night won't change a thing. Because there'll be no way of knowing, not even with the lights off, if she's really asleep.

That's what I've done. I've made sure there's no getting away from Moira.

Is it any wonder my leg begins to ache? As if, beneath all that damaged skin, it knows, as if it can feel it in its very bones. Something is going to happen.

And I'm the one that started it.

❧ Chapter Sixteen

THE OTHER PROBLEM IS LYDIA.

Next morning she stamps past us without a single word, flings her satchel down onto the floor. Which, as a gesture of disgust, is hardly useful because then she remembers what it contains and, humble, has to pick it up for cradling again. But the face like thunder stays in place. And this is the girl who went home last night looking as if she had been standing in a golden shower. Something must have happened.

'Ooh, Lydia, whatever's the matter with you?'

Look at Hilary, all lit up at the thought of trouble.

But Lydia is in such a state she can't answer even a simple question. And it's not that she's trying to be dramatic, the way you would have to suspect of Hilary. Lydia genuinely cannot talk. But it hardly matters. I have a feeling I already know the reason why.

In the end, it comes tumbling out. And I was right. Lydia's mother has announced that she can't come to stay at my house for the weekend.

'And there's no reason,' she keeps telling us, first here in the cloakroom, and later in the classroom, and later still at break time in the queue for the tuck shop. 'No reason at all. She just won't let me.'

But I could tell her. I could tell her the reason. Lydia wants to think this is about her, and having a mother who won't let her do what she likes. *I* know better. Lydia's mother is simply keeping her safe, keeping her home, making sure it all stops here. No more undesired influences, no more forces she can't control. No more of *him*.

'Can't you persuade her?' Is all I can think of to say. And Lydia, who believes I'm being sympathetic, simply howls for the hundredth time. 'But she won't even tell me why. . . .'

Lucky Lydia. Stupid Lydia. Thinking the whole world is against her. Especially, her own mother.

Yet there's something else, something far more important than Lydia not getting her own way. *He* hasn't made up his mind about her yet, Mrs. Morris, I mean. Now he won't have to give it another thought. She won't be amongst the Chosen, not now. How could she be, when she's putting obstacles in his way, interfering with what's meant to be? He'll make up his mind and she will have to go with everyone else, disappear into that long dark night without end.

What would Lydia say about *that* if I told her?

She'd probably say she was pleased, she's so very vicious this morning. But that is because she doesn't understand. There's only one place to go if you haven't been Chosen. And if she doesn't know that, it must mean she isn't Chosen either. You can't go to Heaven if you don't understand about Hell.

She and her mother are going to end up in the same place after all.

Silly Lydia, stupid Lydia. She thinks it's touching, the way that she finds me turning to her, gripping her arm—the way you might if a life was at stake—to whisper in her ear: 'Try again, try to persuade her, one last time before it happens. I won't tell my father yet. I won't tell him anything.'

But as I've said, she thinks this is about her and one weekend, and how we choose to spend it. She doesn't understand that it's about choices, and making the right choice. She doesn't understand that she has to persuade her mother.

BUT the days pass and nothing could be more certain. Every

morning I look at Lydia and every morning she shakes her head.
Then one morning I find I can't even catch her eye. Lydia has
stopped trying. She's given up even attempting to persuade her
mother.

And after that it starts to slip away. Because then, the unbe-
lievable happens. Lydia begins to forget why she wanted so badly
to come to my house.

The first sign was what happened in Greek. Lydia has been all
ears ever since that first lesson about Socrates. But that was for
reasons of her own, and the satchel has never left her lap. And
Jamieson can't say a thing about it because Lydia is the most willing pupil she'll ever have.

Then one day, Lydia leans forward to get a pencil from her desk
and the satchel slips onto the floor. *And she lets it fall.* Doesn't
seem to want to do a thing about it. She just carries on, writes
what she wanted with that pencil.

You'd have to know Lydia to see what it means. You'd have to
have been watching her, remarking the way she has hugged the
satchel that's held the book, never once let it go. Now book and
satchel are on the floor, somewhere anyone could step on them.
And Lydia doesn't care.

Or maybe you don't have to know Lydia that well to see the
signs. Maybe it's just plain obvious to anyone.

In the end, all her mother had to do was put her foot down.
What she says goes. That's what *he* recognised weeks ago. She's a
proper mother. She did what any mother would do. Lydia is safe.

BUT she's not leaving anything to chance, Lydia's mother, I
mean. A day later, Lydia comes into school to announce that they
are going to a hotel for the weekend—the same weekend that she
would have been coming to our house. There's going to be walks
and outings and fancy food. A swimming pool even.

So what about Church? And what about reading Greek, just
the two of them? Lydia doesn't say a word about any of that. She

doesn't even mention Dad now, or not so you'd notice. She has become someone else, if you like. Not our Lydia any more. It makes you wonder if she even realises how all this time she's been a battleground? Now someone else has won the war.

Maybe that's what it means to have a mother. Lydia doesn't even have to think about it. Anything else is just unnatural.

Even Hilary is impressed by talk of the hotel. She spends the rest of the day reminding anyone who'll listen of the fun in store for us at my house, all girls together, tries to remember his exact words and can't. The shine's been taken off. Lydia is going to a hotel, while we get to go home with Moira.

And Moira herself? None of us talks to her. Who knows, if we ignore her enough, she might change her mind. This is what Hilary keeps saying anyhow, making sure Moira can hear every word. But I know better. Moira hasn't taken her eyes off me. Moira knows she's coming.

AND we've lost Lydia completely now.

On Thursday morning, there's no sign of her, not in the cloakroom, or at her desk come to that. It takes a few moments, but then we spot her, over by the radiator, with Fiona McPherson and the others. Lydia is talking and everyone else is laughing, which immediately makes you wonder why. Lydia's never said a thing that was funny, not in all the time she's been with us. At least not that I've heard.

Hilary takes one look and sniffs.

'Just listen to them, laughing their heads off at poor old Lydia.' But there's a note in her voice that doesn't say *poor old Lydia* at all. Lydia is laughing as loudly as the rest of them. Yet when I stroll across the room to use the waste paper basket I can hear what's supposed to be so funny. She's telling them how she doesn't have a thing to put on for dinner at the hotel this weekend, just the frock she used to wear to children's parties when she was twelve. How she's going to look a real sight. Because that's what she'll be dressed in when her father takes her for that first promised waltz, lets her have her first taste of wine.

A Daddy's girl doing all sorts of grown up-things.

What's so funny about that, I'd like to know. It's what I say to Hilary, who starts doing something quite nasty with her compass. And who can blame her? Nothing's the way it's supposed to be. What she says goes, Lydia's mother.

BUT then everything changes. Suddenly, the world swings right back to where it's meant to be. As if nothing had ever happened to turn it off course.

It shouldn't have come as such a surprise. I'm his daughter. All I had to do was remember who's in charge. Who will always be in charge. It's something I should have expected.

I hadn't said a word about Lydia's mother not letting her come. But it was Thursday night and it had to be done.

I told him in the car, on the way home. And it's just as I imagined it would be. He sighed and his hands grew heavy on the wheel. For a few seconds, the car had to drive itself while the news sank in. Then he shook his head and you knew it was all over. He'd read the signs and he'd made up his mind. Now we know where Lydia's mother is headed.

In the seconds that followed I felt as if I was listening. As if something valuable had been dropped into a well and now I was waiting for the splash.

WHEN we walk into the house, he doesn't say a word to anyone, not even Gran. He just carries on into his study. A moment later we hear the music blasting out. He has turned on his record player. Walk along the corridor outside his room and you would be able to see the walls vibrating with the din. But then, quite without warning, that music stops for another kind to take its place. The new music falls on the ears like a lament, watery and final. And in a way, it's something like the noise I was listening for in the car.

As usual, Gran thinks I'm the one to blame. She won't even let me go upstairs, but blocks the door so there's nothing for me to do but stay with her. Then she stands over the stove, never takes her eyes off me, adding extra salt to everything.

He doesn't come through for supper, not even when she's gone to his door twice to tell him that it's ready. She puts his dinner to sit over a saucepan of boiling water, and eats her own with me, watching the gravy form a crust of salt around the rim of his plate. Never stops sighing.

Then the phone rings. Yet it's not even eight o'clock. Too early, surely. The music stops, and this time it doesn't start up again. Something has happened.

Dad is frowning as he steps into the kitchen. He comes to the table and lowers himself heavily into his chair. When Gran brings him his plate, he shakes his head and sighs. Then he signals for me to come and stand next to him.

'Eeeh, Katie love. But it's a funny old world.'

Katie. When has he ever called me Katie? He changes other people's names all the time, makes them longer, shorter—alters them till they could hardly say they were the same names any more, were names *he* has given them instead. Yet never mine, not before today.

'Katie, oh, Katie, people never learn, do they? Thinking they know best, thinking they can go their own sweet way. *Thinking that what they say goes.* But they forget, don't they. They forget there's Someone else in charge. And then they wonder what's gone wrong.'

Is this meant for me? It can't be. It can't be me he's talking about. I know Who is in charge. All the lessons he's taught me I've learned by heart. Besides, he called me *Katie.* It's not me that's done something wrong. Not today.

Why don't I feel relieved then?

Suddenly he turns to Gran and says, 'Put the kettle on, Mother. I feel the need of tea. Hot sweet tea.'

Like people have when they're in shock. Except of course, Dad is not in shock. Nothing surprises him or catches him off guard. Unless you count Moira, just that once by the car. But he turned that around, too, didn't he. Now he can't wait for her to come.

He waits until the tea is in the cup in front of him, sugared and stirred for him by Gran. Sighs again, and lifts his eyes to the ceiling.

'Lydia,' he says slowly, 'will be coming to stay after all.'

He'll be happy with the look on my face. Not even a shred of surprise. It shows I trusted him, that I always knew the right thing would happen in the end, despite everything, despite *her*, Lydia's mother. Somehow he'd make it come about.

But what about the hotel? The swimming pool and the fancy food? What about all the plans? *How did he do it?*

Wait and he'll tell me. He's telling me now.

'Lydia's mother has had an accident. I'm afraid it's serious. It happened as she was peeling potatoes.'

He stops, takes a slow sip of his tea. *Peeling potatoes.* The phrase lingers, incomprehensible, proof that God works in mysterious ways.

'Katie love, it's a reminder. We live by the grace of God, doing even the simplest things. Yesterday Mrs. Morris was peeling potatoes, that's all. Making you ask, where is the danger in that? How can peeling potatoes in the evening bring a woman to the brink of destruction in the morning?'

His voice is rising. Suddenly we could be in church and hundreds of people listening. But it's me he's talking to.

'I'll tell you how, Katie love. The knife she was using slipped, slipped from her hand and cut into her finger. One little cut, that's all it was. But in that sliver of torn flesh, in the ooze of blood, greater forces than she could have conceived were hard at work. Tonight that woman is in hospital, fighting, I say *fighting* for her life with septicaemia . . .'

There's an interruption—Gran banging the table with a

spoon and scowling. He'd forgotten the extent of her ignorance.

'That's blood poisoning to you, Mother.'

But it's me he's watching now. To see how I am taking this. It explains the change of name. He's being extra specially gentle. Extra specially testing. 'Katie,' he says, softly. 'It's a proper case of touch and go . . .'

Oh, he knows, doesn't he? He knows I was never in his drawer in search of chocolates. He knows the value of the horse. He knows why it was precious. And he never said. Gluttony, he was pleased to call it. But he knew all along it was something worse. Now he wants to see what I will do. He wants to hear what I will say. Everything about him is gentle and questioning. And no-one would ever guess. This is the greatest test of my life.

Whose daughter am I?

It takes a moment. Some things will always take a moment. One moment to find the right words, another to find the right face. But it all comes in the end. So he can know whose daughter I am.

'Poor thing' I say. 'I *do* hope she'll be all right.'

Dad smiles at me. There's an ocean of understanding between us.

Gran folds her arms, snaps: 'I'm not having young children here though. I don't want the responsibility.'

Who would have believed it? Gran is the only one to remember Laura. Or so I thought. As it happens, however, Dad hasn't forgotten either.

'The younger sister is off to some aunt, that's what the father told me just now. But he thought Lydia would prefer to come here.'

The father. Lydia's dad, thinking that's what Lydia wanted, letting Lydia down, because he never learnt to read his child. Laura is off to Aunty Jane. But Lydia, Lydia is coming here.

And there's nothing *she* can do about it, her mother.

Something seems to have happened to my insides suddenly. Gran's cooking maybe, all that extra salt scratching away beneath the skin. Luckily I've done so well up to now that no-one stops me or asks the reason why. I can tell them I'm not feeling well and they believe me. I can run upstairs and close the door behind me.

First though, I have to check, just in case. Miracles do happen. One happened just now, didn't it? When I was least expecting it, the world swung back into place. But there's been no further miracle. I feel under the pillow and of course, there's nothing there.

So there's nothing for it but to lie down, try to hold on to the pain in my stomach, keep it one place, in an attempt to stop it spreading.

A proper case of touch and go, he said. And no knowing what will happen. Not even if you have *It*.

NEXT morning there's a yellowish tinge to Lydia's skin. She tells Hilary that she spent the night in the house alone because Laura had already gone to Aunt Jane's and her father was at the hospital. She says to Hilary that she didn't sleep, not even for a short while. She says the house was cold because she didn't know how to work the heating. She says that she has no news.

Lydia tells all this to Hilary. For some reason she doesn't seem to want to speak to me. Or look at me, even.

Later, in history, the tears start to slide out from under her glasses. Mrs. Chatto sees them and the whole lesson grinds to a halt. Lydia looks up to find the entire class is staring at her. But what does she do? Something only I seem able to notice. Lydia leans just that little bit closer into Moira, as if this is the one place of shelter she can find. But Mrs. Chatto doesn't see this. She's sweeping an eye over the class, looking for someone to take charge.

'Kate, take Lydia outside and look after her.'

Well it was only natural. She has seen the two of us together, on the pavement, in and out of Greek. She assumes I'm her friend. It would never occur to her to ask Moira, not in a hundred years.

OUTSIDE in the garden Lydia is still unwilling to look at me; she stands with her face pressed up against the wall of the domestic science block, shoulders shaking with muffled sobs. Mrs. Chatto had told us to go up to the medical room, but it smells of germolene and sick there and personally I can't stand it. There are two of us to think of after all. So here we are, in the fresh air—where nobody can hear us. You see, there are a few questions I want to ask—about the peeling of the potatoes for instance.

The trouble is, it doesn't seem to matter how long I stand here, as quiet and sympathetic as she could wish, the minutes pass and still Lydia won't say a word.

So what would *you* do? Especially when you remember that it is clear as daylight that it's herself she's sorry for. She might have spared a thought for her mother instead, lying in a hospital bed, knowing it's out of her control, and that Lydia is coming to stay after all. A case of touch and go.

'Oh stop blubbing. Pull yourself together.'

I didn't mean to snap, not exactly. It just happened. That said, the whole world has been handling her with kid gloves today so she could hardly complain when one person accidentally loses patience. And it just shows, how you can be too soft on some people, because the second the words are out of my mouth, she stops crying. It must have been the shock. But it does the trick. For not only does it stop her crying, but it gets her talking.

'But it's my fault, you see, all my fault. She wouldn't be in hospital if weren't for me.'

I thought she was going to carry on, but she stops there. And of course, you know why. She's waiting for me to say the obvious. Something on the lines of *how could she think such a thing and everybody knows it was an accident.*

But I don't. I don't say any such thing. Because it happens all the time, discovering you're the one to blame. That's what I've been learning all these years; that there are any number of invisible lines between cause and effect, running and spreading like a spider's web till you see that every mortal thing is connected, till you discover that you're the one responsible for everything, the one who's always to blame.

After that, though, it's only a short step; till you realise that if you're responsible for everything, then it must also mean you're able to control everything. And it's a revelation, something never to be forgotten.

But Lydia is never going to understand that. She hasn't got it in her. Just now it's interesting to see exactly what the connection could be here, between Lydia crying outside the domestic science block and her mother lying in hospital and no-one knowing if she'll ever come out alive. Why is Lydia to blame? So I wait, and I listen as Lydia tells me.

'You told me to ask her, remember? Ask one last time for her to let me come. So I did, I asked when she was making supper and there were only the two of us in the kitchen. But she wouldn't listen to me, she just carried on peeling the potatoes as if they were the only things that mattered. She just smiled and said she had made up her mind, and we were going to have a lovely time at the hotel, just the four of us, and . . .'

But someone has to interrupt here, point out the obvious. 'I thought you *wanted* to go to the hotel.'

For a moment Lydia stares at me, as if I'm stupid or worse. 'Of *course* I wanted to go to the hotel.' She states this as if it's old history, as if anyone could understand. 'But *you* said to ask her one more time. That's what I was going to do. Then, next time I saw *him*, I could have told him that I tried, that I did what you said, that I really made an effort.'

Things are becoming clearer. Lydia is definitely beginning to make sense. She had been doing her best to have it all ways. A case of having her cake and eating it.

'So what happened?' I ask the question, but really it's hardly necessary, is becoming less necessary by the second. It's almost as if I can see it all for myself. Lydia standing beside her mother at the sink, and Mrs. Morris peeling away, smiling, perfectly happy because she knows, no matter how Lydia rants and raves, she's keeping her daughter safe. Lydia's not going anywhere.

'She shouldn't have smiled, Kate.' Lydia's voice, scarcely more than a half decent whisper to begin with, starts to shake. 'She shouldn't have looked so smug, as if she had everything under control. If she hadn't smiled like that, I wouldn't have told her I hated her. And I wouldn't have said I wished I was like you, with no mother to ruin everything, and that I wished she would go away so there was only Dad and me. . . .'

. . . And that's when the knife slipped and Lydia's mother would have cut her finger. And can you wonder, faced with a daughter who says she hates her, and doesn't understand that all she's doing is loving her, and keeping her safe?

Imagine the effect it would have, the shock. The words would have thrown her off guard, at the very second she sliced through her skin. She'd have been like a city with its defences down, just for those few moments, just long enough for the germs to flood in and do their work. I can see it all. I might as well have been there myself, one of the germs, standing aside and watching it happen.

Lydia has gone quiet. She wants me to say something, tell her she's wrong. But what is there to say? We both know. She's perfectly right. None of this would have happened if it hadn't been for her.

Although, there is one thing I could have mentioned to make

her feel better. That is, it was me that told her to ask just one last time. But then again, why should that change anything? I wasn't to know, was I?

Silly Lyddie, stupid Lyddie, who will do anything you tell her. Who never knew when she was lucky.

Who can't blame me for anything.

We go back to the classroom. Mrs. Chatto glances at Lydia, then allows a brief smile in my direction. She thinks I've been a great comforter, saying all the right things to make stop her crying. The fact is, Lydia is beyond tears.

She goes and sits down next to Moira once more. But this time there's no leaning into her. Lydia is by herself, unworthy of help from anywhere.

NOTHING more happened at school. Not unless you count the 'incident' in domestic science. Moira only went and set a chip pan on fire. And it's typical, isn't it? One moment she's making you wonder how she can stare the way she does, how she knows the things she knows. And the next, she's proving that she has no more sense than a plank of wood.

They had to evacuate the whole school, just in case. Moira was the last one to come out, strolling away from the domestic science block as if she hadn't noticed a thing, as if she had nothing to do with the smoke billowing out behind her. As if she had no idea what fire could do.

AFTER school, though, the four of us walk out together. Hilary can barely contain her excitement. What if Lydia's mother were to die tonight? It would be better than anything in her books. *Chums rally round broken hearted school-friend.* She should realise, though, it wouldn't happen like that; Lydia doesn't even know she's there. Lydia is in a world of her own.

As for Moira, she's with us all right, but we don't talk to her.

Today Dad has got out of the car and is standing on the pavement. And this is unheard of. He never gets out to wait. *We* have to come to *him*. This must be for Lydia then, more special treatment, the only thing likely to make a difference.

'Lydia,' he says. 'Lyddie my love.' He puts his arm around her and draws her aside, somehow turning a crowded pavement into a private place containing just the two of them. Yet Lydia doesn't seem to notice him, of all people. As his arm closes round her, her eyes simply drift over his shoulder towards the traffic.

But he's not having that.

He drops the arm, puts up both hands to cup her face, and gently forces her eyes to look into his. Then he begins to speak words to her that we couldn't possibly hear. And it must have been the words that do it, bring about the change. Suddenly her body sags as her knees give out from under her. She can't stand up any more. For a moment then she seems to dangle from his hands, eyes locked into his. Then he lets her go, almost allowing her fall before catching her at the last. He picks her up and puts her into the back of the car, carefully, like something precious.

But when he stands up, he looks at us. And winks.

HILARY gets to sit beside her, which means I can hardly see Lydia from where I'm sitting. But Moira I can see well enough. Moira he has placed in the front seat next to him.

'All present and correct?' He beams.

'Oh yes, Mr. Carr,' sings out Hilary, happy as can be. Then covers her mouth. For a moment there she had forgotten we are meant to be worried.

In any event, the question wasn't intended for her. Lydia is catered for, and he doesn't need to think about me. He was talking to Moira MacMurray. His new special interest.

Is it a shock to him then, when slowly she turns her head, meets his smile with a gaze so completely blank he must have felt he had been beaming at a brick wall? It's not what he is used to, not my dad.

Yet he doesn't seem to mind, not one little bit. If anything, his smile grows warmer, his eyes even more twinkling. I'd say it was like a ray of purest sunshine, that smile, capable of lighting up the darkest night, or penetrating the thickest walls—even the ones made of brick. You'd think nothing in the world could withstand it.

But you'd be wrong. Because the smile has no effect at all.

Moira's face stays blank, her eyes unchanging. The beam flickers ever so slightly, then locks on even more tightly than before. Dad clears his throat, and looks away. But Moira doesn't. Her stare stays exactly where it is, fixed on the side of his face.

It's begun.

Hilary giggles as we move off. She hasn't noticed a thing wrong. What's more, since she isn't familiar with the car, there's no way for her to be aware that there's a new sound to the engine since he started it up, like something over-revving, far too noisy suddenly, for all the world as if its mood has been upset.

But that's only the car. Dad would seem as right as rain to anybody watching. Smiles for everyone, an endless stream of jokes, as though he's determined to have us all rolling in our seats; because laughter is infectious, and some of it might spread to the front seat next to him. But he may as well not bother. Moira continues to sit, as she has sat from the moment she got into the car, body facing the front, and her head turned to face him. Moira hasn't taken her eyes off my dad for so much as a second.

Gradually the jokes fizzle out, and the chatter dies away. In contrast, the noise from under the car's bonnet seems to have become louder still. It sounds downright angry. You could see why you might not want to try talking over it. Since there's no more conversation from the front, Hilary turns to Lydia. I can just hear the question above the din of the engine.

'What did he say to you then, back there on the pavement?'

There's a pause before Lydia says anything. Then in a dull voice that hardly sounds like hers, she replies. 'He said not to worry. She'll be all right. He said he'll take care of everything.'

Then she frowns. 'At least I think that's what he said.'

Hilary takes a moment to look impressed, then says, 'And do you believe him?'

This time Lydia doesn't answer, turns away to look out of the window.

DAD stayed by the car when we got out, pointing to the church and waving us on towards the house without him. If you want to know what I think, I'd say he was tired. All that talk earlier on, all those wasted jokes, taking their toll. And that's not the only reason for being worn out. It can be exhausting too, feeling that someone's eyes are always on you. Sooner or later you begin to wonder if they are seeing things nobody else can. And that's when you remember; some things are better kept out of sight.

He should ask me about it. I know exactly how it feels.

Anyway, when the phone started to ring, he wasn't there to answer it, and Gran never made a move. Gran won't touch the phone. Besides, she had just had her first sight of Moira, and now she was staring at her as if she had never seen the like, with a look that was half horror, half admiration.

So I went. I answered the phone.

It didn't take very long. A few words and a single question on my part, just to be sure. Then it was back to the kitchen.

'It's for you, Lydia. Your father.'

Her eyes went blank, so you'd think she had been taking lessons from Moira. But you could see the elastic in her legs as she walked out into the hall, closed the door behind her. Again it only took a moment. Then the door burst open and she flew back into the room as if she was on wings.

At the very same moment Dad stepped in from outside. He was moving heavily as if he was still exhausted, as if he had been putting his all into something.

Lydia takes one look and runs towards him, flings her arms right around his waist.

'Lydia! Lydia love! What's all this?' Gently he pulls away her arms, unwraps her from his waist. She doesn't know. You don't touch Dad, no-one touches Dad—not unless he decides.

Lydia steps back. Her eyes are shining, brimming with tears. 'You were right,' she says, but with difficulty. It's as if the words are having a happy battle to find their way out. 'You told me you would take care of everything. And you did.'

Dad stands very still, then says quietly. 'I told you *He* would take care, Lydia love.'

But it makes no difference. Lydia has thrown herself at his waist again. *She* knows who is responsible. She knows who is in charge. And this time he doesn't pull her away, but stands there, smiling. Says not another word. Beside me, Hilary is standing, eyes wide, mouth slack, remembering what Lydia told her in the car. Even Gran looks impressed.

There's just one person who doesn't seem to have noticed a thing. Moira is standing next to the stove, at the pan Gran uses to fry chips the way Dad likes them, as if wondering when the next meal will be. And Dad, catching sight of her, turns to her with that same gentle smile. 'Moira?' he says. 'This is glad news, is it not?'

But she doesn't answer. Moira just stares at him, doesn't even blink. And is it my imagination or does his smile once more begin to fade a little bit, just around the edges?

The fact is, whatever the reason, Moira is a distraction to him. Which is just as well since a distraction is what is required. I don't want Dad looking at me, not for a while.

When I picked up the phone, it had indeed been Mr. Morris. Who had said, 'Oh, thank God you're home. Keith will have told Lydia the good news of course. Is she happy now? Poor little thing, she didn't know if she was coming or going.'

Which had given me just enough time to think, and then say, 'No he hasn't told her yet. He wanted to leave it to you.'

Then I had gone to fetch Lydia. Who hadn't been told a thing.

IT'S been a good quarter of an hour but she has only just let go of my Dad's waist. She can't take her eyes off him, not even now. And who could blame her? For who else could turn disaster into triumph? Keep every promise that he makes? And never once let down those who put their trust in him?

❧ Chapter Seventeen

IN THE END THOUGH, EVEN he has had enough. Well, two of them staring, it would wear anyone down. He can't do a thing about Moira, but Lydia is easy.

'Kate love' he says. 'Take our Lydia to the bathroom. Splash a bit of water on her face. All those tears have made those bonny cheeks downright ugly. See what you can do.'

So off we went, Lydia and I, to the bathroom.

I only turned my back on her for a second, long enough to turn on the tap. But when I turn round again, something seems to have snapped. Lydia has begun to cry all over again. And this is worse than at school even. She is being shaken by huge hiccuping sobs that look as though they could choke her. For a moment all I can do is wonder what's gone wrong. Then it comes to me. It's the shock of course. Shock and tiredness and relief, all rolled into one.

And it's strange, how it's only now I seem to feel sorry for her, when it's over and we know she has nothing to cry about, not any more.

'Come on, Lyd,' I say. I even put my hand on her shoulder. 'Don't cry. She's going to be all right. Remember?'

Lydia looks up slowly. 'What?' she says, blinking. 'Who?'

Again it must be the shock. Because it's as if she hasn't understood a word I've said. She has taken off her specs and her eyes look unexpectedly large with all those tears, the lids swollen with so much crying and lack of sleep. Seeing her now, you'd think she was five years younger than she actually is.

All at once however she pushes me away and runs to peer into the mirror hanging over the washbasin—though what she could expect to see without her specs and all those tears is beyond me. One glance and she then slumps, all but falls into the sink. Another flood of tears sprinkle the water that she was meant to wash her face in.

'Lydia . . .' I begin to say. Only to be rudely interrupted.

'He says I'm ugly. You heard him. He told you so just now. *Ugly*, that's what he said.'

Now it's my turn to be confused. Then the penny drops. She hasn't been crying about her mother. Her mother isn't the reason for those swollen, damaged eyes, not any more. And there I'd been . . .

. . . There I'd been, actually feeling *sorry* for her.

Do you know what it makes me want to do? Walk straight out and leave her to it, to the silliness of how she thinks she looks and what he's going to say about it. But I don't. I'm here because he told me to come. And for another reason that has nothing to do with him. I came because it's the ideal opportunity. This may be the one chance I have. It's the reason I've closed the door. And locked it. Some things have to be kept quiet. Some things he must never know about.

'Listen,' I say. 'Listen. Do you realise you don't have to stay here now? Not now she's better. You could ring your father and get him to take you home. You . . .' I don't know why this last part is so hard to say. 'You could go back home to your family. To her.'

Lydia frowns. For a moment she doesn't say a word. Then:

'But why, Kate? Why should I want to go home?'

Is she not all there? Doesn't she understand a word I've said? So I try again, thinking this time, surely I'll get through.

'Well,' I say, and it's wonderful really, how calm I sound, how patient. 'You would be able to say you were sorry for one thing.'

'Sorry . . . ?' She repeats the word after me, mystified. Lydia doesn't have the faintest idea what I'm talking about. She's forgotten everything. Put it all behind her. Every word about it being her fault. Her fault that her mother hurt herself. Her fault that a simple cut went and turned into a full blown case of touch and go.

That's what he's done; he's made her forget everything.

So what is there to say? I might as well stop here. She wouldn't listen. She wouldn't even understand. There's nothing more I can do. And there's no-one even to tell her mother that I tried.

'Wash your face,' I tell her, adding, 'You'll look better then.'

That cheers her up. She nods, then turns to splash the water where it's needed. And when she straightens up, she is actually smiling.

'You know what, Kate?' Her eyes, still wet, are shining again. Eyes that can't see past the end of her nose. 'Your father says he's going to take me into his study after supper. We're going to read Greek together, like he promised. Tonight, just the two of us.'

So saying, she pops her glasses back on to her nose, beams even harder at me. And it's a relief. Without the specs, she had looked hardly older than Laura, too young to realise what she was doing, too little to know what was important. Now with the glasses back where they belong, she looks quite her old self.

In other words, old enough to look after herself.

DAD must have had a word with Gran about what to put into the supper. Maybe he explained how some folk are different and not everyone likes their vegetables to taste of the Dead Sea. The result is a meal that even Lydia could have managed, leaving only Gran to push the food around her plate like a sulky child. The salt cellar stands sentry beside her and she resorts to it constantly, scowling and shaking it over her food as if defleaing a dog.

Strangely enough, Moira does the same. Or maybe it's not strange after all. Salt on her crisps, sugar in her sweets. Maybe it has to be one or the other, something extreme. Everything else probably just tastes of herself. Anyway, Gran approves. In fact,

Gran seems to like everything about Moira. Perhaps it's the silence of her, or else the sheer size of her. Or the way she doesn't take her eyes off Dad.

Lydia scarcely eats a thing. Even before we are half finished she's watching our plates for the first sign that the meal is over. 'After supper' he had said to her. But this is a supper that seems to go on for ever. It's the silence at his end of the table that does it, something neither Hilary nor Lydia could ever have expected, not before today. Yet now neither of them seems surprised. If Dad sits in our midst, too weary to speak, they can understand. Miracles don't come from nowhere. Someone has to make them happen, give up something of himself.

They think all they have to do is wait, and in a little while he'll be his old self again. But you know, I'm not so sure. Right in front of him, Moira sits, working her way through supper, demolishing second helpings, and even thirds. The food seems to find its own way into her mouth, fork after forkful without pause. Apparently Moira could eat a ten course meal with her eyes closed. But of course they are not closed. They are wide open, unblinking—and haven't once left his face.

The phone goes. It must be the silence, because tonight even he jumps a little, as if startled. Yet it's eight twenty-eight exactly. What must he be thinking of?

As he heads for the door, Lydia, very daring, pipes up: 'You'll come straight back, won't you, Mr. Carr?' But she doesn't get an answer. I don't know that he even heard her.

What's worse, he doesn't come back. We clear the table, we do the dishes and we put away. We even get out the Scrabble board so that when he does come he'll see we've been keeping ourselves occupied. But he doesn't reappear. And now Lydia is starting to flag. It's a wonder she's lasted this long with no sleep last night. Whisper *Greek* to her, though, and she'll spring right back to life again. Behind the yawns and the lids that look as if they can scarcely stay open, she's ready; she thinks it's still going to happen. He's kept one promise after all.

Then, long after anyone else would have given up hope, the door from the hall opens. It's ten o' clock and even Hilary is looking heavy about the eyes.

But now here's Dad and everything changes. Lydia's eyes snap open, ready for action. But there'll be no Greek, not tonight.

'Girls,' he says, with a voice so weary that just hearing it makes you feel tired for him. 'Ah, girls.' And he begins to walk—straight past us to the back door.

'Oh, Mr. Carr, you're not going out. Not at this time of night.' This is Lydia of course.

He sighs, but doesn't look at her. 'Duty calls, Lydia love, you should know that.' Then he stands back to allow Gran to unbolt the door. And that should have been the end of it.

But no-one has reckoned on Lydia, and the effect of no sleep and promises not kept. 'But *why*, Mr. Carr?' Her voice is petulant. 'No-one's been here, no-one's called.' (Not since eight twenty-eight, that is.) 'We were going to read Greek, remember? You can't go out now. You *promised*.' And, then, the most shocking thing of all. *Lydia stamps her foot.*

Oh, oh this is something new. Something I've never seen before, not in this house. People don't tell my father what to do, not even Gran.

But I know the feeling that comes with it. That's not at all new. A prickling on the backs of my hand, a rush of cold as if with opening the door, Gran has let half the night flood into the house.

Even Lydia feels it, starts to shiver, knows straightaway that she has done something wrong. She just doesn't know how wrong, not yet. She stays where she is, staring up at Dad, who is looking at her with an expression she couldn't possibly recognise. Because no-one will ever have looked at her like this before, not even her own father. Especially not her own father. It's the look reserved for the Stranger in your midst.

And here come the words, so soft as to be almost a whisper. But she can hear them all right, hear them and understand that words are only the beginning, the tip of the iceberg. My father begins to speak.

'You're telling me not to go? You're telling me to stop at home when there's one poor soul out there crying to me for help? Pardon me, but I have to go where I am needed. Nothing, *nothing* gets between Keith Carr and his duty. There's a world of suffering out there, Lydia, and you are telling me to turn my back.'

The worst of it is that, as he speaks, he appears bewildered, as Jesus might have looked if Lazarus, raised from the dead, had then asked for eternal wealth as well. A wondering look that wants to know—hasn't he done enough? And Lydia, seeing it, understands what I learned years ago. Ingratitude is the greatest of sins, for which there can be no forgiveness.

And here it comes, the worst bit of all. The final whisper. 'Child, I thought I knew you.'

Lydia goes white. Because this is what Dad does. He shows people how to see themselves. Now, after tonight, she won't be able to look at herself, because she'll only see what he sees. Ugliness, inside and out.

'Please, Mr. Carr,' she whispers, but not so it matters, not so anyone's going to listen. 'That's not what I. . . . I'm so sorry, Mr. Carr.'

Watching her, you could almost feel sorry for her. Until you remember that people have to learn; everyone has to learn. You don't talk to Dad as if he was just anyone.

I'd say she was learning now though. And no chance of her forgetting. For the rest of her life, Lydia will remember how in one evening she witnessed a miracle beyond description—and then lost it all through the wickedness of ingratitude. The memory will be there when she wakes up in the morning, the last thing she knows when she goes to sleep. . . .

. . . Or will it? Because then something happens, bringing it to an end, that education, that learning, stopping the process.

Something so unexpected it turns her head, turns all our heads. A sudden noise, that takes a moment to recognise, and pin down for what it is; a gurgling, high-to-low-pitch yodelling sound, that could be anything on earth, until you realise that it's somebody laughing.

In fact, it's Moira, laughing and at the same time pointing at Dad, as if he's something she's spotted up on stage, an act, a comic turn.

A donkey braying, that's what she sounds like. Something that falls short of human. Except for the words, listen to the words. *Some poor soul*, she's saying over and over again, as if that's what's making her laugh. *Some poor soul*. Gurgle gurgle gurgle.

And the result? Lydia is looking on in amazement, shocked—but definitely not cringing, not any more. Hilary's mouth has dropped open. Even Gran appears shaken. But Dad is the one to watch. He seems—how can I say this and have anyone believe me?—terrified. Like a man reeling from a blow he never saw coming. He's standing there, trying to regain his balance, and he can't. Because Moira just keeps on laughing, as if he's the funniest thing she ever saw in her life.

So what's wrong with me? Why am I not in the least bit shocked? No-one is moving, or seems able to move, not Lydia, not Hilary, not Gran. But *I* can move, past them, past them all as if they were no more than waxworks. Until I come to a halt in front of Moira.

And slap her hard across the face.

The laughing stops abruptly, like the needle knocked off a record. Moira's eyes close—and open again, fast as the shutter of a camera. Then her face goes blank once more, eyes turned not on me, standing right there in front of her, but past me. I really am invisible it seems. Moira has gone back to what she was doing before, looking at him, at Dad.

Hilary, as usual, is the first to recover.

'Well,' she says, and turns to Lydia, but she gets no satisfactory response there. Lydia just blinks and shakes her head, as if she has been dreaming. 'Well,' Hilary says again, and looks across at Dad instead.

But that's no use either. Dad hasn't even begun to recover, not yet. He is still staring at Moira, and the look on his face tells you he's wondering if there's something else, something even worse to come.

But there isn't. Moira is quiet. A whole minute passes and nothing happens. And that's when you have to hand it to Dad. He lets out a long sigh, followed by a little shake of his shoulders—and suddenly he's the old Dad once more, the proper Dad.

'Why, Moira,' he says quietly. 'Moira love. I think I might have to find the time for a little talk with that old granny of yours.'

And that's all he needs to say. Reproach couldn't come any gentler. He might have been talking to a child. Yet his words bring us back to normal. A moment before the kitchen had been like nothing so much as a ship, threatening to capsize. Now it had righted itself. Everything is all right again.

Just the same, I thought he might have something for me, a word or a look. A glance to show he recognises the strange truth; that I was the one who silenced her, the only person able to stop the laughter. But there's nothing. He doesn't even glance in my direction. The back door opens for him and he's gone.

The very second the door closes, Hilary turns on Moira. 'Moira MacMurray, what is the *matter* with you? That was . . .' she stops, poor unimaginative Hilary, at a loss for words, '. . . disgusting.'

Moira looks at her, eyes mild, and shakes her head ever so slightly. Then she opens her mouth, and it's clear that she is about to say something. For a succession of seconds we wait, on tenterhooks again. The kitchen sways a fraction. The ship could go belly up after all.

And what does Moira have to say?

'My granny, she always makes me a plate of chips before I go to bed. She knows what I like.'

And that's all that Moira has to say. Gran throws up her hands and Hilary rolls her eyes. But me, I'm already rising to the task. Or as close as I can get. The chip pan will have to stay cold tonight. But I can do the next best thing. Butter bread, cut cheese. Anything to keep Moira fed.

Well, why shouldn't I? I had been so sure she had been about to say something else, something that might have explained the laugh, that would have explained *him*. Moira had laughed as if she had known him of old, longer than me even, as if she had known everything about him. At any moment she could have told us exactly why she was laughing. But she didn't. She didn't say a thing.

So I pile the cheese on the bread, spread the butter thick. You have to show gratitude one way or another.

IT was crowded in my room with the four of us. Hilary had made doubly sure *she* got the other bed, covering the pillow with all the cuddly toys and mascots that she normally keeps on her desk. Which left Lydia and Moira with the two camp beds and just enough space to get undressed. Suddenly Hilary nudges me, and nods her head towards Moira. And sure enough, it's a sight to behold; Moira has expanded into a huge flannel nightie that can only have belonged to her granny, something only an old lady could possibly wear.

Still, she might need it, every bobbly yard of it. Her bed is as far away from me as it could possibly be, right under the window where it will get all the draughts.

We're no sooner in bed than *my* gran stamps into the room and cuts off the light. Hilary giggles and pretends to be indignant, but Lydia you could feel welcoming the dark, snuggling down and sighing happily. Somehow, Moira and her laugh have wiped out all memory of what passed between Lydia and Dad. If she remembers it at all, she'll think she imagined it.

Is she sparing a thought for her mother, though? I hope so. I hope they were careful at the hospital, when they told her where her daughter was. I've heard the least thing can cause a relapse, even when you think the patient is getting better. I hope they told her gently.

I wish they could have told her Lydia was coming home. Or at least that I tried to make it happen.

Now, one by one, everyone is falling asleep, Moira being the very first to go. You could hear the change in her breathing almost right away, each breath sounding longer and wheezier than the last. A person could use up half the air in a room that way. Then there's Hilary. Five minutes after she falls asleep she starts to snore and doesn't stop. Only Lydia drifts away discreetly. Little tiny mouse sighs that wouldn't disturb a soul.

And she doesn't wake up. Nobody does. I lie here and listen to the sound of so many different people breathing. Yet if you asked me, I would say there really is only one other person in this room. One other presence, separate from the rest, wide awake and watchful. A silent presence that is not only there, but growing. Becoming bigger and bigger until I feel I could stretch out and touch it. And I know where it's coming from; it's coming from under the window, where it's refusing to stay.

Here in the dark, even when she's asleep, there is a part of Moira that is everywhere. No getting away from her.

And getting bigger by the minute, closing in around me like a hand, blotting out the dark. Which brings me to the strangest thing of all. This is what I feared, what I somehow knew would happen. Yet now, with Moira all around me, I discover that I don't mind. This must be what it's like for Lydia, discovering that you can lose yourself in her, if you only let yourself. If you only take the chance.

Is Moira the reason that I dreamed?

Standing in *his* room again, staring at the picture of the dancing girls with their offerings, and the Golden Calf. And waiting. This time the footsteps take no time to arrive, are already there, right outside the door. So close now, it seems I can almost hear her breathing on the other side. Now she's stopped, is waiting there, on her side of the door. But why doesn't she open the door? *Why doesn't she come in?*

Then suddenly it becomes so clear. She's waiting, too. For me to let her in.

The sound of her breathing grows louder. It's filling the whole room. And still growing. The breathing has turned into the very air that I breathe. *I am breathing in another person . . .*

And then here I am again, in my own room, wide awake. His desk, the picture, the girls have all gone. But the breathing is still there—as well as something that's just been learned.

She. I dreamed a person who is *she*. I know who is on the other side of the door. But don't say her name. Don't even breathe it. Remember the rule.

❧ Chapter Eighteen

I'VE SAID IT BEFORE; NO-one knows how to rouse a room like my dad. First the explosion of the door, then the blare of music from the wireless to make an unsuspecting sleeper's hair stand on end. And *then*—as Lydia and Hilary are sitting up in bed, eyes sleepy but already lit up at the sight of him—the small remark.

'Eeeh ladies, but it's whiffy in here.'

So saying he marches over to the window and flings it open, as if the air is tainted. As if everything in the room is tainted. Lydia and Hilary immediately lose the lit-up look, and stop breathing altogether. Only the one person is unconcerned. I can see her from here. Slowly, belatedly, Moira opens her eyes. And already they are trained on him, as if she could have found him with her eyes shut.

And just see Dad shiver.

But he opens the window still farther, so the wind rushes past him to get to Moira. Yet she doesn't turn a hair. Apparently Moira doesn't mind the cold.

Dad turns down the music, rearranges the lines of his face. 'Bad news, girls. Old Keith Carr has discovered he has to work today. You're going to have to have fun all on your own.'

When did he discover? Last night? This morning? Whenever it was he realised that Moira is never going to look away?

But the effect is exactly what you'd expect. 'Oh, Mr. Carr we can't possibly have any fun without you.' This is Hilary—though not questioning, you understand. Hilary is voicing regret not criticism.

On her camp bed, however, Lydia doesn't say a word. It's a question of good manners now. She's forgotten the rest. But it's Lydia that Dad is turning to.

'You see how it is, Lydia love. Duty is duty and Keith Carr has never been a man to ignore his.'

If he's trying to remind her of something worse, then he's failing. She only smiles vaguely, flattered by the attention. And that's Moira again, making sure that what's forgotten, stays forgotten.

But when he leaves the room both she and Hilary are cast back into gloom. Again it's not what they expected. When had he said anything about leaving us to our own devices? Lydia looks positively tragic. Could it possibly be that we don't like each other enough to be able to have fun by ourselves?

'What are we going to do then?' Says Hilary, glumly. 'Go somewhere?'

'I don't have any money.' This is Lydia answering. 'No-one remembered to give me any.' Well, they wouldn't, would they. Pocket money will hardly have figured large in anybody's mind in Lydia's house these past few days. Although maybe I'm wrong. You never knew with Lydia's mother. Lydia is always on her mind, isn't she. It's only Lydia who doesn't know it.

'I've got money.'

Now here's a surprise, Moira suddenly speaking up. Moira making out she has the answer.

You should have seen Hilary's lip curl. 'Oh yes, and how much would that be?'

The answer comes as Moira reaches under her pillow and brings out a fat, fake crocodile wallet, the sort that will hold a pension book and TV stamps and pictures of your grandchildren. Peels it open. Hilary's eyes grow large. Inside are notes. Pound notes, five-pound notes, ten-pound notes even. Lydia puts on her specs and gives a little gasp.

'Moira!'

Despite the exclamation, Moira just looks blank. Yet it can't be what she's used to, finding herself the centre of attention, and all eyes on her. Or maybe she realises it's not herself that's surprising, but the wallet. There must be a hundred pounds in there at least. All kinds of possibilities spring to mind.

But it's Hilary who speaks up first.

'I know, we can go into town. To the café.' She looks at me meaningfully. Cafés represent just the one thing to Hilary, and it's definitely not coffee.

Yet is that all she can come up with for an idea? Going to a café? With a hundred pounds a person could leave home, go any-where, live anywhere. Become invisible. And all Hilary can dream up is going to a café.

Still, I can give it some thought. It would mean making a phone call, but apart from that, there seems no urgent reason to disappoint her.

Typical Hilary though, there's not an ounce of gratitude. Turning back to Moira she says, 'How did you get the money then?'

There's no mistaking the suspicion in her voice, but Moira doesn't seem to mind. In fact she doesn't even appear to be aware of Hilary. When she answers it's me she talking to, as if I was the one doing the asking.

'My mum. She sends the money to my gran to pay for me. But Gran says she doesn't want it. She says she wouldn't touch it with a barge pole. She says no-one has to pay her for looking after me.'

There's a silence. Even Hilary looks embarrassed. It's that men-tion of her mother. It's almost indecent somehow, the thought of Moira as a little girl, of Moira with a mother. Indecent to wonder about what her mother must think of her so as to have left her.

But then, no-one seems to wondering about what her gran must think of her so as to be willing to look after her. And for nothing.

Surprisingly, it's Lydia who asks the question, the one that's on everybody's mind. 'Moira, where *is* your mother?'

There's another silence as Moira considers. You'd swear she was trying to remember. 'Abroad,' she says finally. 'With him. And them.'

Hilary makes a face. She's letting it be known that it's not her fault she's confused. But I know what Moira means. Her mother is in another country, as far away as she can possibly be, with a man who's not Moira's father, and children who aren't her brothers and sisters. Or not properly. A whole family then, but no place in it for Moira, not the way she is. No-one wants Moira—except her gran of course. Who won't take a penny for her.

Moira's gran won't touch the money because Moira's worth more than that. You don't have to have *It* to work it out. It's the sort of thing even Lydia could manage.

MY gran has made porridge for us—although Moira and I are the only ones to eat it. That said, Gran ignores me to watch Moira eat the equivalent of a bucket of it, salted and sugared in equal proportions. Gran is still fascinated by Moira, can't seem to hold a grudge against her, even after last night, and the trouble she caused. She probably blames Lydia for that.

And of course it helps, having a distraction. While Gran watches Moira, tries to take her all in, I can creep out to the telephone, make the one necessary phone call. Plan the day that Moira has provided for us.

WE make the journey into town by bus. Hilary sits next to me, and Lydia beside Moira. As soon as the bus moves off, Hilary begins applying mascara, and doesn't seem to realise the result is pure disaster; her eyes look as if they have been joined in dot to dot by a furry felt pen. Then, silly girl, she offers it to me, as if I'd want it. You don't need make-up when you have *It*. People look at you for other reasons. And for the colour of your hair.

Meanwhile, Lydia has returned to the book she has neglected lately. Even so, she must be on her third or fourth reading by now. What she'd like is to have him test her on it. She could recite his entire life back to him.

And Moira? She just looks out of the window.

Has anybody noticed the change? Dad's not here. But I am, sitting not six feet away from her. Yet Moira is looking out of the window. She's not looking at me any more.

'Moira,' I say. 'How about a toffee, Moira?' But she doesn't seem to hear. Doesn't even look round.

IT was raining by the time we got to town. Not just raining, but bucketing. Hilary immediately gets into a flap because she's worried about her hair getting messed up before anyone else sees the trouble she's taken with it. Then all at once she stops fussing, and stares. We *all* stare. It's Moira. She has drawn a flat fold of clear plastic from her pocket, is busy opening it out like a giant sweetie wrapper. Then it dawns. Moira is about to put a plastic rain hood over her head, the sort her gran would wear every time she goes out in the wet.

'Moira, you're not going to . . .' this is Hilary. But Moira *is* going to. She's tying the ribbons under her chin, making sure everything stays in place. Now her head looks like something bagged up by a butcher. What's more, if you listen carefully, you can hear the patter of raindrops bouncing off the top.

Seeing her like this, you don't know whether to laugh or cry. There was I, thinking there was something special about Moira. Something that sets her apart. Then she puts on a plastic rainhood and I'm the one that ends up feeling like a fool. This is the real Moira, then, the Moira everyone sees. The Moira even her mother doesn't want.

When we walk away from the bus, there's no doubt about the way we must look. Three girls and an old lady out for the day. Twenty yards from the bus station, Hilary can't stand it any more. She grabs my arm, starts pulling me through puddles at top speed, barging through people on the pavement and sending them flying. And all in an attempt to get away, to put a clear distance between the two of us and Moira and Lydia. But the other two are surprisingly fast. The crowds seem to part for Moira in a way they never did for us and the result is that we arrive at the café practically together.

And there, Mark and Owl Boy are sitting at a table, waiting. Just the way I told them to. Not that Mark is looking in the least bit happy. It's another one of his precious Saturdays, when he should be on a playing field somewhere, leading the pack. Instead he's here. But that's Mark for you, remembering the last time, and the accidental squeeze. Some people are just born hopeful.

Still, it's always useful to know who they are, the Born-hopefuls. It's so easy to waste your time otherwise, trying to make the wrong folk realise what they are missing. It's why I've never bothered with the Fiona McPhersons of this world, or the Mrs. Chattos. They are so convinced they have it all, there's nothing you could promise that they would possibly want.

Well, we know where *they* will end up. How often has Dad said it? People who think they are happy aren't ever going to be Chosen. You can't like what you've got and expect you are going to get more. That would be seeing things the wrong way. People who are chosen are the ones who look around them and say; this is not enough. People who are chosen are always going to want more.

And that's where we come in, Dad and me. Always holding out promise.

All you have to do is find out what they want. In the meantime, there's Mark. Folk like Mark are easy, no prizes for guessing what he's after. And that's the glory of it. Most people are no different from Mark.

It's a cheering thought, that. It almost makes up for Moira and her rainhood. In fact, I'm halfway to smiling at Mark when something beside me catches my attention. It's nothing really, just the movement of something large, shifting its weight from one foot to the other. But it makes me lose my drift.

Makes me lose more than my drift.

Funny how the oddest things can change a mood completely. Half a minute ago I had been on the verge of feeling cheerful, thanks to Mark, sitting where he's been told to sit, ever hopeful, a shadow of what everybody thinks he is. And all because he's convinced I've promised him something he can't get from anybody else.

Look at him, not daring to take his eyes off me, not daring to say a word either. Mark is easy. And you can see what's wrong of course. He's *too* easy.

Back to Moira, then. No getting away from Moira, shifting her weight, shifting the way you look at things. Maybe I'm like Dad. Maybe I like a challenge.

It happens very quickly after that, the way things do when you forget to stop and think. There are two empty seats at the table. Two quick shoves then, and Hilary and Lydia find they are sitting down, opposite the two boys, both of them blinking and wondering how they got there. Which leaves just Moira and me.

Everybody wants something. The secret is to find out what it is. That's the challenge. Even if it's Moira.

Especially if it's Moira.

She's the easiest person ever to take by the arm. When I start dragging her towards the door she comes as sweetly as a ship through water. Just as on the way here, crowds seem to part for her. The only problem is the door itself, not wide enough to take us both at once, slowing us down, when I needed to make a quick exit.

Out in the street though, we can go as fast as we like, Moira doesn't mind, never complains even though we are practically running. Doesn't even get out of breath. And when we have to stop, it's not her fault.

You can blame Lydia for that. Two minutes out of the café, and I can hear my name in the crowds on the pavement behind us. The thing to do is ignore it. But then a mob of people ahead, waiting to cross the road, means we have to slow down. After that there's no chance. A few seconds later, Lydia is beside us, red faced and out of breath.

But the running has hardly a thing to do with it, I mean the colour in her cheeks. It had already arrived when we left her sitting in my seat, right opposite Mark. Which was where she should have stayed. It was her big chance. Because you never know, she might have stumbled across something to say, something to make him notice her for more than three seconds.

But no, here she is instead, impossible to leave behind. Perhaps it's Moira she's following. Not that she says as much. 'What on earth . . . ?' she begins, and she's off, launched into some long half-tearful tirade about being abandoned. Typical Lydia, not knowing when she's in luck, blaming me for doing her a favour.

It's not all bad though. At least there's no sign of Hilary. You won't catch Hilary walking away from the opportunity of a life-time, just because she's shy and because she's never learned how to take what's on offer.

I could have said as much to Lydia, but where would that have got me? And besides, she has a point. Mark's never going to look at her. So there's nothing for it but to wait while she drones on, and let the noise of the traffic drown out the worst of it. And think about Moira. And what Moira wants.

'Well,' I say at last, bright and breezy. 'What shall we do now?' I'm trying to get Moira's attention, you see. She's looking out along the street, taller than both of us. But she's not listening. Something has caught her attention in the crowd across the road, drawing her eyes after it the way they might follow a sweet trolley on the other side of a room. But when I look, I don't see it, whatever it is. Just a hotel and people going in. Probably it was nothing. Who knows what Moira sees?

'Well?' I say again cheerily. And all at once there's something familiar about this, the way I'm talking. Then I remember. I sound like Dad sounded yesterday, trying to make headway with Moira in the car—and failing, the way I seem to be failing now. Moira turns, not to me, but to Lydia and, ignoring the fact that I'm still talking, says something that I can't hear. I have to get Lydia to repeat it for me.

'Moira wants to go in there.' She points to the Woolworth's standing behind us.

I should have known. Woolworth's will be where her granny buys her crumpled bags of toffees and who knows what else. Moira must have run out of things to suck. She needs a visit to the Pick'n'Mix.

Or that's what I thought. Yet inside, Moira ignores the Pick'n'Mix, and heads straight for the hair products. And this where she stops, in front of shelves and shelves of different dyes, boxes and tubes and bottles, all promising to transform the colour of your hair, just so that no-one would ever remember the colour you were born with. And once stopped, she doesn't move. It's embarrassing. People have to walk around her, as if she was one of the red and gold pillars holding up the shop.

'What?' I say. '*What?*'

Lydia turns, surprised to hear me snap like this. You see, she doesn't mind. She never seems to mind what Moira does. But it's not Lydia I'm concerned about. It's Moira. Only Moira.

But at least she heard me, because this time she actually stirs. Her eyes flicker from the shelves to the top of my head, and rest there for a moment, as if contemplating something, perhaps the colour of my hair. Moira is about to speak.

'What I want is . . .' She is talking in that slow, creamy voice of hers, the one that makes you want to shake her till the words fall out faster. '. . . What I want is to work in a place like this. One day.'

And that's it. The answer to my question, the one that made me take her and run with her out of the café, away from where we should have been, away from where everything was nicely under control. And what does Moira want? She wants to work in Woolworth's, amongst the Pick'n'Mix preferably. And again it's enough to make you want to laugh—or cry. Because even Dad can only promise the gift of the world to come. But he can't give her this. He couldn't get her a job in Woolworth's. They wouldn't have her.

Now she's moving away, away from the hair dyes, drawing Lydia after her, and not another word to me. Not that I care. I'm tired out suddenly. Having It is draining in itself; using it to read other people can take up more energy than anyone could guess. But imagine trying to use it to see through people like Moira. You might as well try making sense of a book that has no beginning or end or any logic to it whatsoever.

I wait until they are past the checkout before I join them, then almost wish I hadn't. Because now Moira is carrying a two pound box of chocolates—with that picture of kittens in bows on the lid.

'Oooh,' says Lydia. 'They look nice.' But what does she know? Then her eyes grow wide as Moira passes the box right under my nose and puts them in her hand. 'You have them,' she says. 'Give them to your mum.'

So Lydia takes the box. Puts it under her arm where it stays, jutting out, making her twice as awkward as before—if that were possible.

OUTSIDE the rain is beating harder than ever, blowing straight into our faces and trickling down our necks, a reminder of the danger of doing things on the spur of the moment. We could have been sitting in the café all this time, the way Hilary is now, warm and dry. Instead we are here, getting soaked, going nowhere.

And all Moira really wants is a job in Woolworth's.

To cap it all, she has started gazing across the road again, towards the same spot as before. And still there's nothing there, nothing to see; only folk passing back and forth in front of the hotel, bumping into each other in all the rain, blind under their umbrellas; a miserable river of people, no more interesting to watch than the wet granite front of the hotel itself.

At which point Lydia says, 'I'm hungry.'

How she can say that? We are standing here, apparently hale and hearty, so you'd never guess that Gran's porridge is still having its effect, a dead weight to carry around. How can she be hungry? Then again I was forgetting, Lydia didn't eat any porridge. She has a reason to be empty.

But it has a result, that mention of hunger. Moira stares down at Lydia, opens her mouth, as if about to say something—then closes it again. Instead she begins to move off, slowly, but then with gathering speed. Unable to do anything else, we follow her, right across the road, through the traffic, to the spot that has been catching her interest for the last half hour—and there we stop. But even here there is nothing to see, only the hotel and a set of revolving doors.

But wait, Moira hasn't stopped after all, she had merely been slowing down to let Lydia catch her breath. Then she's off again, upwards this time, right to the top of the steps leading to the hotel, pausing by the revolving doors before pushing on through. Lydia giggles, gets herself tangled between the doors and the box of chocolates, and almost ends up in the street again. But finally she makes it inside. And then here we all are, the three of us, standing in the middle of the hotel lobby. Over by the lift, people are looking at us, wondering what's happening, what we are doing here.

Or are they? Moira hasn't taken off her plastic rain hat. People glance, then look away again. And it's obvious; Lydia and I are with her. The old lady in the hat. She's in charge.

Lydia giggles again, louder this time, for nervousness' sake.

'Moira, what are you doing? This is a *hotel*.' Even the word makes her excitable, with all its associations. Grown ups, three course meals, rooms with bathrooms.

Moira blinks, just the once. Answers in tones of mild surprise: 'Dinner.'

Lydia then turns to me. Giggles again. 'Kate, tell her. We can't have lunch here. I mean, how on earth would we pay?'

But it hardly seems worth answering if she's been so stupid as to forget. Moira has her wallet, full of her mother's ten-pound notes. Silly Lyddie. Stupid Lyddie. The question isn't so much *how* we are to have lunch here, but *why*?

A waiter is standing at the door to the dining room. He glances at Moira the once, and doesn't even raise his eyebrows; leads us across an acre of carpet spread out beneath dull chandeliers. There's a smell of Sunday lunch, damp coats, and dust. Lots of dust.

It must be the smell catching the back of my throat that stops me, dead in my tracks. Really, it has to be the smell, making me halt, right here, in the middle of the floor, suddenly unable to take another step. I'm going to have to tell them this is silly, that we need to go back to the café, find Hilary.

You see, it has to be the smell. What else could be the reason, making me think this is the last place we should be?

I'm opening my mouth to say just that, when suddenly it's too late. The only person who notices I've stopped moving is the waiter, who turns to me, a question in his eyes.

And he looks like Mark, not much older even, despite the bow tie. It could be Mark I'm looking at.

And I can't help it. I can't help *It*. The smile seems to come from nowhere, nothing to do with me. A quick flash, that's all it was. But a moment later, his expression changes and despite himself, he moves closer, so that we are almost touching as he takes me to the table where the others are already sitting.

Even Lydia notices, and gives another giggle, her hallmark sound for today. 'Oooh, Kate. He must think you're a VIP.'

But what it means is, there's no escape. Not when you've been noticed. You have to carry on, keep flashing the promise you've shown so far.

So it's me that orders the meal—vegetable soup and chicken and chips all round. He writes down the order with his head so close to mine I could say everything in whispers. And it doesn't stop. I take sips of the warm dusty water, and he comes and tops up my glass, every time. And every time Lydia giggles. She'd like to be noticed, too.

And in all this, nobody seems to have the feeling that I have. The feeling that, despite the smiles and Moira's living disguise, we shouldn't be here. That this is the last place we should be.

Still, maybe they don't have the feeling because there is no reason for it. We eat the soup, and nothing happens. Then we eat the chicken, and nothing happens. We order chocolate ice cream with Italian wafers, and nothing happens—unless you count Lydia fretting about some spots of gravy she's left on the tablecloth. We sit here and for a whole hour nothing happens. It's an ordinary lunch in a hotel.

So why do I feel the way I do?

Then Lydia bites her lip, jiggles in her chair. Leans to me and whispers, 'Kate, I need the loo.'

So I just look at her.

Well what did she expect? She's told me what she needs, but I know what she *wants*. She wants someone to come with her, as if she were a child, no older than Laura. But I'm not moving. So far, nothing has happened, but that might be because we have done nothing but sit here, out of harm's way. In the end, Lydia gets the message and she walks off, face red, head down, avoiding the eyes of the waiter—who wasn't looking anyway.

Five minutes later though, she is back, redder than ever.

'Kate,' she says. 'Kate, I can't find it.'

Pointless to ask what it is she can't find—or if she had bothered asking anyone how to find it. They must have heard my sigh on the next table, but up I get, to take Lydia to the bathroom. Otherwise she might just wet herself.

I never thought it would be this hard however. Not far from our table is an exit, but all this does is open onto some stairs leading up to the bedrooms. And it must be the thought of bedrooms that makes Lydia blush even harder, as if by coming through this door we have wandered into somebody's home. So it's back to the dining room, this time to follow the path beaten into the carpet by years of footsteps. A moment later we are in the lobby. But although there's a door that reads *Gentlemen*, there's nothing else that we can see. So it's back to the dining room again, and a glimpse of Moira sitting in the distance staring fixedly at a series of screens along the far wall, set up one beside the other.

Relief may be at hand. It only takes a second to discover that these screens make a kind of corridor which is bound to lead to somewhere. Lydia looks hopeful. But in vain; after running a few yards, the corridor opens out into what is virtually a separate room with space for just the one table. And it is here, well away from the eyes of other diners, that a couple appear to be coming to the end of their meal. She is eating trifle and he is busy with the last of his apple pie and cream, something I noticed on the menu and decided not to order; it seemed too much, somehow, after everything we'd had already. But he's enjoying it. Another spoonful, and there—now it's all gone. Only the wine left. And not much of that either.

As he is lifting the glass to drain the last few drops, his companion, plump and handsome, and dressed all in pink—again—leans across to say something I can't hear, not from where we are standing. Something about coffee perhaps. And liqueurs. Things we don't have at home.

But that breaks the spell, because it means that any moment

now he'll have to turn round. How else will he summon the waiter? He'll turn round and then he'll see us.

Now I know exactly why I didn't want to be here. Why it seemed safer to stay in our seats and never wander.

So it's round to face Lydia—try to fill the space between her and the table at the far end of the corridor, blocking her line of sight. 'Move,' I say. 'Move.'

'But . . .'

Silly Lyddie, *stupid* Lyddie, she doesn't understand. We have to get out of here, before they, before *he* sees us.

'But . . .' she says again, and this time I give her a push, so hard that a look of anger sweeps over her face—Lydia's, of all people—and before I know what's happening she's gone and pushed me back, all but knocking me over. And that leaves the way clear for her to see right past me to the far end of the corridor and its single table. And the people sitting at the table. A moment later, her mouth opens. And she understands.

We only just made it in time. It seems they hadn't wanted coffee after all. There must be something else they have in mind.

Crouched in a corner of the lobby, under the stare of an astonished woman at the desk, we see them, making slow but dignified progress upstairs to the bedrooms. My father and Mrs. Forbes White.

AND would you believe it, behind us is a door marked *Ladies*. It must have been there all the time. But Lydia doesn't seem to care that we've finally found what we were looking for. I have to push her inside, close the door behind us.

'Go to the loo,' I say to her. But Lydia doesn't move. She stands, back up against the bathroom door, eyes fixed on the opposite wall.

'Go to the loo,' I say to her again. Someone has to remind her of the reason we are here, the reason we've been running all over a hotel, ending up in places we were never meant to be. Seeing things we were never meant to see.

Look, we wouldn't even be here if it weren't for her.

But still Lydia doesn't move. She's thinking. I've seen her like this before, in maths for example. Sitting at her desk with a problem that she can't quite work out, not straightaway. It's been almost comical watching her in the past, lips moving, eyes staring but seeing nothing, working out the alternatives. And I haven't been the only one to think so. It happens every time. Gradually other people start to notice her, to stop what they were doing and nudge each other, so that in the end everyone in the class is watching, and waiting—even the teacher—to see if Lydia will be able to come up with the answer.

What will Lydia come up with this time, I wonder. And what is she going to do about it? Clever people don't like thinking they've been fooled. They get nasty, start looking for all sorts of ways to get their own back.

I have to guide her back to the table. She'd never have made it by herself. Meanwhile, Moira is exactly where we left her, this time staring towards the lobby, and the stairs with its people going up and down.

So what does Moira see when she stares? Things that other people miss, that's what. Folk entering a hotel for example. Seeing them, but never thinking to say a word to others.

Time to go. Moira passes a handful of crumpled five-pound notes over to the waiter, who glances at her as he takes them, then stands, frozen to the spot. At last he's noticed, has finally looked at her long enough to see. The person paying isn't our granny after all. She's just a young girl, no different from us.

Except that's exactly what's wrong. Moira's not like us. She isn't anything like us. Moira is completely different, and it's only now he's realised.

IT's as we are coming out of the hotel that we bump into Hilary. No sign of Mark, though, or Owl Boy. But she must have had a reasonable time there in the café, because she's all smiles and coy blushes. Yet it's no use her trying to tell us all about it because nobody's listening, least of all Lydia. She's still thinking hard, working out the alternatives. I have to help her onto the bus.

In the end, it's Moira who almost gets left behind. Standing on the pavement, about to follow us on board, she suddenly goes from being merely still to statue-like. Something has caught her eye. Again. But this time I don't look. In fact, I do more than simply fail to look, I turn my back, to make sure that I see nothing, nothing at all. The way I should have done before.

HALFWAY home, Lydia jerks back to life. With a sudden feverish flurry she starts delving into her satchel to locate the book. There follows a short frantic search through the pages, and then . . . and then she's found it. Lydia reads what's there, then looks up. Her eyes are shining, triumphant even. And quite peaceful.

She doesn't seem to mind when I take the book away from her, to run my eye down the page. And, sure enough, there it is. The paragraph about the righteous man who must rise above the judgement of others. If folk choose to misunderstand him, then so be it. In judging him, they judge themselves. But they should remember that Our Lord talked to his flock in all kinds of different ways. In other words, it's the message that counts, not the way it gets across. And then it goes on to talk about Jesus with the prostitute, and the things people had to say about that.

But there's no need to read any more. My dad, he's covered every eventuality, just with this one book, explained everything in advance. And now it's all there in black and white, a reason for everything. Lydia doesn't have to bother herself thinking an more. He's done all her thinking for her.

And look at the result. She's humming a little tune as she looks out of the window, a small half-smile curling up her lips. She's like someone who has been let in on a secret, and in consequence is sitting there hugging it to herself, completely happy. Not because of what she knows, but because she's been trusted to hear it in the first place, because she's special.

Silly Lyddie. Simple Lyddie. Somehow she's forgotten the most important thing of all; that what we saw was never intended for our eyes. We weren't meant to be there. Hotels, with their three course dinners and their rooms with bathrooms, they are for grown-ups and the games grown-ups play. And nobody else.

IT'S a long time before Dad gets home, and when he does, he appears completely drained. Of course it's no surprise. Every day carries its own hardship, he has always said that, but Saturdays are especially hard, the reason he invariably returns looking as if something vital has been sucked out of him. It's what we've come to expect.

Gran leaps up and brings him his plate from the oven where she's been keeping it warm for the best part of three hours. Dad takes one look and shakes his head.

'I'm sorry, Mother. I couldn't eat a thing, not tonight.' It's the same every Saturday.

'Oh, Mr. Carr, whatever have you been doing today? You look absolutely worn out.' This is Hilary, anxious as usual to make the right impression.

All the more touching that he can find a smile then, even for a girl who hasn't done a thing to deserve it, who has sat in a café all day making eyes at small boys.

'You don't want to know, Hilary love. Believe me, it would break your heart. Just think of folk in need and you can guess the rest.'

'But you helped them, Mr. Carr? You've been doing all you can?' Hilary's eyes are shining.

'I hope so Hilary love. I hope so.'

As he speaks he glances at Moira, perhaps to be sure that she's hearing all this—then tries not to blink when, just as he should have expected, he finds she is already staring at him. Yet why should it bother him? Lydia is gazing at him, and so is Hilary. So is Gran, come to that. It's only natural. When Dad is in the room, all eyes are drawn to him. It's part of having *It*, the secret of everything.

But now suddenly he has Moira and her stare. Because of her, his hands come out of his pockets, he has to clear his throat, glance at the ceiling, then down at the floor, hum a little tune.

Nothing strange about any of it. In fact nothing could seem more ordinary. He could be anybody. Except when has Dad been just anybody?

It makes you wonder how Moira does it, how it is she cuts him down to a size he's never been before, simply by the way she stares. It makes you wonder how, but then it makes you wonder why, why she only does it to my father. Whatever I thought of Moira and her stare, she never looked at me like that.

❧ Chapter Nineteen

BUT OH, MY DAD, HE'S not just anybody after all.

Last week, Miss Jamieson told us about the Hydra, a mythical beast, more powerful than anything that tried to take it on. The Greeks knew about it. You'd cut off a head, and another would grow in its place. Nothing could measure up to it, and brave men died in the attempt. But what is it that makes me think of that now?

A minute passes, perhaps two, then suddenly Dad has raised his head, is looking straight at her, at Moira. And he's smiling. And it's the smile that lets you know everything is back to normal.

A smile that tells you who's in charge.

'Moira love.' Suddenly I never heard him so jaunty. 'How about stepping into my study for a few moments? We can have a little chat, just you and me.'

Lydia's head shoots up. Already a wave of colour has swept over her face, faster than a rip tide. Well, we know why. This is what she's been waiting for, the summons to the study, the promise of togetherness. Now it's finally come—but it's not for her. And it's interesting. Because look at her face. Which one is she going to be angry with: Dad or Moira?

And what about Moira? Dad is waiting, yet she stays exactly where she is, eyes locked on to his.

'Moira?' He calls her name again, but quietly. 'Moira love.'

And now you would never dream there was a battle taking place. Perhaps it's because there's only the one of them fighting and his expression is so mild. The other continues to sit as if nothing is happening, nothing at all.

Slowly Dad gets to his feet. Everyone looks at Moira, expecting her to get to her feet, too. And she doesn't. Again Moira stays where she is. Now Dad's face has begun to change colour, tiny pinpoints of blood stippling his cheeks in faint blotches. But he doesn't look away. And he doesn't stop smiling.

Then an unexpected thing happens. Gran gets up and taps him briskly on the shoulder.

'Leave her, Keith, there's a good boy.'

And it's proof, isn't it, of how partial Gran is to Moira. And proof of something else as well. That she recognises something in Moira that has escaped him, something he might do better to leave alone. But it makes no difference. Dad pays no more attention to her than he would to a fly buzzing along his arm. Less, in fact. He'd kill the fly.

He's started heading for the door now, but only so as to stand there, to show once more that he is waiting. Smiling while he waits. Proving that no-one smiles like my dad.

Then, without any warning Moira looks away, does more than simply look away, turns her gaze from him—to me. And that's not all; a moment ago her eyes were blank. Now they are not empty any more. Now they contain a question, so unexpected it takes a moment to understand. Then it hits me. Moira is asking me, *me*, whether she should go with him, is watching and waiting for an answer.

Yet there's not a thing I can say to her. Because he is there and so is Gran. Nothing will go unrecorded. Nothing. But saying nothing is just as bad. Because as long as my mouth stays closed, Moira will sit where she is.

Then something stirs. Not Moira, not Dad, not Gran even.

'Moira MacMurray, you stupid pig! Why can't you just go when you're asked?'

It's Lydia exploding at last, too furious to care what she sounds like. She's telling Moira to go ahead, take her place in my father's study, but is full of rage about it, at Moira, who is too stupid to recognise her luck.

But it works. It breaks the spell. Lydia's voice snips the invisible ribbons that connect us, and Moira's eyes fall away from mine. There's a slight pause, then slowly, like an old lady, she hauls herself out of her seat and lumbers off to join him at the door, her face expressionless once more. Dad beams and places an arm around her shoulders, guides her gently out of the room.

And that is the last we see of her.

YET I could have stopped her. One word, one glance and Moira would have come back, she would have stayed with us and never have gone with him. It's me that let her go.

Then again, why should she *not* go with him? It should be obvious, surely. Lydia is right, and Moira is luckier than she could ever imagine. This is Moira's chance. The greatest prize she could ever hope to win. Dad is going to turn things around. He is going to change her life. He's done it before, time and time again. Alcoholics, fishermen, idiots, thieves, they all have something to live for now. They all love him. The way Moira will after this.

I thought I was the reason she was here. But I was wrong. This must have been what he had in mind from the moment he saw her on the pavement. Now he's taking her into his study. And tomorrow will be the day Moira begins to be like everybody else.

Moira is going to be saved from herself.

It's his job. A good shepherd will bring every one into his fold, right down to the last lost sheep. In fact, it's that last sheep which is the most important, the one that poses the challenge. And my Dad likes a challenge. He'll rise to it any way he can, in any way that's possible. No-one gets past Dad.

Stupid, stupid of me not to have remembered. What could I have done but let Moira go?

Upstairs, getting ready for bed, Lydia and Hilary are peeved at having been left out, sneaking furtive, sulky glances at their watches. A few moments he said, yet Moira has been down there an hour already. They are probably thinking it would almost be worth being her, just so that they could be saved too, by him, my dad.

Then another hour goes by. Hilary and Lydia fall asleep. Lydia is making small, grumpy noises under her breath, still furious, even her dreams.

It must be taking him a while then, turning Moira around, definitely longer than he's used to.

I didn't mean to fall asleep myself, though. I wanted to be awake to see the new Moira, the Moira he's just made, nothing like the old Moira. Witness the miracle of what can be done with old material. A person doesn't necessarily have to approve, but she can admire the newness, the effort that has gone into the creation.

I didn't want to miss any of it. I wanted to stay awake. But sleep crept up on me as if it had been waiting, as if it had something else in store.

SLEEP put me back where it has always put me, night after night, locked in my father's arms, as he carries me through a house, with the light shining out around us. But more than ever now, the light is coming from him, streaming from his arm as he strides between creaking walls that are beginning to fall like trees. He is singing, at the very of top his voice, a hymn to the power of the Lord. It looks like a rescue. But it feels like . . .

. . . It feels like I don't know what. And there's no chance to find out, because then, without warning, the dream falters, turns back on itself. Suddenly the light and the din fade away, and so does my father. The dream has shifted, time has shifted.

Now everything is peaceful. I am in his room, by myself. No more light, no more heat. And no more Dad. Now there's nothing to worry about.

All I have to do is wait.

And it's easy, because I'm used to waiting, used to keeping the silence. *Pretend we're mice*, she would say. *Pretend it's a game.* So very important never to disturb. Noise is what he can't stand. If we remember to keep small and quiet, he'll be pleased with the both of us.

So it's not hard to remember now, to keep quiet while I wait. Especially here, in his room. Look instead of talk, isn't that what I'm used to doing?

Look at my feet then, ten rosy little toes. And look at the picture, at the Golden Calf gleaming like polished spoons. *Wait*, she had said. In the meantime, count the teeny tiny dancing girls with their trays of fruits and smoky offerings, their flimsy skirts lifting in transparent swirls about their legs. They look ready to dance all night, until they drop, till there is nothing of them left when the morning comes. Same girls, same moon-struck faces.

Except for one. Suddenly in the middle of all that arrested movement, is a girl I have never noticed before—larger, older than the rest, almost matronly. And it's as I'm staring at her, trying to remember if I've seen her before, that she turns and looks straight at me. For a moment we stare at one another, then slowly, she raises a finger to her lips.

Hush, that's what she's saying. Not a word to be spoken. Really I should ask her what she's doing, how something that's only painted can come to life. But there's no time, not now. I can hear the footsteps outside the door. *She's* coming, just like she said she would.

So you see, it's time to go. The waiting is over and nothing is going to be the same.

The handle on the door begins to move. I can ask *her* about the dancing girls. Ask her what everything means, the waiting and the watching and the need for hush. Why it's so important never to disturb. Never to speak aloud. I can ask her where we are going after this. All I have to do is wait for the door to open. I can hear her breath on the other side. In a moment I will feel it on my face . . .

. . . And again I wake up.

SOMEONE is crying. Is it Lydia? No, not Lydia. Someone else.

It takes a moment to realise. It's me, crying the way I used to cry before I grew up, before I learned all sorts of lessons. In the beginning, crying because I'd lost something. Then later, crying because I couldn't even remember what it was I'd lost. And after that, finally, no more crying.

Now it's started again, after all these years. Crying with the disappointment that comes with waking. Crying because I came so close. Tonight I almost touched her. Another moment and I would have seen her face. It's been so long since I cried, I didn't even know it was me.

This isn't a dream I want to have, not if waking has to be like this. Better not to dream.

Better to sleep the way he sleeps, silent, dreamless. Safe amongst the righteous men.

Better still not to cry. Because what is it he says about tears? That there are good tears but there are also bad. Crying for the wrong reason is almost the worst sin, he says, because tears signify a protest against His will and the way things are meant to be.

Find a way to stop crying then. Look on the bright side, Kate. Try. Try hard. Think of every lesson he's ever taught you. All these years of learning how to see the world the right way. But it's hard. If it were easy there would have been no need for him to keep teaching. I would be the daughter he always intended me to be. Take the blind intelligence of Lydia, the blind faith of Hilary. The silence of Moira–and there I would be: Perfection. The daughter of his dreams. The child he can trust to carry on.

Instead he has me, still dreaming the wrong dreams. No wonder I'm a disappointment. No wonder I wake up crying. What would he say if he knew I was crying even now?

Maybe it's time to try harder. Time to think the way his daughter would think. I could start by looking for the bright side. *His daughter*, remember, so there is always a bright side. Try, Kate, try hard . . .

. . . .And there, it's not so difficult after all. Because he's right. There always is a bright side.

Listen to the sounds of breathing in the room. There are only two other people here. You wanted to see the new Moira as she arrived, but she's not here. Which means she is still downstairs. The bright side is that you're awake to see the miracle after all.

And anyway, who needs to dream? Or to cry, for that matter?

It's only children who cry, thinking dreams are better than the real thing. I bet you there's no end of tears when Lydia's little sister wakes up after dreams of flying or being a princess, when she discovers she's just plain old Laura. Tears and tantrums all 'round.

Dreams are wicked. They fool you into thinking that things can be different.

Maybe it's time to stop dreaming.

I could do it. I'm his daughter. There is a way to make sure I never dream again. But it would mean committing murder.

You see, I know where the dreams have been coming from. There is only one place. A little part of me that never came from him. I'm talking about another Kate, a different Kate, no bigger than a baby eel, curled up in a place he has never touched, deep inside. A Kate he never even knew was there. That's where the dreams are coming from, causing all the trouble.

I've never told him. I wouldn't have known how. But it's not right, is it? Keeping it a secret, letting it stay alive, asking its questions, dreaming its dreams, and all of them about *her*. Letting it cause all kinds of problems. But it's time he knew. It's the last precious thing I have. Now it's time to let it go. Hand the secret over. Let him put it where it belongs, in safe keeping.

Or better still, just kill it. He has given me everything I need. There's nothing else I want. There's nothing else I need to know. I am who I am. His daughter.

And what did he say after the last time? When the last chocolate was gone and my body was burning with sweetness? Only a question of time now, he says, until I am ready. All I have to do is try. Be the daughter I was meant to be. That's what the teaching has been leading up to.

But something else has to happen first. I have to grow up. No more questions. No more wanting to know who made me. No more wondering about *her*.

And no more dreams.

Kill it then, the part that's been causing all the trouble. It's easy if you know how. Think of it like that eel. Something you can crush under your foot. Kill it, Kate. Like that, just like that. No more dreams. No more crying. Ever.

Is it done? It must be. Why else should suddenly I feel so different? Where there were questions, now there is . . . nothing. No more questions, only him. I am full to the brim with him.

In other words, I am happy, ready for anything. Ready for what he has planned.

Maybe I should tell him now. Or does he already know? He knows everything else about me. Maybe this is why he's been taking so long with Moira. He's been waiting for me to come and take my place, to be there at his side.

Isn't this what he has always promised? I am the Future. I am the What Will Come After. Why else would he have a child— unless it was to help him in his work, to make a difference? To make sure that he lives on in me.

I never really believed him, not before tonight. But I've seen him take on Moira. I've seen the uselessness of dreams. I've killed the part that wasn't his. Now I feel as if my soul is bursting out of me. I am his daughter.

A place for everything, and everything in its place. I should be downstairs, not sleeping, not dreaming, but by his side. Helping him, now and forever.

Get out of bed, Kate.

And so I do. There's nothing to stop me. The old Kate is dead, crushed underfoot like that baby eel. And now it's a minor miracle in itself—the way I float, fly, rather than run downstairs. Quieter than thought I go, happier than the day I was born. This must be the feeling that comes over you, when you say goodbye to obstacles and contrariness and dreams, and give yourself up to what is meant to be.

Happiness like this could send a person skimming over miles and miles of space. But tonight, his door is far enough. And here I stop. It's very slightly open, with just enough light escaping to welcome me, his daughter. And invite me in.

So I give the door the gentlest of pushes and smiling, stand there.

And stand there.

AND all I can think is that the miracle has failed. Moira hasn't changed a bit. Her eyes, trained on mine as if they were expecting me, are without expression, empty. Her face is a perfect blank. The only remarkable thing about her, as she stands facing me, is her stillness. Even now, after so much time, I cannot believe the stillness of Moira.

Next to all that stillness though, is movement, a busyness of sorts. Dad is bent with his back to me, face level with her chest—like a man stooping to a keyhole, trying to see through a door that is closed to him. His whole body is intent, twitching with the smallest of movements, vibrating to the motion of his hands. Not that I can see them. They are thrust deep inside Moira's blouse.

But you can see the shape of them easily, shifting, scrabbling just about where her heart must be, as if he were searching for something that's been lost.

But it's no good. He's not going to find what he's looking for, and he knows it. You can tell from the noises coming from his throat, small desperate moans, the same whimpering sounds a man would make when flailing through muddy water for something precious that has fallen in a pond and is dropping farther and farther out of reach.

Of course you know what's happened. He must have tried everything else with Moira, and this was the only way left. Working through the flesh to reach the soul. It's what he calls it. So it must be true. Everything he says is true. He says.

But the work is coming to nothing. He set out to save Moira, but now he's scrabbling for something that will save himself. And he'll never find it. Moira is keeping it from him. Moira is in charge.

Meanwhile Moira looks at me as if nothing is happening, as if neither of us is really here, as if this is someone's else's dream. Then slowly, very slowly, she raises a finger to her lips.

But it's too late. Because although I should know the truth, although I know everything there is about righteous men, something inside has suddenly decided not to believe it. The small part of me I thought I'd left dying has found a voice, and it won't be quiet.

In fact, it has started to scream. Is screaming and screaming, as if it would never stop, as if all this time these screams have been waiting for one particular moment of release. Happy to scream the house down if necessary. Happy to wake the dead.

Happy? That can't be right.

Happy. In this house the dead are already awake. How else to account, finally for Moira and her stare?

Dad's head swings up, and he tries to turn around. But what can he do, with his hands still there, caught up in Moira's clothes? Nothing. And the screaming just goes on.

Inside me though, despite the screams, inside that little space that was always there, everything is perfectly quiet. I'm even able to think, to observe the event with something close to wonder. For the truth is, there has been a miracle. Moira is the same, yet Dad—he is completely changed. And not just for now, but for ever, I'd say. After all, no-one ever talked about the wine turning back to water, not so much as a drop of it.

And what did I say about screams to wake the dead? Here's Gran now, standing beside me, mouth hanging, a black hole where her teeth should be. And the ruffle around her neck looking more like a shroud than ever.

Then her mouth snaps shut like a trap and she lays her hands on my shoulders, fingers like old dry bones as she begins to shake me, hard as she can. But that doesn't stop the screaming. Quite the opposite. The shaking, it just turns the screams into accidental howls of laughter.

Eventually it's too much, even for her. Out of the blue, Gran begins to scream herself. There must be something in the air tonight, having its effect, because once she starts, she can't seem to stop either.

'Stop that, you little bitch. Stop the row.'

But of course it doesn't stop me. It would take more than Gran to stop me now.

So she shakes me even harder, and with the shaking a babble of words streams out of Gran, not making any sense. 'I said stop that or what happened to *her* will happen to you. You'll learn your lesson just as she did. Do you hear me?'

Yes. Yes, of course I do. It was that mention of the word *her*. But I don't stop screaming. The more I scream, the more Gran will forget to think what she is saying. And I need to hear what she has to say.

'*She* thought she could scream as well, make all sorts of noise. *She* thought if she made enough noise she would have the whole world running to see what she was screaming about.'

'Mother . . .' This is my father, but his voice sounds odd. Gran doesn't even hear him.

'*She* thought she could run out of the house screaming all those lies, spread them around. Ruin everything he'd done, pull it all to pieces, and for what? Because she wouldn't understand a man like him and his needs. All that work, all that sacrifice, it meant nothing to her. The bitch, she had her bags packed that night.'

'Mother . . .' Dad is doing his best, but it's still no good. He remains trapped, in all the different layers of Moira.

'But you listen to me, my girl. *She* had her mouth stopped didn't she, that night. She learned, oh yes, she learned. She had me to contend with, didn't she. Do you know what she had in her bag? Children's clothes. All those little pairs of socks. First things I put my hand on. And they did the trick, my God they did the trick, stopped the screaming, stopped the lies. She should have shut her mouth. One pair of cotton socks shut it for her. Put an end to all that racket. One little pair of socks stuffed where . . .'

But here it's Gran who stops. There's been another sound, another movement, one that neither of us saw coming, ending in a small explosion. My father has somehow freed himself from Moira, and the sound was his hand catching Gran full on the side of her face. The blow jerks her head away from mine, so now it's him she's staring at, standing there with his hand still raised, ready to strike again.

'What?' she screams. 'You thanked me for it. You got down on your knees and thanked me, remember?'

Then she stops. For the first time she hears the silence, realises that no-one is screaming, not any more. Her breath fails and her mouth opens and closes, like a sea anemone swallowing stones. Then her hands dart to cover it up, so nothing else can escape.

Dad steps back. 'Mother?' he says, in a way that shows he's not yet sure of her. He'll use that hand again if he has to.

Gran looks at him, then slumps. 'Son,' she moans, 'oh, Son . . .' Then remembering, swings round to see who else was in the room. Who else could possibly have heard?

But there's only me. Moira has gone, which suddenly explains why Dad is free. Yet I never even saw her leave.

'Son,' she says again, reaches out with her hand, tries to catch his arm, but he takes a step back. Her face crumples. Next she's turning to me, to show him there's no harm done. She even attempts a smile, which is worse than anything.

'Kate love.' There's a tone in her voice I've never heard before, wheedling, almost pleading. 'You don't want to listen to your old gran talking her nonsense. You just made her cross, that's all, wandering about in the middle of the night, making that noise. You don't know what it does to my nerves. See?' Her voice hardens, begins to sound more familiar. 'It's you that's caused this, making a poor old woman come out with all kinds of rubbish. You're a naughty little girl, Kate, that's what you are. Tell her, Keith. She's a naughty little girl. In need of another lesson, isn't that right, Son?'

But Dad doesn't stir. He's staring at my hair, frowning, like a man trying to remember what he was looking at before. I feel my hand go up, both hands, trying to cover what's there. But it's no good. His eyes stay where they are, until finally the frown disappears. And that's how I know. At long last, my father has noticed the exact colour of my hair. Now Dad is looking at me, but he's seeing somebody else.

'Keith,' snaps Gran.

'What?' His voice seems to be coming from far away.

'I said she's a naughty little girl, who needs to learn her lesson.'

But he's not listening. His eyes are still snagged by the colour of honey. But here's the most surprising thing. The look on his face is almost tender. What is it he's remembering then? Who can he see? If I looked in a mirror, would I see her, too?

And just for a moment, watching his face, I can't help thinking, perhaps there is an answer, things don't have to be like this . . .

Then the look disappears. So fast, so abruptly, it's like a window slamming down. To be replaced by a new expression, one that even I have never seen before. And that's when I know there is no answer. My father's hand drops down to work at the buckle on his belt.

So now I know what's going to happen next. It's going to start again. All that education. All that punishment. But this time it's not only me. Someone else is going to be punished all over again. He was looking at *her* just now.

And this time, who knows where it will end?

I have a feeling it will end in here, in this room. There is no place for me any more. There is no future, not for me. And suddenly, I feel so tired. So very tired that even the end seems too far away.

But then, something catches his attention and his hand stays where it is. He's listening. Now we can all hear it. From the other side of the door, the sound of whispering, of feet shuffling, the tell-tale signs of a nervous discussion.

And finally a voice, tremulous, not even sure that it wants to be heard.

'Mr. Carr, oh, Mr. Carr. Is that you? Please, what was all the noise, Mr. Carr? Has something happened?'

The voice belongs to Hilary. Gran frowns at Dad and shakes her head, ever so slightly. He sighs.

And buckles up the belt again, though tighter than it was before, as if he were girding himself for another challenge. Then he raises his voice.

'Nothing to worry about, Hilary my love. You get that sleepy head of yours back on to the pillow where it belongs. Lydia, too.'

There's a silence. I can't see her, but I'll bet you Hilary is biting her lip. Because it's not enough, is it? It doesn't explain a thing. And here she comes again.

'But the screaming, Mr. Carr, it was so awful. We didn't know what to think.'

Dad closes his eyes, and when he opens them again, it's there. The twinkle is back, right where it belongs. The room feels warmer suddenly. He rubs his hands together, then walks briskly to the door. On the other side I hear him begin the long process of explaining. He's telling Hilary and Lydia what happens when a person, an unstable person, sleepwalks and wakes unexpectedly. He—*she*—becomes terrified, even violent. They listen as he tells them it was my screaming they heard, waking up to the unknown.

Another silence as Hilary digests this. Then a final question, sounding embarrassed. 'Where is she now then, Mr. Carr. Where *is* poor Kate?'

Patiently, infinitely kind, he explains that all is well. How I was comfortable as could be, in the study, with his best rug over me to keep me snug. Best not to disturb me any more. And best not to mention it to me in the morning either. In fact, better not to mention it to anyone. People might think there had been something wrong with me, something not quite right.

Listen, he's beginning to talk about me in the past tense. As if already he doesn't have a daughter any more.

I can hear his voice on the stairs. He's taking them back to bed himself. He sounds so gentle, so soothing, they'll be half asleep by the time they reach the top. Meanwhile, downstairs, on the other side of the door, someone is turning the key in its lock, making sure I stay where I am. Gran makes so little noise as she pads off to bed you would think there was nothing bigger than a rat scuttling along the corridor.

That's the drawback, isn't it, of all girls together. Dad and Gran are going to have to wait. As he says, if a thing's worth doing, it's worth doing well.

UPSTAIRS the talking dies away. Doors close. Presently there is no sound at all. Everyone has gone to bed. Including Moira, I imagine. Will she even dream about what happened? In fact, does Moira dream? Somehow I can't believe she does, not exactly. Something understood now—or something imagined: Moira's entire life is nothing but a waking dream belonging to somebody else. I believe this because I saw her face just now. Wherever Moira was tonight, it wasn't here.

Socks though. Gran mentioned socks. Whose socks if not my socks? Whose bag, if not *her* bag? *She* had it packed and everything, that's what Gran said. But she would never have been leaving by herself, not with a suitcase full of children's clothes. Socks could only mean one thing.

She never was going to leave me. She was never going to leave me behind. She had been going to take me with her. My mother.

My socks, though. My socks, and something that Gran did with them, that stopped my mother's mouth. Stopped the screams for ever. Something my father got down on his knees and thanked her for.

What did Gran . . .?

Don't ask a question if you can't bear to think of the answer. But it's too late, the answer is there. I know what they did to my mother.

I don't think my legs are willing to hold me any more. I have to sit down, in his chair, where I've never sat. And this I can't believe—as I sit here, my eyes are beginning to close, as if nothing could stop them. This is a tiredness I've never known before. It must be the reason that despite everything, despite the words and the sights, I have the feeling that sleep is going to steal over me and carry me away.

It's as if nothing else can happen, not while I'm awake. A waking Kate would just be in the way. I have to be asleep, go to a place where none of the usual rules apply.

BUT this time I don't have any sort of dream. This is nothing but simple sleep, empty and without thought, like Moira's stare. A sleep that comes from elsewhere, as inexplicable as Moira herself.

The dream doesn't come until later, when I am awake.

I open my eyes and here I am again, still sitting in his chair. Yet the sleep must have done me good because suddenly I feel wide awake, more awake than I can remember. Wide awake and waiting.

And straightaway I know. In the time that I have been asleep, something has happened. Something . . . invisible.

You can tell just by breathing, by listening to the sound of your own breath. Then by stopping breathing altogether, to listen to what's left.

The house is quiet but, at the same time, not quiet. Behind the stillness, you might almost imagine you hear something like the sound of whispering. A sort of rustling, as if the air had turned to paper. As if the entire house had been given a stealthy life of its own, had life running through its walls. Not here though, not in this room. This is his place, the heart of the house. Everything in it belongs to him and has no life of its own. It couldn't possibly make a sound without him.

The rest of the house though, that's different. Outside his study, I would swear the house is trembling. Not so violently that it could wake anyone, but delicately, so you would hardly know it. Like a violin perhaps, still vibrating minutes after it has been put down. A silent humming of the tune just played.

And it makes it all so difficult. How am I supposed to tell the difference, between what's real and what can only be a dream? In front of me is the picture of the dancing girls, but that doesn't tell

me anything. Except that I can't see her now, the girl who signalled to me before.

It can't be real. Houses do not tremble. Houses don't hum, not
even silently, to themselves. Houses don't make you feel as if you
are encased in the dead heart of a living thing. Not real then. But
still I can't believe it, not until I get out of his chair, walk across
the floor and touch the wall.

And that's when I feel it. The wall is alive. The wall feels
warm.

It's then that something stirs, not in the house, but inside me.
A kind of answering hum. Something is beginning to wake up.
Something about to be remembered. It tells me where next to
look, although not what I should expect to see.

So I turn from the wall to the door. And what should be a
shock is no shock at all. Folds of smoke, paper thin, are slowly
curling through the crack between the floor and the door, hovering, then billowing upwards like grey, delicately shaken scarves.

But even then, I don't understand. Not straightaway, not even
as I stand and watch more smoke enter the room and climb the
walls, run along the angle between the ceiling and the walls in
pretty spirals. More and more of them, beginning to weave a pat-
tern of smoke overhead.

I'm wide awake but, oh, I'm slow. Try the handle of the door.
And of course, it's locked. Yet still I don't remember what there
is to be frightened of. It's not until the first tickle in my throat,
the same feeling you have when you swallow a hair, that it all
comes back to me.

This has happened before. In this very room, or a room almost
exactly like it, all but identical, right down to the dancing girls on
the wall. Smoke about to blot out any differences. Such a long
time ago that I'd forgotten. All I ever remembered was the room
and ten rosy little toes, and even then, only in my dreams.

Try the door again. Call out a name. But the tickle turns into
a cough, swallows up the sound. Just like it did all those years ago.

Try to think, watch the smoke, see what it does. And see, it's exactly as I've just begun to remember. There's more of it finding its way in now, creeping not just underneath, but through the sides of the door; and not in tendrils any more, but in sinuous waving limbs like the long searching arms of a ghost. I remember them, arms stretching through space to reach me. Meanwhile, above me, the spirals have come together to make a fragile, floating ceiling. Presently it will begin to sink under its own weight. I remember that, too. Got to get out before that happens.

Beat on the door. Cough. Beat and cough. All the good air escaping from that small space that's left inside. Three deep breaths, the space fills up and the room begins to disappear.

Last time this happened, I was a little girl.

Tired, tired again suddenly.

I have to lie down, the way I did the first time, underneath his desk, on the floor, with his carpet pressed against my face. This is where I'll have to wait, there's nothing else I can do. Too tired to think, suddenly, too tired to remember why it is I'm waiting. The simplest thing is simply to sleep. Simplest of all, to dream.

Then. Then on the very edge of sleep, it comes to me, the reason I am waiting. Of course. *She* brought me here. *She* told me to wait. She said, wait and she would come for me. *Just wait, Poppet.* That's what she said.

So I've been waiting all this time, for years, it seems. Ever since the first time when I waited, and listened, and wondered about the noise that broke out after she left me here to wait. The sound of screaming. It came from far away in another part of the house, yet still deafening, as if, for the first time, someone didn't care how much noise she made. I'll have to ask her about that when she comes. *We* have always tried to be quiet, she and I. She says *he* wouldn't like it otherwise. Not with all the work he has to do. So we are like mice, little mice, trying to do the right thing, doing our best never to disturb. To make him pleased with us.

But after this, we are leaving and everything will be different.

After this I'll be able to make as much noise as I like. That's what she told me. But until then, I have to wait. Never move a muscle, never make a sound.

Which makes you wonder why, if I had to be quiet, *she* was making so much noise. I never heard my mother talk in anything but a whisper before. I was almost glad when it stopped as suddenly as it did. If she'd finished screaming, it must all be over. Soon she would be coming back. All I had to do was wait.

But I waited so long I fell asleep. I was only little.

And when I woke up, she still wasn't here, and the room had disappeared in a grey fog that somehow meant I couldn't breathe. Like now. And there was nothing I could do about it. Except to wait. *Don't move a muscle*, she had said. *Wait until I come.*

So that's what I do. I wait. Besides, I've become so tired now, I don't believe I could move. There's only that small part of me that remains awake. Wide awake and waiting.

But then, at long last, I hear it, the sound I've been waiting for all this time, all these long years. Footsteps in the corridor, getting closer, brisk but unhurried. You see? There was never any doubt. She made a promise. All I had to do was wait.

And now it must be time to go. The footsteps stop, they are right outside the door. I'd like to be readier than I am, but somehow I can't stand up, I've forgotten why. I can't move a muscle.

But it doesn't matter. A disturbance in the smoke shows the door is opening. Light pours in, framing her shape against the solid air, all shot with more light. And there she is, waiting, her arms held out to me. It's the sight of her that lifts me to my feet and carries me across the room to her. And as I arrive at the door, her hand takes hold of mine, and keeps it fast.

She has come for me, my mother. At long last. It's time for us to go. Together.

But before we leave, she opens the desk, takes something precious from inside, and tucks it safely in my hand.

❦ Chapter Twenty

AFTERWARDS EVERYBODY SAID HOW TERRIBLE it was, history repeating itself like that. How unnecessary.

'*Midnight Feast goes tragically wrong,*' was the headline in one newspaper. They re-printed Moira's school photograph, where it seems as though the photographer has done his level best to make her seem as fat and pasty as anyone could possibly be. Just the sort of person who would be frying chips in the middle of the night.

STILL, she redeemed herself, didn't she, almost made up for having been no oil painting to look at, for never being exactly popular. That's the part the papers tend not to dwell upon, the part that might put off the readers. Who wants to read about fat girls who can't get through the night without a plate of chips?

Instead the newspapers are calling her a heroine. First she came and led one young friend through the flames of a burning house. And then, after leaving her confused but safe outside, went back to rouse her two other pals, led them to safety, too. Yet even that wasn't the end of it. As the newspaper put it, heroic teenager, Moira MacMurray, 14, then went back into the house one last time. Because upstairs, still asleep, had been popular Man of God, Keith Carr, and his elderly mother.

And this time, Moira failed. In the terrible chaos of a house on fire, she must have turned the keys in the doors the wrong way. Smoke does that, suffocating the brain, making you move in the wrong direction, do the wrong thing. And that's how the doors were found later. Locked. No-one else came out of the house alive, including Moira. But she had done her best.

No wonder the papers had a field day. It made you proud to be British. Editorials carried her name, recommending that her photograph be pinned up in every youth club and guide hut in the country. It would have been all wrong to dwell on just the one unhappy fact.

That none of it would have happened if Moira hadn't been trying to fry chips in the middle of the night.

Only the woman's page in one particular newspaper paid any attention, to ask what it is that drives some women to eat forbidden foods in secret. It went on to wonder what kind of compulsion drove Moira that night, into the kitchen, into the dark, reaching for the chip pan, while everybody slept.

Besides, there was that other point of much greater interest. Of history repeating on itself, regurgitating events in a most spectacular fashion. Journalists picked over old cuttings and found they had another story on their hands.

It had happened before, in another part of the country, to this self-same family. My family. A previous fire that started whilst everyone was sleeping. But then only the one person had been unfortunate enough to die, a young woman. They had found her, much too late, lying in bed with her arms by her side. The peaceful, undisturbed, completely burned shell of what had been my mother.

Luckily there had been Gran then, making sure it all made sense, telling the papers how my mother had always been one for her bed. Telling them how she would sleep through church, sleep through the long nights when *he* was working, sleep when she should have been up making his breakfast. It was the drink, she said—and being a secret smoker with it. That's where the fire started, in her bedroom, with a cigarette among the bedclothes.

But there are lots of things I remember now. And I don't remember my mother smoking, or drinking. I only remember her trying to do her best for me, trying to keep me quiet. Trying to keep me safe.

Yet it means it's all on record still. 'Facts' about my mother; too lazy to put out a cigarette, too drunk to wake up. That's what Gran told them. And they must have believed her. After the flames had finished with her, there was nothing left to say any different.

My father though, that was a different story. For a short while he was famous. Famous for running through the flames that same night with his tiny daughter in one arm, and a picture under the other. A lucky little girl, the newspapers called me at the time. Except for the damage to my leg of course.

Lucky this time round as well.

THAT'S the stuff that people read about. But it was nothing like that.

That first flight from a burning house, for instance; I remember it now. My father snatching me up and striding, *not running*, with me through the flames. As we went, he seemed to be carrying his own flame, his very own lighted brand, lighting his way through the lesser light of ordinary fire. It proved we were not alone and fitted with the prayer that he was reciting at the top of his voice, loud enough to fill a church, louder than the crackling of flames and timbers crashing. His voice only broke as he reached the *Amen*, and handed me into the arms of a neighbour.

Naturally, I thought he was God.

I never realised the flames that followed us were all mine, that it was my own leg burning. I had been screaming all the while, but that was because she wasn't with us. Because I hadn't waited as she had told me to wait. Now he was carrying me away, and I was leaving her behind.

It was me. *I* left *her*.

But it's only now I remember this. All these years I thought my dad was the source of all the light. And all the time it was me, burning.

Later in the ambulance, he held my hand, cradled my head, stroked me—until he was sure that nobody was looking, and took his hand away. Less than perfect now, you see. I remember it all.

BUT the newspapers were wrong; history didn't repeat itself. It was different this time round. This time, we walked from the house the way we would have done the first time, the way *she* had planned. Hand in hand, no screaming, no burning. Nothing touched us, nothing even came close that I knew of. I heard the flames and I breathed in the smoke, but I saw nothing. Then again, I only had eyes for her. We walked and I wished the walk could last for ever.

Outside she took her hand away. Stay here, she said. So what could I do but stay? At first then, I stood in the rain with the cool drops falling on my head and heard the sound of car doors slamming in the lane and people shouting. Minutes later Lydia and Hilary arrived outside, shocked and shivering, but I didn't even look at them. I was watching for her. For Moira to come back.

But Moira didn't come. I don't suppose I expected her to. But they should have let me back in, those people who came running. They should have let me try. Instead of holding on to me as if I was a mad thing, as if I was doing something wrong. Stopping me from going back inside, and finding her. Again.

SO.

I've been staying with Lydia and her parents for a while now. No-one quite knows what to do with me. They think I've changed of course. But I haven't, not enough. Not yet. I'm sitting on *It*, keeping it under wraps, doing everything I can not to let it show. I got it from him, you see, and it's never going to go away.

It used to keep me awake those first nights, lying in their lemon-coloured bed, worrying about it. Having *It* means he is still inside me. Because of me, he'll live for ever.

I am the future. That's what he said. And that's what I thought. He will stay alive in me.

Or will he? Now I'm not so sure. He reckoned without the past, didn't he, and what happens when you begin to remember. And I'm remembering everything. Thanks to history 'repeating' itself, I remember more and more of her each day, and the more I remember her, the less there is of him. He is not the only one who made me. He is not going to live through me. I don't have to let him, not now.

And to help me I have the horse, the crystal prancing horse she took for me out of his drawer. It's still missing its leg. But it's perfect. Absolutely perfect.

LYDIA'S mother cried at Moira's funeral, even though she had hardly known her. She kept saying what a terrible thing it was, a mother who wouldn't come to the burial of her own daughter. But Moira's gran, she didn't seem a bit surprised. She didn't even cry, which Lydia's mother says she simply cannot understand, since Moira must have been everything to her.

Lydia's mother wasn't with me when I walked up to Moira's gran outside the church. And if she had been, I don't think she would have understood, even then.

It was raining and Moira's gran was wearing the same plastic rainhood that Moira wore that time it rained on us. Listen and you could hear the rain drops pattering in just the same way. Her eyes were a light, faded blue, sharper than Moira's.

They rested for a moment on the top of my head, as if recalling someone else. Then she said: 'I knew your mother, of course. Right from when she was a girl, from the time when she was your age. She'd come home with my daughter almost every night after school. Years ago that was.'

And I nod. As if nothing could surprise me. As if this was something I had known all along. As if, years ago, when I first came to my school, a girl called Moira with a slow creamy voice had once told me exactly this—and I had put it out of my head. *Don't talk about her. Don't even think about her.* That was the rule. The rule that never once got broken.

'I didn't want her to marry him. He was whipping people up in church even then. It made you wonder what he'd be like in his own home. It's what I told her, it's what her mother would have told her, if only she'd been alive. But she wouldn't listen. Girls don't listen.'

And again, I nod.

'She married him and I never saw her after. Not once. He closed the doors and never let her out. I'd ask to see her, and that mother of his would send me away with a flea in my ear. But when I heard you were at the school, I told my Moira she should keep an eye on you. I thought one day you might come and see me. And I thought it would make Moira feel . . .'

. . . Needed. That's what her gran had tried to do for Moira. And this is what Moira had done for me; she did as she was told. Moira kept an eye on me. Exactly as her gran had said to do. And then something happened. And it wasn't *just* Moira, watching me.

Moira's gran doesn't smell like Moira. She smells of loose powder and rain and resignation.

I didn't cry when it was the day for Dad and Gran.

Apparently, it was only to be expected. I heard Lydia's mother whispering to Lydia's father, asking if he thought I was still in shock, and he nodded, as if he had seen it all before. As if experts in Trompetto know everything about everything. I almost shot him a smile then, the sort I would have treated him to before, just to see his face.

But I didn't. It's not the kind of thing I would want my daughter to do. Not at a time like this, not at a funeral. Daughters should think what their mothers would want and try to act accordingly.

That's what I've decided. Since there's no-one left I'd want to listen to, I'm going to listen to my mother.

Which is why, here, in this lemon-coloured bed, I wait for her, night after night. If I am quiet enough, I can almost hear her talking to me, deep in that small space inside where he never was able to reach. She is always there. I am not alone.

All the same, I can't stay here forever, going to sleep each night in someone else's bed, tucked up in sheets that don't belong to me. I'm upsetting the balance of everything. Lydia's father is still worried that he's going to find me looking at him the way I did before. And he has a point. Old habits do die hard.

So I'm going to have to tell them about the letter that came this morning, from Moira's gran. Describe rather than show it to them, perhaps. They might be taken aback by the spelling, think the less of her, and her offer. Some people believe that if you can't spell, you can't think. Which has to be wrong, because Moira's gran must have thought hard about what to put in this letter.

She wants to know if I would consider going to live with her, now that she doesn't have Moira, now that she's alone. Now that we both appear to be alone.

So I'm thinking about it.

Of course, you know exactly what he would have thought, my dad. *He'd* have said it was a disgusting idea. There's nothing spe-

cial about Moira's gran, nothing to suggest that she's been chosen—apart from the fact that she didn't cry at Moira's funeral.
He'd say no daughter of his would so much as think of it, even for
a second.

And he's right of course—no daughter of his ever would.

WHICH is probably one reason why I shall be writing my own
letter in the morning, to tell Moira's gran I'm coming. Drink a
cup of tea with her and listen to the world swing full circle.